Must Love Dukes

Elizabeth Michels

sourcebooks
casablanca

Copyright © 2014 by Elizabeth Michels
Cover and internal design © 2014 by Sourcebooks, Inc.
Cover illustration by Jim Griffin

Sourcebooks and the colophon are registered trademarks of Sourcebooks, Inc.

Published by Sourcebooks Casablanca, an imprint of Sourcebooks, Inc.
P.O. Box 4410, Naperville, Illinois 60567-4410
(630) 961-3900
Fax: (630) 961-2168
www.sourcebooks.com

Printed and bound in Canada.
MBP 10 9 8 7 6 5 4 3 2 1

For Mr. Alpha Male—for the hugs when things don't go well, the cheers when they do, and the football-themed pep talks in between. You are my big fish. I love you.

One

London, England
Spring 1815

As Devon paused to allow a carriage to pass, a heat spread across his back. Someone was following him.

Turning, he cast a quick glance down the street toward Habersham's shop. He would not be at all surprised to see old man Habersham running after him to continue their chat of the Mad Duke's antics. Yet all that met his eyes was a group of austere-looking ladies ordering some poor footman to load their packages into a carriage.

Then he noticed a set of ladies' boots scurrying around them before disappearing behind a food vendor.

He was being ridiculous. Why would anyone be stalking him? He shook off the thought and continued down the sidewalk. The clean buildings of Bond Street began to diminish, making way for simple shops, taverns, and the occasional brothel. The crowds thinned and the people traversing the area now were common folk out running errands.

A comfortable feeling of peace filled Devon as he left

the trappings of wealth behind, favoring the simplicity of a society revolving around trade. It was as if two separate worlds inhabited the city. As usual, he wanted nothing to do with the world to which he belonged.

Moving onto a side street, he strode into the shadows of stone buildings that grew closer together as he progressed. He had just rounded another corner when he heard footsteps at his back. Being followed in this section of town was never a good sign. He'd only needed to lose all the money in his pocket once to discover the truth of that sentiment.

He spun, determined to catch whoever it was off guard. The only movement that met his eyes was the swirling edge of a blue dress as it whipped around a corner.

Was that a woman following him? Why? He didn't want the answer to his question as much as he wished her to stop. He had endured enough for one day and wanted nothing more than to have a drink and escape life for a few hours. He passed onto a wider street and continued walking, still aware of a heated gaze across his back and quick footsteps behind him. This had gone on long enough. Someone would surely be missing the lady back at the shops where she belonged.

He turned, ready to confront her and send her on her way, but saw no one. Good. That was done. Yet, as he was pivoting to continue down the street, some-thing made him look back once more. It was then that he caught sight of the voluminous skirts of a blue dress extending from either side of a light post. The occupant of the dress was carefully hidden from view, but she was no spy. She had clearly underestimated the size of the dress she was wearing. He hadn't seen a dress that large in ten years. Devon smirked. Perhaps she was stalking some other prey, but glancing around the empty street, he knew they were alone.

Devon decided to ignore her. She would give up her quest soon enough. He was heading into the darker side of London, after all. Surely, she would not dare follow him there. He passed the window of a small shop and saw the reflection of the hem of her dress behind a horse tethered across the street. What did she want of him? Could she not see that he was in no mood to entertain ladies?

Lengthening his stride, Devon soon neared the entrance to the Stag and Doe. The tavern was seedy enough that no lady in her right mind would pursue him inside, yet it offered the highest quality drink on this end of town. Best of all, within these doors he was a nameless, untitled man and nothing more. Whatever the lady in blue wanted of him, she could damn well wait in the street surrounded by dirty sailors for all he cared.

He was finally free—free of whispers behind his back, free of his own identity, and free to spend the evening drinking his problems away.

Pausing as he opened the door, he smiled at the thick smell of lager and smoke hanging in the air. As he breathed in the sweet smell of anonymity, something careened into his back with a small "Umph."

He turned and looked down into the face of the woman in blue. "Woman in blue" indeed, for staring up at him were the purest blue eyes any man could behold. Her golden hair slipped from its elaborate style where it was topped with a hideous hat covered with several large flowers. She was lovely in an unconventional way. Perhaps he was in the mood to entertain women…one woman in particular. He grinned.

"Is there a reason you're following me, ma'am?"

"Following you? I'm not following you! I'm simply entering this fine establishment for some refreshment on a warm afternoon," she blustered.

"Yes, the Stag and Doe does often draw the Bond Street shopping crowd on warm afternoons." Whatever the reason this vision in out-of-date fashion had followed him here, it was certainly not for afternoon refreshments.

"I can see why, with its convenient location and inviting décor. Now, if you don't mind, I would like to go inside." If her chin tilted any higher, she would be thrown off balance and fall into the street behind her.

Devon quirked a brow and gave a tip of his hat as he motioned her inside. "By all means."

She paused just in front of him and appeared to be admiring his waistcoat with odd intensity. He glanced down but only saw the gold chain of his new watch glinting in the sun. She gave him an assessing stare, shot a quick glance down the street they had traveled, and then entered the tavern. Who was this lady? And what the devil was she playing at?

The same elderly man who always tended bar set a glass down on the long wooden surface that ran along one side of the room. A wall covered in bottles of spirits stood at his back. He nodded in Devon's direction, eyes lingering on the lady standing frozen beside him. She had the look of a wide-eyed fawn in a room full of hunters.

A few brave women were in the tavern, all drinking merrily, yet from the look of her, this lady was just that—a lady. She most likely had never been inside a tavern and had chosen a poor time to follow him, for this was where he planned to while away the remainder of his afternoon.

"It is customary to continue walking through a door and then sit at a table," he rumbled over her shoulder, causing her to jump.

"Of course. I was merely assessing where I might find the best table."

"I'm planning to sit there by that dirty window. I always find the afternoon light to be the nicest when viewed through a hundred years of grime." He took a few steps across the room before turning to look at her with an easy smile. "Care to join me?"

He moved past barmaids stepping around them as they dipped between tables serving drinks. The men in the room sat gathered, laughing and telling stories, while swirls of smoke rose from their cheroots.

He pulled her chair out and watched in amusement as she dusted it off before sitting. With her back straight and her hands folded neatly in her lap, she looked more out of place than a fish resting comfortably on a grassy hill. He sat opposite her with the hint of a curious grin lingering on his lips. Her hand darted to the pearl necklace around her neck. That piece of jewelry was a bit too fine for this part of town. She would likely be set upon by thieves if she was found alone. He said nothing, only watched her, willing her to speak and tell her reason for following him through the city.

"I do believe I should know your name if we're to have refreshments together."

A smile curled the corners of his mouth. She made the Stag and Doe sound like the finest of London salons where they would chat over a cup of tea. She was in for a rude awakening when the drinks came, if that was her anticipation. "That may be the first time drinks have been referred to as 'refreshments' inside these walls," Devon mused.

As a barmaid approached, he ordered something potent and equal to the task of erasing the day he was having.

"I'll have one of those as well," she offered politely.

"It appears the lady will have one as well," he repeated with a smile aimed at the barmaid.

When they were alone again, she added, "I have heard that they are well known for that drink here. That's why I came."

"A sangaree?"

"A what?"

"The drink you ordered. Your reason for coming here," Devon supplied.

"Yes, I've heard that, um, sangarees are delicious." She was clearly bluffing, because her cheeks were turning deeper shades of pink by the second. "You never said your name."

"That I did not, did I?" He stretched his legs, crossing them at the ankle, and narrowed his eyes on the woman across the table. The irony was not lost on him of having traveled this far into the shady side of town for anonymity, only to be asked who he was upon arrival. Of course she would want to know his name.

Although, if she had followed him from Bond Street as he suspected, then she most likely already knew the answer to her question. Therefore, he looked her straight in the eye and lied. "Mr. Grey. Since we're on such friendly terms as to share a few sangarees, you may call me Devon."

"That doesn't seem quite proper. Calling you by your given name, I mean."

"Will you tell on me?" he asked with a conciliatory tone, granting her the roguish smile that tended to make ladies swoon.

"No, I won't be telling anyone of this." She smiled a quiet, secret smile, clearly delighted with the idea of sharing a secret with him. Some part of him was enjoying this clandestine meeting as well, which was odd since he grew bored with all females within seconds of being introduced. Surely, the same would be true today. Perhaps what held his attention were the mystery surrounding her arrival and the low point in life at which she had found him.

"Devon." She tried his name out tentatively. "It's nice to meet you. I'm Lil—" She paused to clear her throat before saying, "Lily Whitby."

"A pleasure, Miss Lily Whitby. Are you from London?"

"No. Are you?" She still sat with her hands folded neatly in her lap as if they were at tea and half the *ton* were present. Would she ever reveal her interest in tracking him through the streets of London today? She didn't seem disposed to offering any information about herself.

Perhaps if he spoke freely, she would as well. "God, no," he said. "My home is in North Yorkshire. I've only been forced to endure the city recently."

She was looking like a tightly bound ball of nerves as two large men sat down at the table beside theirs and began a loud conversation about bosoms. He shot one of the men a look that could slice tough meat and they quieted down. Lily, unfortunately, still looked ill at ease. She would never confide her reasons for following him if she felt uncomfortable. He sighed, not sure how to calm her.

She looked like a bird about to take flight as she asked, "Say, do you have the time?" Her eyes flitted across his chest for a moment before returning to his eyes. What was that about? He supposed he would find out soon enough. How odd this encounter was becoming.

"Do you need to leave so soon? Our drinks look to be arriving."

Just then the barmaid set two large tankards on the rough wooden table between them. He watched Lily's eyes grow wide. She leaned forward and took a tentative sniff of the brew. Being made of Batavia Arrack, citrus fruits, spices, and sugar, it was a sweet drink, thick and soothing after a long day. This little tavern was the only place he'd managed to find rack punch outside the Antilles.

He took a swallow. It could also knock you on your arse if you had more than one. He smiled. This little meeting could get very interesting if she took a sip.

Her gaze turned thoughtful as she took in their surroundings once more and then glanced at him. What was she considering?

With a nod of agreement over some unsaid inner battle, she lifted the tankard to her lips and began to drink. "Gulped" was a more apt word because she did not come up for air for quite some time.

Devon chuckled. "Easy. It won't grow feet and walk away. You don't need to down it so fast." He watched as she drained half of her glass. "Or perhaps you do."

"Perhaps I do." She smiled. "I confess that I have not had the opportunity to do…" She broke off to wave her hand in the air indicating their surroundings. "Things like this. My home life, such that it has been, has not allowed for freedoms like time with friends or…" Her voice disappeared into a bubble of laughter that overtook her for a moment before she could continue. "It has not allowed time for me to eat or sleep. No, beverages partaken with strange men in taverns simply do not happen. Not to me."

He could see that the liquor she had just ingested was taking effect because her posture had relaxed a fraction. She glanced out the grimy window with a pensive frown. "This city doesn't seem at all bad to me. Then again, a crossroads with a flock of ducks would be more exciting than my life as of late."

"To be entertained by London, you must be easily entertained by society." He repeated the word, grinding it out with a clenched jaw: "*society*." He looked down at the table, studying the beverage in his hand. "I much prefer a life lived outside its constraints." He spun his tankard around in a slow circle on the table before him.

Glancing up, he noticed she was watching him. Wasn't he supposed to be interrogating her? He blinked away his disparaging thoughts about the London peerage and got back to his task. "Where is your home? Or do you no longer live there? You spoke of it as if you had moved away."

"Oh, I live there still. In a small town with no society to speak of. This is practically the first time I've left home, other than my time at finishing school." She tipped up her tankard, looking into its almost empty depths. "I used to look out at the sea that borders our estate and dream of traveling to distant lands." She set the stein down with a clink on the wooden table, looking at him with a dazzling smile. "You know, if a book exists on the subject of travel, I believe I have read it. However, London is as far as I have gotten as of yet."

His eyes flashed at her mention of travel. "An affinity for travel is something I can relate to." That was an understatement. "I spent five years on an expedition to Africa studying native plant life and geographical mapping. That was after a Himalayan Mountain excursion but before a brief stop off in Spain." But now he was home. His jaw clenched and he worked to keep the frown from his face.

"You have truly been to all of those places?" Her eyes widened and she leaned in toward the table with interest. "Tell me, are the Himalayas as magnificent as Mr. Childers Caldwell describes in *Flora and Fauna of the Himalayas*?"

"Ah, Mr. Caldwell. I met him once at a base camp." He shook his head over the memory of the obnoxious man. "He complained incessantly. It's a wonder he traveled anywhere beyond his own garden with the way he went on about the poor quality of the food, the cool weather, and the dirty, uneducated people. Quite annoying, really." He took a sip before continuing. "I later read his book and, to this day, suspect it may have been written by his traveling companion and passed off as his own work. But, yes, the descriptions of the grandness of the mountains were quite accurate."

"Have you written anything on the subject I might have read?" Lily asked.

"No, I haven't the patience to write a book. I presented the Royal Society with several plant specimens upon my latest return and wrote an article for a journal. It was a fascinating trip."

"I should read your journal article," she offered.

Was she truly interested in his travels? Who was Lily Whitby and where had she been hiding? He had decided all ladies were only concerned with hair ribbons and retelling the latest on-dit. How refreshing. Of course, she had followed him, so was she speaking the truth? She was still talking, he realized as he snapped his attention back to her.

"That was when I began to read every book in our library on farming techniques. Since then, my life has been completely absorbed in the workings of the land. So, clearly by this point, I could use some reading materials about unknown plants, as mine are a bit too known."

He laughed. She continued to surprise him at every turn. "I apologize. I'm only trying to picture you as a farmer."

"I do play a large role in the management of crop yields and plantings. But no, I do not reap the harvests with my own hands. My skills are better suited to poring over journals for modern farming techniques than digging in the dirt." She quirked the corner of her mouth in thought. "I would hate to see the state of things if I didn't do so."

"You are quite unexpected, Lily. Tell me more of your life." She was quite unexpected indeed. Wasn't he supposed to be gathering some information from her? Oh, her arrival, with the following business. Yes, he needed to get around to that eventually. For now, he wanted to hear of a life not lived within the bounds of London.

"My life is rather quiet. I won first prize for my La Belle Sultane roses last year at the parish rose festival. And I..." She grew quiet, looking down at her hands. Her gaze turned to his as she said, "I haven't lived a large life. Not like you. My adventures have all taken place between the pages of a book. Tell me more of your travels."

"I don't know. Your death-defying defeat of your enemies to claim first prize for your roses sounds fascinating," he quipped, taking another sip of his drink. "That breed is beautiful. They deepen to a dark purple with growth, don't they?"

"I can't believe you know of them," she said in amazement.

"Have you ever seen an African daisy? They grow wild on the plains. Their deep violet petals are pinched together in the center to make them look like tiny spoons around a black center."

"I would very much like to see that one day." She had a wistful look in her eye that he wished he could harness and hold in his palm forever.

"I had one brought back and placed in my gallery with the other plants and artifacts from my travels. When I long for a place other than London, those specimens of exotic culture keep me sane. I could show it to you." How ill-advised were his words? Would he scare her away or draw her in with his invitation? He waited for her reaction.

She blinked in surprise. "I meant that I would like to see it in its natural setting. I couldn't possibly go to your home. It wouldn't be…"

"Proper? Lily, haven't we covered this ground already? Consider it an open invitation from one plant admirer to another."

"I will consider it. Perhaps with an escort?" She took the last drink from her tankard, setting the empty vessel down on the table. She appeared to be lost in thought for a moment. When she looked up, she asked, "What made you return from your expeditions if you enjoy them so?"

He signaled the barmaid for two more drinks before answering. "Ah, um…there was a death." He dropped his gaze to the table for a moment. "I returned for the funeral services. Sorry to be morbid when we are just becoming acquainted."

"Duty to family is something I quite understand. My father passed recently, though I don't wish to speak of it now, either."

"It was my father's death that brought me home as well. I had to…take care of things here." Bury his father, take up his title, survive the ridicule of the *ton*…indeed, he'd been busy.

"One is never quite the same after a loss such as that. You have my condolences."

He dismissed her comment with a wave of his hand. He had no desire to discuss who he was—and who everyone in the *ton* perceived him to be.

"Life goes on and the sun still rises on us," she offered with a sympathetic tilt to her head.

"Yes, it does, but enough of this melancholy conversation." Two fresh drinks were placed before them. "Shall we?" he asked.

"Oh yes, another drink would be lovely."

Devon shook his head, wrapping his hand around the fresh tankard of sangaree before him. "This hasn't been the afternoon I'd imagined, yet I can't say I'm regretting it."

Lily grinned in return. "I had thought to do some shopping today. I don't know that I would have had the nerve to leave my home if I had thought this was where the afternoon would find me."

Holding up his tankard toward her, he offered, "To unexpected meetings and exotic flowers. Or should I say unexpected meetings *with* exotic flowers? Either way, it is a fine way to spend the day."

Devon watched as her blush deepened, spreading up her neck. She smiled a smile that would keep him warm on endless damp English days.

"To exotic flowers and strange men," she returned between laughs, then took a drink. "This is really quite delicious. I had always thought liquor to be harsh, dark brews of liquid fire."

"You must keep strong spirits in your home. Some liquors do seem to be constructed of nothing but fire, not all though." He leaned one forearm on the table with a grin. "I once had a sweet wine made from small blossoms of a tree that grows at the base of the Himalayas." He lowered his voice as he continued, "I woke up a day later in clothes I didn't own, hanging upside down bound in tree vines." He sat back, smiling at her astonishment. "Trust me. It doesn't need to be a harsh, dark brew to throw you for a loop."

"Oh my! How'd you find yourself in that predicament?"

"Although I'm sure it is an exciting tale of drunken debauchery, I regret to say I have no memory of it." He shrugged. "I later found out that the wine I was served was typically used in small doses for ceremonial purposes to introduce young warriors to their spirit companions. I, however, had a guide with a regrettable sense of humor who plied me with the concoction the night before we were set to leave camp."

"Oh dear." She laughed, her blue eyes dancing at his story. He would tell a thousand stories a thousand times over only to watch those bright eyes laugh. By the third tankard of drink, she'd removed her hideous hat and laid it on the table. Her golden blond hair was tumbling down around her face. He had never seen a sight so beautiful. Perhaps she had followed him here for some unknown reason. Yet, those reasons were lost at the bottom of their empty steins.

The afternoon turned to dusk over stories of his adventures and hints of her serene country life. Soon the tavern grew louder as more patrons entered and more drinks were poured. He really should escort her back to her home for her own safety, yet he could not bring himself to end their afternoon together.

"Lily, how is it that we've never met until this day?"

She paused, her smile fading as her eyes dimmed to a thoughtful expression. "Devon, the truth is this. I have spent the past six years tending to my—"

She screamed as one of the large men from the table beside them descended on her, taking one of her breasts in his filthy palm.

Devon was out of his chair and over the table in a heartbeat. He and the man toppled to the floor together. His fist connected with the man's jaw.

How dare he touch Lily in that manner?

Devon swung again, hearing the snap of the man's nose breaking as blood flew everywhere. But the contact with the man's face didn't ease the rage that coursed through Devon's veins over this stranger laying a finger on Lily.

Another blow blackened the man's eye. He should have been more aware of his surroundings.

Picking up the limp body under him by the shirt, Devon pummeled him another time. He should have known that something like this would happen in such a hovel of a tavern. If he had not been so starry-eyed over his drinking companion, he may have noticed the man approaching.

How could he have allowed that to happen? The man's friend was now pulling at Devon's shoulder.

Through the haze of anger and splattered blood he heard, "Just a bet, gov'na. Meant no offense." Devon released the shirt held tightly in his grasp, dropping the man's limp weight to the floor.

Standing, he glanced around at Lily to find her standing pressed against the dirty window, her eyes glazed over in shock. He spun on his heel, threatening the man at his back, "Next time you choose to wager, choose someone else's lady. For if you or anyone else ever lays a hand on her again, I'll come back here and kill you with my bare hands."

"I don't doubt it, sir. I'll never disrespect your lady again, sir."

"See that you don't," Devon sneered as he turned away.

He stepped over the unconscious man on the floor and held his hand out toward Lily. Pausing for only a moment of indecision, she laid her hand in his and allowed him to lead her to the door. Her hand trembled slightly in his. Had the man hurt her? Was she traumatized by what she had seen Devon do? Now she would think him a brute. They didn't speak a word to one another as they walked past the bar, back to the entrance.

The sounds and smells of the tavern died instantly as the door closed behind them, replaced by the musty scent of coming rain and a baby crying somewhere on the next block. He looked down at Lily standing at his side. Her hand was still wrapped in his and he did not want to let it go. Not now. Not here on the street. Perhaps not ever. She stared straight ahead without a word.

"Are you injured?" When Lily didn't answer, Devon turned her cheek so that she was looking into his eyes. "Lily, are you injured?"

"I don't think so." She licked her pink lips. "But I do feel a bit off."

"A bit off," he repeated. "Not hurt?"

"No, but I'm dizzy and my head feels rather hollow." She tapped the side of her head as if checking it for fullness.

"Do you mean you're foxed?" He couldn't help the grin that tilted the corners of his mouth up.

"Is that what I am? My, but I have never experienced this before." A bubble of laughter escaped her as she began to list sideways into him like a ship on stormy seas.

His arms rose immediately to steady her. Where was a hack when he needed one? She was in no condition to walk back to Bond Street. Glancing up and down the street, he assessed which direction would take them out of this area of town the fastest.

They had spent longer inside the tavern than he realized, for the sun was beginning its descent, gleaming off windows on the opposite side of the street while they stood in the shadows. Before long, these streets would begin to crawl with pickpockets and light skirts out to make some coin. It was no place for a lady, and certainly not one who was foxed for the first time. Had she said "the first time"? How was that possible?

Then, as if conjured by a magician, a hack rattled around the corner. Devon's arm flew up in signal and the carriage slowed. He opened the door and led her forward toward the step.

"You've never been foxed before? How old are you?" His curiosity over this woman was mounting, which was a bit disconcerting.

"Three and twenty last month. But there was never any time for that, and…" She turned to him, shaking her finger in imitation of some apparently extremely crotchety old man as she said, "…young ladies don't do that." She giggled. "You know what, though? I don't know why not. This is terribly fun."

"I am in complete agreement with you there." He half assisted, half hoisted her into the carriage. "It makes all of life's ugly realities disappear. For a few blessed hours anyway.

"Where should I tell the driver to take you, Lily?" Devon entered the carriage after her, sitting on the seat to her left. She widened her eyes a fraction but said nothing. He supposed the gentlemanly thing to do would have been to sit opposite her on that large, empty bench seat, but he wasn't feeling very gentlemanly at the moment. Too many sangarees would do that to a man.

"Oh…um…I'm not sure where to go from here."

"I find that I'm not ready to return home, either," he agreed.

"Yes. That must be it. Too much fun and all."

"I'll instruct the driver to take a turn around the park for a bit while we come to our senses, shall I? I can't very well deliver you to your home in this condition anyway."

"To my home, yes. I couldn't possibly go there just now. I didn't realize how much I'd consumed until I stood up when that man grabbed me. By that time, the fight was all around me and…" She looked down and instantly went into alarm. "Devon! Your hand! You're bleeding!"

"That does tend to happen when you punch a man in the face. It's only a scratch." He inspected the back of his knuckles with a frown. "I believe I removed his tooth, if that brings you any comfort."

She pulled open the reticule at her wrist and retrieved a small square handkerchief. "Give me your hand."

When he hesitated, she held out her hand and motioned for him to comply. Something in the tilt of her head and the look in her eyes made him wonder if she had played nursemaid before. He had been bandaged as a boy too many times to count and knew the look of efficiency and experience at once.

Who was she and who had she cared for before?

An odd sense of jealousy bit at him, which was completely irrational since he had only met her today. Whoever had benefited from her care in the past was irrelevant. Bringing his mind back to the present, he offered her his hand with the bloody knuckles.

As she began to wrap the handkerchief around his hand, tying it neatly at the corners, he could not pull his focus from the feel of her fingers on his palm. The light, glancing touches made him want more. He cleared his throat. "I cannot imagine what gave him the idea that he could take such liberties with you. That oaf in the tavern, I mean."

Her face flooded with color as she looked down at herself in an assessing manner. "I don't know, either! No man has ever tried to do anything like that. Although I have never before squeezed into one of Mama's old dresses." Her mouth closed abruptly, and her eyes widened as if she realized she had said something inappropriate.

"This isn't how you usually dress?"

"Heavens no," was her only response, clearly closing the door on the subject. "There you are. You will want to clean that and bandage it properly when you get home."

The handkerchief was wound and tied neatly around his hand with a perfect knot in the center. He couldn't imagine that he could do a better job of it once home. He tended not to bandage his scratches anyway. Life aboard a ship had taught him that fresh air and sunshine healed better than any bandage. He shrugged off the advice and lifted his gaze to Lily.

His eyes lingered on the view of exposed pale skin her dress offered before meeting those clear blue eyes. Her breasts were displayed like delicious cakes in a baker's window. He kept his eyes on hers but could not seem to control his fingers as they greatly desired to dip into the cake frosting before him and take a large lick.

"I rather like your dress." He ran his fingers over the row of lace that trimmed the deep neckline, skating one finger along the creamy skin it exposed. He watched as she swallowed and looked back into his eyes. She did not flinch or pull away as he had expected her to. Even when foxed, ladies tended to attempt an air of propriety, in his experience. But Lily was not like other ladies. That much he knew.

"Did he bruise you here? When he grabbed you?"

"No," she whispered.

"Good. I would hate to have to return to the tavern to kill him." His finger traced back across the lace, almost touching her skin but not daring to do so.

"Don't leave."

She had only spoken two small words, yet they pounded in his ears with joy. She wanted him to stay. She wanted to be with him. It took every fiber of his control not to dive onto her right there, in the back of a hired carriage as it jostled down the street. But Lily deserved better than that. She had recently been mauled by a drunken ruffian, and he didn't want to be the second in line for that honor this day. No, he would take his time with her. They had all evening to be together, after all.

"I won't leave. You've been through quite a trial. And I'm not inclined to leave you just now anyway." Emboldened by her words, he trailed the backs of his fingers over one creamy mound and watched as it rose and fell with her quickened breaths.

Lifting the pearl necklace from her throat, he ran a finger under it, gently pulling her closer. Her eyes blinked once, then twice, before fluttering shut as his lips met hers.

It was a sweet kiss, the innocent kiss of someone who'd only read and heard of kisses but had never experienced one firsthand. He almost chuckled. Kissing her once more in the reverent manner she must have envisioned was appropriate, he allowed her to grow comfortable with his closeness.

Sliding one hand around the back of her neck, he held her still while he increased the intensity, his lips searching hers, his quiet request becoming a demanding growl. She made a small squeak of alarm as his tongue slid past her teeth. Then she leaned into him in a blatant plea for more. Her citrus-flavored mouth was soft and willing under his lips. He felt her hand reach for his shoulder, landing light and shaky as if she was afraid to touch him.

His arm slipped around her waist, wrapping around her, pulling her closer. The contact was not enough. He needed more. She must have felt the same, for she pushed closer to him, her breasts pressed against his chest. In that small motion, she seemed to let go of all pretense of ladylike behavior, because she then slid her hands into his hair and began to kiss him back, mimicking every flick of his tongue and press of his lips.

He lifted her and set her on his lap. Breaking contact with her lips, he trailed kisses across her cheek to tug on her earlobe with his teeth, kissing his way down the slim column of her neck. Her hands wound around the back of his neck, twining his hair between her fingers.

His lips paused at the base of her throat to suck on the point where her pulse pounded wildly. Her head fell back on a moan.

He kissed his way down the expanse of exposed skin at her neck, wanting to feel her body, to taste her. The contact was not enough, but her large dress would not allow him the access he so desired. He pushed down the piles of fabric bunched between them to run his hands over her thin yet curved frame, only to have her skirts bounce back to block his path. He groaned in frustration only to hear her giggle over his difficulties with her dress.

"You find this amusing, do you?"

"Only a bit." She offered him a dreamy smile as

her eyes dropped to his lips and her smile faded. She kissed him again, the intensity growing with every passing second. The carriage hit a bump and their heads collided, breaking the moment that could have drawn out forever.

He chuckled and set her back on the seat at his side, watching her rub her forehead with a frown. "The back of a carriage is no place to do this."

"Yes. I can see now the dangers involved," she said with a crooked smile.

"Lily, you have no idea the danger you are in at the moment." He ran the backs of his fingers down the line of her jaw, watching as she tried to decipher his words of warning.

"Am I?"

"Only if you wish to be."

A silence fell between them as they gazed into each other's eyes. All that could be heard for the next few minutes was the gentle clip-clop of the horse's hooves hitting the cobblestone road. He did not want to leave her on some doorstep and have this day end.

"I want to show you my gallery this evening. Come home with me."

She sat watching him for a moment with pursed lips. "What if someone sees me? Sees us...alone...in your gallery?"

"I live alone and have well-compensated servants. I'll show you the findings from my travels." *Please say yes*, he pleaded in silence.

She took a deep breath, her eyes never leaving his. "Yes. To see your plantings and artifacts, I will come."

Devon released the breath he'd been holding as a smile spread across his face. He would not have to leave her. Not yet.

Two

Her hand slid across the sheet to remove the hot blanket placed on her during the night. Why was her pillow fluffed so high? When had her bed become this soft? Nothing felt right. Just then her hand encountered the thickly muscled forearm wrapped around her body.

"Blast it all." Lillian murmured the pained whisper into the darkness. "What have I gotten myself into?"

The sinewy man at her side shifted in his sleep, sliding his hand across her skin to rest his warm fingers over her breast, anchoring her to the bed and pulling her closer. She inhaled a quick breath as the previous night's activities came rushing back to her mind in sharp relief. Bond Street, the tavern, the drinks, Devon. That was his name, was it not?

Yes, Devon Grey, that was it. The way he kissed her lips, her body, and, oh my, she had allowed him to… She glanced down to confirm the disturbing fact that she had on not a stitch of clothing.

How had she let this simple plan go so horribly awry? The warmth of his body seeped into her spine, his deep breaths fanning over her hair where it spilled onto the pillow behind her. Something hard ground into her back. Mortification flushed her cheeks at the thought of what it must be. Before last night she would have thought he slept with a pistol, but this morning she knew differently.

She needed to be gone from this place soon, away from his sinful kisses, away from the reckless behavior he encouraged and the risk of falling back into his arms again. She had already allowed things to go too far. Who could blame her? But an evening together was all that could ever be between them. This was certainly why it was not advisable to drink large amounts of liquor with a man.

Lillian shifted in the largest movement she dared, a minute shiver, moving away from the man at her side. When he did not stir she wiggled again, sliding gently to the edge of the bed. Kicking with one foot, she tried to untangle her bare limbs from the sheets. Yet they held her, binding her to his bed. With another swift thrust, she found herself falling to the carpeted floor. Landing on her hands, she winced at the sharp pain stabbing through her wrist and mouthed a silent "ouch" in the darkness.

After hanging there by her ankles with the cool morning air chilling her skin and her rear exposed to anyone who happened to be peering in the windows, she pulled her legs free and began to crawl toward the foot of the bed. This was certainly a new experience, creeping out of a man's bedchamber before dawn in the buff. She'd claimed to want more adventure in her life, but somehow this was not what she had in mind.

The sound of a carriage rolling down the street quickened her pace. Soon the muted glow of daylight would spread, spilling its warmth across the city. She must get away before one of Devon's household staff caught sight of her. They would certainly be up soon. She gained her footing and rounded the corner of the poster bed, still crouching low—as she imagined was the proper way to sneak about a strange man's room in the dark. Lillian spotted her chemise where it had landed in a heap by the door.

Rounding the far side of the bed, she searched for her corset. The floor creaked under her bare foot, freezing her movements.

Holding her breath, her eyes shot to the bed, but Devon had not heard the noise. Taking a shallow breath to steady her nerves, she took another step, willing the floor to allow her a silent escape.

Where had she left her corset? Her eyes searched the darkness, yet saw nothing. For that matter, where were her half boots and reticule? And more importantly—where was her dress? Her fingers slipped around one stocking, pulling it from the bedside table. Where was the other? None of her clothing seemed to be in the room. Last night's events were a bit blurred by the pounding in her head. She rubbed her forehead in an effort to make sense of her jumbled memories.

Last evening we paused on the landing of the stairs.

❦

He'd kissed his way down her neck, his lips lingering on the base of her throat where her pearls encircled it. She arched into his body, the masculine feel of his hands on her more intoxicating than the drinks they had shared. There were too many layers of clothing between them, even with her dress gone. She wanted to feel his skin against hers. Her fingers clutched his dark hair, pulling him closer. It wasn't enough. She strained against the bounds of her corset with a shallow breath and exhaled on a quiet huff.

He chuckled against her skin, the sound rough and enticing as the deep tone reverberated through her body. "Patience, Lily. I'll have you free of this contraption in a moment."

There was a yank on her corset ties, pulling her back toward the edge of the stairs, accompanied by the sound of ripping fabric. He flung the garment away and gathered her to his body. Her hands slid to his chest as she gazed into his stormy blue eyes. His lips descended on hers again, kissing her with growing need.

She slipped the wool coat from his broad shoulders with frantic movements. She could feel his hot, muscled skin beneath his shirtsleeves. *More*. Her hands tangled in the knots of his cravat as their kiss deepened, tongues tasting, demanding. Her fingers skimmed his exposed neck, and she heard an answering growl from deep within his chest.

He lifted her straight up, her toes just touching the edges of the stairs as he carried her. She wound her arms around Devon's neck, his shirt gently abrading her taut nipples with every step. She wanted something, some indescribable something. All she knew was that he could provide it. His kiss. His skin. His hands. She needed him.

She bit at his lip and he turned in an instant,

pressing her against the wall of the stairs. He held her suspended there as he pressed his body against hers. "Lily." He murmured the name against her lips. "If you keep that up, we will not reach the top of the stairs."

"Oh, I don't want us to fall. I only…" She became lost in the thought as she stared at his lips inches from hers. She kissed him again. He ground his hips into hers in a way that made her breathless and flushed.

"It is not the fall that has me concerned," he said, thrusting his hips into hers once more and watching as she gasped. She wanted to wrap her long legs around him, pull him in, and keep him there. What was he doing to her?

Confusion fell away to sensation as his hands skimmed down the outsides of her breasts, slid over her waist, and drifted down her hips to her bottom, lifting her to him. Only the thin film of her chemise separated his large male hands from her. How did he know what she wanted? He took a few more steps up with her anchored to him, kissing his way up her cheek and into her hair. She returned the favor, kissing the side of his neck before biting at his ear.

In an instant she collided once more with the wall as he slashed his lips across hers in a deep, demanding, ravishing kiss. He pulled back to smile at her. It was a roguish smile, the smile a wolf might give a small rabbit just before dining on bunny ears. "As much as I enjoy these stairs, darling, I would like to see the top of them eventually."

"I thought you scaled mountains for sport. This is but a little staircase."

"I scaled mountains for science, and I was not hard as rock for a minx I carried in my arms at the time."

"Your muscles feel quite pliable to me, not at all like rock." Her hands skimmed his arms with gentle grasping motions, trying to feel the rock he was speaking of.

He laughed as he began to climb the stairs once more. "You are delightful, Lily Whitby."

She was confused by his remarks but had no time to consider them for they had reached the second floor of his home and he was kissing her again. They stumbled past a table and she heard something fall. He dropped her onto a settee and bent over her with a bright gleam in his eyes.

"We survived the stairs, perilous journey that it was. We must still venture down the hallway. I promised to show you my gallery. Of course my bedchamber is also down that hallway."

"The hallway just there?"

"Yes. Where shall I take you, m'lady?" Devon waited, looking deep into her eyes as the question he was truly asking sank into her bones.

This had been a grand adventure that kept lasting just a bit longer, then a bit longer after that bit. Yet it all had led to this moment. She felt her head nod *yes* with a nervous smile before she could think it through further. He brushed the backs of his fingers across her cheek in response as a smile creased the corners of his eyes. Some emotion lingered there. Was it hope, or longing? Perhaps something else she did not recognize. Before she could analyze it, his head bent.

He kissed her wrist, her shoulder, her collarbone.

Moving down her body he suckled her breast through the chemise, nipping at its peak with his teeth. "So beautiful." His voice rumbled through her body as his hands skimmed her waist and hips.

He pulled at the lace edge of the thin garment with his teeth. She felt the cool air hit her skin as he gathered the chemise around her waist. His fingers slid up the inside of her thigh to come to rest on the apex of her legs.

She took a shallow breath. Their gazes connected, neither daring to look away.

He kissed her gently as his finger slipped into her depths. She clutched his shoulders, wanting more but scared to ask. He coaxed her, his thumb gently rubbing as his finger slid farther into her.

Her thighs fell apart on a moan. *Oh my.* Had she made that sound? She would be embarrassed if he would stop to allow her to think. "Oh Devon," she said against his lips.

"Yes, Lily. That's it, Lily. God, I want you, Lily." He said her name like a prayer in the candlelit hallway.

A maddening tension was building within her. She arched her body into his wicked hand. His fingers worked in ceaseless thrusts. They pulled her asunder into scattered pieces of her former self. She clung to him, anchoring him to her as she splintered apart and collapsed under him.

He smoothed her hair from her face with a reverence that made her melt into the soft settee. The look of promise and compassion in his eyes had held her captivated as he carefully righted her remaining clothing. His fingers had threaded into the laces of her boots as he pulled first one, then the other from her feet with care.

❧

She blinked, and the memory slid away like a dew droplet rolling from the petal of a flower. It had been the most marvelous night of her life.

If memories could be trusted, her clothes were not in this room. She grimaced at the delay. Devon turned in his sleep, his hand resting where her hip had been only moments ago. If only things were different. Deciding to abandon her corset to get done what must be done, she turned, searching in the near-dark room for Devon's discarded clothing.

Spying his waistcoat, her fingers frantically dipped into his pockets and grabbed at the fabric until she found what had brought about this entire incident. Yes, that was it. That was the way she would think about last evening. Incidents could be ignored as if they never happened. No one could ever find out what she'd done. If only she could forget.

Lillian grasped his pocket watch in her fist and breathed a sigh of relief. Running her thumb over its cool surface, she took comfort from the weight of it in her hand—solid, heavy, and hers. A grim smile tugged at her mouth in the darkness. Finally. Now all she needed was to find her dratted clothing and flee.

A grumble sounded from the bed as Devon rolled over in his sleep. She stood watching him for a moment, knowing that with every passing second the sun rose a little higher in the sky and her ability to vanish into the night was becoming more difficult. However, she found it hard to turn away from him.

His coal-black hair curled ever so slightly across his brow, and the strong features she remembered from last night softened with sleep, giving him the face of innocence on a world-hardened body. It was too bad that she would not be able to gaze into his eyes once more. She wanted to solidify the look of storm clouds rolling in over the sea forever in her mind. How she wished she could talk with him once more and make him understand.

Her eyes raked over him, memorizing every muscle, every inch of exposed male skin. The sheet had fallen to show the thin trail of dark hair that led to...well, best not to think about where it led just now. Lillian scolded herself as she turned to leave. Scooping up her chemise from the floor, she slipped it over her head as she took one more step closer to the door, closer to escape.

Last night with Devon would no doubt be her one and only experience with a man. Things should never have gone this far with him, but since they had, she would silently cherish the night they spent together. He would live forever in her memories as she went quietly into spinsterhood. Clutching the pocket watch in her hand, Lillian gazed one last time at where he lay on the bed before closing the door to his bedchamber with a soft click.

This was the beginning of the rest of her life. So why did it cause this tightening of her chest? *What a mess you are, Lillian.* She shook her head and looked around to gain her bearings in the dark house.

Tiptoeing down the hallway, she was keenly aware of her current state of undress and the potential to be discovered by a maid lighting a morning fire.

Rounding a corner, she spotted her half boots beside the settee in an alcove opposite the stairs. Sticking her feet inside them, she paused to right a vase of flowers on a nearby table. Most of the flowers were scattered across the floor, but time could not be taken to tidy all. She compromised her need for order by straightening the paintings knocked askew on her way down the stairs. Grabbing her corset where it lay draped over the banister on the landing, she continued down, spying her dress piled on the third step from the bottom.

She'd managed to gather the dress around her slender frame, with buttons splayed open down her back, and was stuffing her one stocking and the pocket watch into her reticule by the front door when the butler rounded the corner into view.

She spun, keeping her back to the door so that the open buttons would not be visible. He froze. They stood staring at one another for what felt like an eternity. He appeared not to know what to do, and as it happened, neither did she. However, the longer she stood there in a staring contest, the more likely they were to be found by another servant.

Was exposing one's back to an unknown butler in London the worst crime in history?

She took a slow step sideways for the door. His eyes widened. He took a step forward. Lillian inhaled a shallow breath. It was now or never, and never was not an option. Another moment ticked by before she turned and flung the door open, fleeing into the cool morning air.

With the last rebellious fiber of her body, she flung her corset high into the air in farewell and looked back over her bare shoulder at the scandalized butler before hitching up her skirts and running toward the open garden gate.

❧

Devon woke in his bed just as he did every morning. He swung his legs over to find the floor with his feet. It was only then that his mind caught up with his body.

He had not been alone last night.

As the memories began to fall into place in his mind, he turned to find the bed empty at his back. The rumpled indentation marking the place where someone had slept beside him was all that remained. She was gone. He glanced around for a note or some token from her, feeling like a disappointed light skirt as he did so. Rolling his eyes at his own sentimentality, he got to his feet.

It was then he saw the edge of lace peeking out from under his pillow. Perhaps she had left some memento for him. His chest tightened at the idea. Pulling it free, he let the thin silk slide across his fingers. The smell of rosewater filled his lungs.

"Lily," he mumbled. Only a single cream-colored stocking remained as evidence Lily even existed. A grim smile curled his lips.

Lily had been the perfect distraction to his sour mood. He could not remember a time when he had enjoyed anyone as much. He never brought a lady back to his residence, wherever that may be, but somehow Lily had slipped past his guarded exterior. Even in his drink-fogged head, he could remember laughing with her and seeing her intense blue eyes bright with excitement. Then, the night with her had come.

Devon sighed, remembering the feel of her lips, her reaction to his kisses, and the curves of her body pressed against his. Now, she was gone. She had vanished like the memory of a dream that would not quite remain within his grasp. How could he find her?

Dragging a hand through his hair, he staggered across the room, gathering his discarded clothing as he went. His head felt as if it had been trampled by a coach and eight. He would have to get Cook to fix some of her special tonic. That and a cup of coffee, and he might survive the day. How late was it, anyway? The sun was up. He began digging in his pockets for his new pocket watch and came up empty-handed. His gaze turned to the rug under his feet, but the watch was not there, either. Stooping to look under the bed, all he saw was the dark floor. He could remember its weight in his pocket last night, yet it was no longer there.

His watch was gone. "What bloody time is it, then?" His voice echoed off the walls of his bedchamber.

For a moment he stood thinking through the possibilities of where it could be. His mind steadily avoided one obvious conclusion at least three times before settling there with some resentment. Lily had stolen it. And now she was gone.

"That little thief!" he grumbled, gazing once again at the empty bed where she had lain only hours earlier. Had that been her plan from the beginning? Something akin to hurt unfurled inside Devon. He brushed the emotion away, concentrating on how she had accomplished this feat.

No one took advantage of him, and certainly not a woman such as Lily Whitby. Had she known he was going to the Stag and Doe? Had she spied him there in recent weeks? Perhaps she had followed him all the way from the shop where he purchased the damned watch. He was dressed before his thoughts were even in order. With his headache forgotten, Devon strode out the door. Lily would rue the day she tangled with the Mad Duke of Thornwood.

⤳

The laughter was still bubbling up in her throat as Lillian turned the corner onto a street already bustling with early morning activity. What a reckless trollop she was turning into. The cool air whipped through her loose blond hair. She breathed in great gulps. This must be the feeling of rebellion. My, but she could see its appeal. Yet rebellion did not seem to encompass what she was experiencing.

"Freedom." The word tripped from her tongue with an answering smile. A hack was rumbling down the street toward her. Throwing up a hand, she watched as it slowed to a stop beside her and the driver jumped down.

"The Cross Keys Inn, north of the city, to reach the stage coach before it leaves in two hours, if you please."

"Ma'am," the driver offered in response as he opened the door to the conveyance. Then he tipped his hat and raked his eyes over her in an assessing manner that made her all too aware of her attire.

As she climbed up, she looked back in the driver's direction to add, "Make all haste." She really should try to pull herself together before arriving at the inn filled with travelers.

Settling onto the carriage seat as the door closed, she was thankful for every turn of the wheels that took her farther from Devon's home. It was done, the ordeal concluded. And now she was alone, as always. Her lingering smile faded as she watched the buildings move past the window.

There was no reason to ever think about last night again—except that she could not tear her mind away from it. There was a certain soreness between her legs, and the memories of his hands on her skin remained like ink on paper. What had she done?

She hadn't even used her real name. Shameful. Miss Lillian Phillips. Was that so very difficult to say? It was a good thing she *had* used a false name, now that she'd had relations with him. She gave the empty carriage a satisfied huff. Devon would never find her now.

Only, a wave of grief washed through her, filling the place where relief should be. She had lied to him. She told herself last night that if her name was false and no one found out, it didn't matter. None of it mattered. None of it was real. Why then did everything that passed between them feel so real?

In any other circumstance, she would go immediately and apologize. Yet that was the one thing she could never do. No. She had deceived Devon and stolen from him. Stolen! She ran a shaky hand over the pearl necklace at her throat. She should have found another way. She should have discussed it with Devon last night. She should have done anything but what she did.

She was unsure what had been in those drinks at the Stag and Doe, or how she had let things go so far with a man she did not even know. Devon Grey. She knew little of him aside from his name, for goodness' sake. What had she been thinking?

An incident such as this would obviously not happen at another point in the future. She would never see him again. No one knew she had even gone to London, and no one would ever find out. She made a vow there on the carriage seat that she would take this secret to her grave. She alone would know of her actions. She alone would remember the feel of his hands on her body and his lips on hers. He would forever be her private thought.

On lonely nights when the moon stretched long shadows across her bedchamber floor, she would think of him. She knew now what it was to desire. She knew the taste of a man and the uncontrolled pleasure that could be found in a man's skilled hands. She knew what it felt like to sleep curled within strong arms.

The memories of him were enough to last a lifetime. They would have to be, for she would never allow it to happen again.

She set the memories aside to pull her hair into its customary tightly knotted style at the back of her neck and buttoned her dress as high as she could reach at her back. That would have to do for now. Hopefully she would have time to change back into her black mourning dress at the inn before the coach left for Whitby.

She pulled the pocket watch from her reticule and opened it. She had an hour and forty minutes. The steady tick-tick-tick reminded her of why she had traveled so far, why she had abandoned her morals and allowed life to sweep her away like yesterday's ashes.

Her situation could be worse. With none of her family around Bixley Manor, she was free to live her life as she pleased. She would spend the rest of her days eating only the foods that she liked, reading only the books that she liked, walking to only the destinations she liked... Her mind grew quiet around the thought that she would be doing all of those things alone. Forever.

Nevertheless, she would not have to bend to the wishes of any man. Of that she was quite certain. Perhaps spinsterhood would be just the thing. With a nod of agreement, she looked down at the open pocket watch held in her tight grasp. It was the only piece of any man that she would ever need.

Yet, as she gazed down into the sapphire eyes of the fox engraved into its surface, it seemed to be mocking her. "I know your secrets," she could almost hear the fox say. "It was only last night that you were in the arms of my true owner. Thief! You were not so independent then."

"Hush now," Lillian spoke clearly to the small golden fox. She could not dwell on last night just now.

Jostling and bumping down the road, the carriage tossed Lillian across the thinly padded seat. The chain of the pocket watch slipped through her fingers as they rounded a corner. Tightening her grip, she braced her arm on the window of the carriage. The sun caught the watch face, filling the carriage with dancing circles of light. Happy, twirling, rainbow-filled circles.

Surely it was a sign of good things to come. A promise. The backs of her eyes stung with unshed tears but this moment was no time to allow them to fall. Sniffing, she snapped the pocket watch closed, shutting the door on her emotions and the source of lighted dots in the carriage.

Slowly, the stone buildings of London grew sparse as they left the city behind. The morning sun streamed in the carriage window beside her as Lillian gazed out across a field of grazing sheep. Stone walls lined the pasture land as if squares had been drawn in chalk across the vast green of the earth.

Her eyes grew hazy as the scenery streamed past and she became aware of her own reflection in the window. Touching her mother's pearls visible at her throat, she began to feel more confident. It was as if generations of feminine strength passed into her fingertips as they slid over the strand. Bump, bump, bump under her fingers, her courage rising with every pass of her hand.

With the pearls at her throat, the watch held securely in her grasp, and her secret held safe in her heart forevermore, she faced forward into her future.

❧

After a trip to the Stag and Doe tavern to no avail, Devon slowed his steps before the Bond Street shop. He would rather be pecked to death by waterfowl than return to Habersham's Antiquities and Fine

Artifacts that afternoon. Unfortunately, that was the only way he would ever discover where to find Miss Lily Whitby. She had taken something from him and he wanted it back. After all, he didn't know the time, thanks to the damned chit.

Certainly it had nothing to do with being bested by a mysterious woman with whom he had shared an amazing night. She had stolen from him! From him, Thornwood! No one in their right mind would dare do such a thing. He was the Mad Duke after all, or so all of London society said. Grimacing over the source of his so-called madness, he entered the shop prepared to deal with the nosy shopkeeper once again.

His booted feet landed heavily on the floor in long, angry strides. The small bell on the door was still tinkling in the background as he approached the jewelry display case at the rear of the shop.

"Good afternoon, my lord. You have returned," the shopkeeper intoned as he laid aside the necklace he had been polishing. He pushed his glasses up from where they hung on the end of his long nose as he asked, "Was the watch not to your liking?"

Good afternoon…how late was it? Was it not still morning? "Afternoon," Devon conceded. "I find myself in need of another watch."

"Another watch, my lord? What drama has befallen you today?" the man asked with an edge of eagerness to his voice.

Devon had endured enough. His patience snapped. He wanted answers, not more questions. "You may call me Thornwood or Your Grace, thank you. I would like to purchase another watch."

"Your Gr…" The man seemed to choke on the words, flushing a brilliant red. "Certainly, Your Grace. Anything for you, Your Grace."

That was more like it. Perhaps his title did have its uses on occasion. "I would like to see that watch there, and this one as well." He pointed at the display case before him. It was hard to believe he was revisiting this process only a day after he found a watch he was quite fond of. All because of her!

The shopkeeper retrieved the watches and laid them out on a piece of velvet for inspection. His mouth, unlike yesterday, was silent.

"This one will do." Devon indicated the watch on the right, with small scrollwork etched into gold around its white face.

"Very well, Your Grace." The man gave an excessive bow from behind the counter before wrapping the package with care.

Devon methodically rapped one long finger on the glass surface before him. There was no discreet way of asking if the man knew of Lily but to ask it. As much as Devon disliked the idea of the shopkeeper knowing anything of his private affairs, he alone might hold the knowledge of the whereabouts of one Lily Whitby, seductress and thief.

Resigned to the fate of conversing with the man who had proved quite annoying yesterday, Devon heaved a sigh before uttering a word. There was nothing for it; he must ask. "Was there a woman in blue in your shop after I was here yesterday?"

"Why yes, Your Grace," the shopkeeper returned, a frown forming on his face.

"Does she come here often?" Devon leaned in, anticipating the answers he sought.

"There was something familiar about her, but perhaps she has one of those faces that one sees everywhere about town."

Devon did not think there was anything common about Lily's face, and he'd never seen anything or anyone like her before. "She was familiar to you, then? She has purchased things from you before, perhaps?"

"No, not until yesterday. And she only paid for half of the pearls she ran out of here wearing."

Devon remembered the pearls at her throat last night and quickly suppressed the distracting image. "Ah, she stole a necklace. Have you reported the theft?"

"No, Your Grace." The man paused, loosening the collar of his shirt with one finger in his discomfort. "I had just put those pearls out on display, you see. I received them as part of an estate that was let go. I put a…well, a rather high price on the piece because I was hoping the family would choose to buy it back."

"Why would they do that?"

"Pardon me, Your Grace, but if you had seen the fit the lady threw when I came to appraise some of the furnishings, you wouldn't be asking that. Half my storage area behind the shop is filled with their treasures at the moment. Just didn't have the heart to sell it off without giving them a chance to reconsider."

"That's…kind of you," Devon responded cautiously. He had never known a shopkeeper to be accommodating in such situations and had doubts about the honesty of the man's words. There must be some hidden benefit to his actions. "It's too bad, then, that the necklace was stolen by the woman in blue."

"'Stolen' is a strong word in this case since she paid about the price of its actual worth. She wasn't a true thief, if you look at it in that light."

"Yes, indeed. She's not a true thief at all." Devon bristled at the words but did not want to tell the man the woman had followed him and stolen from him. He certainly didn't want to cover the details that came somewhere in the middle of this story.

"It is odd that you would ask after her, for she described the very watch you purchased. She wanted to purchase something with a fox decorating it—for her brother, I believe."

"Is that so?" Devon's jaw clenched. Her brother, indeed. Some man was now wearing his pocket watch. Anger bubbled beneath the surface of his skin but he suppressed it.

The shopkeeper nodded. "She ran from the store after I told her I had sold just such a watch only minutes prior."

"Did she? Interesting. Did she leave behind an address or a way she could be reached with you? A card perhaps?"

"No, I never even caught her name. She was in a terrible hurry, from the looks of it."

"I'm sure," Devon replied wryly. "I won't take any more of your time, then." He nodded his thanks, dropped a pile of coins on the counter to cover the cost of yet another timepiece, and turned for the door. His new pocket watch was in his hand, although he could not find any enthusiasm for the piece. His mind still lingered on the sapphire eyes gazing his way last night, and those of the small fox's as well.

He had nowhere else to look. Lily Whitby was gone and his property with her. He walked out into the weak afternoon sun much as he had the day prior. Yet it seemed like his life had altered in drastic fashion from the previous day. He shook his head and started for home. Why could he not easily shake her hold on his memories?

Three

Bixley Manor, Whitby
One year later…

"THANK YOU," LILLIAN SAID TO A PASSING FOOTMAN as he took her hat and the basket filled with fresh flowers. She dusted off her skirts and patted her hair into place as she added, "The tulips are finally blooming. Aren't they lovely? I think they'll be perfect in the drawing room."

The weather seemed to have forgotten to be warm this spring. The months moved by on the calendar, yet the garden had remained frozen in a winter that would never end. When Lillian woke that day to find brilliant sun pouring in through the windows, she was outside in the garden within the hour.

With the basket now laden with cut flowers to cheer up the inside of her increasingly dreary home, she planned to get a bite to eat before returning to the garden with a good book. Having read all the available travel journals, she had moved on to a borrowed gothic novel. She simply had to know if Victoria would be rescued from the clutches of the madman keeping her in her tower. With her mind lingering on foreign castles and cloaked dangers, Lillian made her way toward the drawing room where she could have some tea.

It was only then that she heard male voices drifting from behind the mostly closed door to the library. She paused. Her eldest brother, Josiah, could occasionally be found skulking around the estate, but who was with him today? She stepped closer to the door to find out.

"She interferes with every change I put into place around here. Does she not know it is not her place to do so?" Josiah's voice rang out in indignation.

"Calm yourself, Josiah. Lillian is but a girl."

Lillian's reaction to the voice slid down her spine and landed like a rock in her stomach. Solomon. There was no mistaking the sound of her middle brother's distinctly cool tones.

When had he arrived?

Why were they discussing her behind mostly closed doors? She was bristling with anger as she inched closer to the doorway, being careful to stay out of sight.

"Calm? Do you know what she forced me to spend on Christmas gifts for the servants? It's their privilege to work in a house of consequence. That should be enough for them! They should consider themselves fortunate." Josiah paused to take a draw from his cheroot. His next words became thick around the smoke in his mouth. "Only last week, she used household funds to purchase shoes for a stable hand who is but eleven years of age. His feet will grow still. Why am I to be held responsible for the shoeing of neighborhood children?"

"Does she still receive the pin money that Father used to give her?" Solomon asked.

"Yes, of course she does." Lillian heard Josiah's chair slide away from the desk as he stood. "She should pay for her charitable works around the estate with her own funds."

Solomon's voice was quiet and sharp as its sound slid into Lillian's ears. "She does seem to have outlived her usefulness at Bixley Manor."

There was a pause in the conversation during which Lillian held her breath before Josiah asked, "Solomon, you aren't thinking of having her…done away with? Because even I couldn't go that far."

"No, I only suggest that we make better use of her life," Solomon replied cryptically.

No matter what was being discussed, Lillian was sure that it would in no way improve her life or better serve others. Her breaths were shallow and her heart pounded as she forced herself to stay and listen to more. She needed to know their plans for her so she could prepare to fight against them.

"How do you propose we do that?" Josiah asked.

"I've made some friends while in London. It may serve our purposes quite well to see her wed. She would no longer be a burden to you, Brother."

Josiah paused before answering while Lillian stood rooted to the floor in the shadowed hallway. "That idea does hold some appeal. Although, we know nothing about the business of marriage."

"Ah, yet it is business, and as in all things business, I will see to the arrangements."

"Are you sure this is the right course of action? She's quite on the shelf as it is. Who will you find to marry her?"

"I have a few ideas." Solomon paused for a moment. "It's past time Lillian married. Her leisure time at the estate has come to an end. She will go to London next week. I'll handle it from there."

Lillian couldn't think. Her breath caught in her throat. She needed to get away.

Time to plan, that's what she needed. Her feet were moving toward her bedchamber before she could direct them where to go. Marriage. She was four and twenty. This could not be happening. Her quick steps turned into a run as she disappeared around a corner, slipping into her private chambers.

She paced the floor, her mind racing. How dare they? After all she had endured! She should have known they would concoct a scheme such as this. The past year had been much too quiet, with Josiah only showing his face at the estate to empty its coffers of more family heirlooms. If only Papa had stopped him, perhaps her circumstances would be different today.

Going to her vanity table, she slid open the top drawer and reached her hand inside. The cool surface of the pocket watch slid under her fingers, yet she drew no comfort from it. She gave the trinket a quick squeeze before replacing it in the drawer. The memory she fought to keep at bay settled around her like a chilly morning fog.

Had it been a year since that dreadful day? It was odd how time slid by, passing like water through her fingers. She was unable to contain it, no matter how tightly she held it. A year ago she would have thought the sun would never rise again. And yet it did.

Now a year later Josiah was poised to upend her life once again. She squeezed her eyes shut, pushing the thoughts of her past away, but they would not budge. Sinking to her vanity chair, she allowed the memory to consume her. Perhaps some knowledge could be gained from her past.

⁓

Her steps had slowed as she neared the bottom of the staircase. She had seen her oldest brother greeting a man she had never met before as the butler disappeared around the corner. "Josiah, I didn't know you were still about the estate. Who is our guest?"

"Mr. Habersham, m'lady. Habersham's Antiquities and Fine Artifacts, of London," the man had offered with an outstretched hand and a thin smile.

"Mr. Habersham, this is my sister, Miss Phillips," Josiah had interjected.

"Pleased to meet you, Mr. Habersham. May I inquire as to what's brought you all the way from London?" At the man's brief pause and sideways glance at her brother, Lillian's gaze also turned on Josiah, who immediately adopted his superior stance.

His hands were folded behind his broad back, straining his waistcoat buttons as a knowing gleam filled his dark eyes. She knew that look well, and it was never a sign of good things to come.

"Mr. Habersham has come to look at a few pieces I see no need in keeping about this drafty manor. If you will excuse us, Lillian, we have some business to attend to. Right this way, Habersham." Her brother turned on his heel to lead the way down the large central hall toward the back corner of the house where it overlooked the rose garden.

Her heart skipped a beat as she realized he was walking toward Mama's private parlor. Lillian hurried after them, lengthening her stride to catch up with Josiah's heavy steps as he neared the end of the hall. "You cannot be considering touching Mama's things!"

"Mr. Habersham, will you excuse us for a moment? I need to have a word with my sister," Josiah tossed over his shoulder. He lowered his voice and leaned in before saying in a dismissive tone, "It is time you moved on from the past, as I have, Lillian."

"Moved on? The furnishings in this house are Papa's property, not yours. And Papa still lives. He is just upstairs. Shall I show you?"

"He has not visited this room since Mother's funeral," Josiah stated as his hand rested on the doorknob. "It is wasteful to leave things lying about when they would fetch a fine price in London. Don't be such a foolish girl. Next you will be spouting poetry and offering sentiment over a mother who has been gone some twelve years. Do you even remember her?" He opened the oak door and stepped into the sun-filled room.

Every inch of the room was exactly as her mother had left it. The book she had been reading lay beside her embroidery basket on the sofa amid flowery cushions. Lillian ran a finger across an unfinished letter that sat beside an inkwell on the writing desk. If she closed her eyes, she could still smell her mother's perfume clinging to the air. The room always gave Lillian the impression that her mother had just stepped out for a moment and would return at any time.

On some of the harder days over the past six years of caring for her father, she would wander the house and always find her way here. She found strength in the light feminine room, knowing that if her mother were still here, she would be brave and hold the family together. Now, in her absence, that duty fell on Lillian.

"Certainly I remember her. Her memory lives on today in this room. And yet you seek to sell it off to the highest bidder."

"Lillian, the affairs of men are truly none of yours. Now run along. I have business to see to with Mr. Habersham." Josiah's plump fingers wrapped around her upper arm as he pushed her back toward the door, past a stunned Mr. Habersham who had wandered into the room.

"Who do you owe money to this time, Josiah? Is it Lord Harrow again? Lord Hingsworth?" She pushed back against his forceful grip and looked her brother in the eye as he propelled her toward the door. "Will you never learn you're a dreadful gambler?"

"You presume too much, Sister! I will soon be Lord Bixley. It will be best if you become comfortable with my authority. Occupy your time with tea and needlework like every other lady, because this," he indicated the room at his back before continuing, "is none of your concern."

The door slammed in her face. She shook the sleeve of her dress back into place and exhaled on a puff of defiance, fighting her desire to scream through the door. How could her brother have no concern for their family history? He truly had no care for the place that seven generations of their family had called home.

Josiah was heir to Papa's title and estate, and this was how he respected the family name? Selling off Mama's belongings was unthinkable. But that was the problem: Josiah never thought. He hadn't given it a thought when he'd gambled away his own allowance or Papa's gun collection or Mama's parlor furnishings—or so it seemed. He obviously had no issue with selling off property that was not yet his. And Mr. Habersham clearly had no issue with it, either.

Lillian despaired at the thought that she could do nothing to stop him. Soon Bixley Manor would be empty, her family's legacy gone to pay for racehorses, loose women, and drink. Surely if she appealed to Papa's sense of honor, he could put a stop to this shameful situation. Yes, Papa would force her brother to see reason. She was at the top of the stairs and striding down the hallway with her fists clenched before she had even thought of what she would say. All she knew was that she had to try. She swung the door open and was greeted by her father's thin voice.

"I thought we were reading that dreadful novel of yours. I looked up and you were gone."

"I apologize for leaving you, Papa. We had a caller downstairs," Lillian explained as she returned to her chair by the bed.

"Oh? Who has come to visit? One of the neighbors, I suppose." Papa coughed lightly and rested his head back on the pillows again.

"No, it was a Mr. Habersham of Habersham Antiquities and some such. He is here at Josiah's request. It seems he is selling off the furnishings from

Mama's private parlor." She paused a moment, allowing the words to sink in.

"Josiah is still here, eh?"

"Yes. He's still here and selling off the furniture from downstairs." Lillian tried again to drive her point home.

"I'm sure he has his reasons. Bright boy, Josiah. He always has a proper handle on estate business."

Lillian bristled at the idea that her brother had anything to do with estate business. She had handled the running of the estate for years, as well as caring for her ailing father. "Josiah is not here often enough to handle estate business, Papa. He is selling off the family heirlooms."

"Now, Lillian. Josiah is a busy man. He has great demands on his time that keep him away. If he feels the need to thin the manor of a few pieces that are not to his liking, so be it." Her father coughed again and waved a hand toward the table of tonics.

Lillian rose and measured a dose of thick, foul-smelling syrup, handing it to her father. "He is thinning the house of Mama's belongings as we speak!"

Her father took the medicine and lay back on the pillows, closing his eyes. "Lillian, your brother knows best. I have been blessed with two wonderful sons. I am truly fortunate."

Did he not understand? Josiah was an arrogant imbecile. There was no possibility of him ever knowing best. In her opinion, only one of her father's *three* sons even approached wonderful, and he had been banished from the estate years ago. She was losing any grain of patience she had left for the men in her life—or men in general, for that matter.

"Josiah is selling Mama's things to cover another gambling debt. Do you understand that?"

"Hmm, well, if you had married someone of consequence and had a home of your own, perhaps you could have had your mother's belongings moved there and this would not be an issue." He closed his eyes as if to close a door on the conversation.

"I…I was…I couldn't," Lillian stammered, outraged that her father was going to sleep at a time like this instead of putting an end to her brother's plans. How could he place the burden of saving her mother's belongings on her shoulders? This was truly unfair.

"Stop your stuttering and speak properly, girl. Where were you raised, in the stables? Three and twenty, unmarried, and complaining of the actions of the gentlemen of this family. You are truly a disappointment." He drifted off into a heavy sleep, his lungs rattling with every breath. Although he had voiced his disapproval of Lillian in the past, this time his words seemed to hang heavy in the air, decisive and final.

And his words had been final, although she hadn't realized it at the time. He was gone an hour later, and she was left to deal with Josiah alone.

❦

She pulled her gaze away from her vanity mirror and the memory of that horrible day. Now, a year later, she was to be hauled against her will to London to be married. Her fate always came back to Josiah, with Solomon urging him to do his will. There was no distant relative to turn to.

No aunts. No uncles. How long would she last on the road—alone?

She rose from her vanity chair and brushed a tear from her cheek. What was she to do now? Stepping toward the window of her bedchamber, she leaned her forehead against the glass. The cool pane soothed her rampant thoughts, while her shaky breaths created puffs of fog in a stilted rhythm before her.

Only an hour later, and with not nearly enough time to think her way out of this mess, she was summoned to the library. She knew the conversation that was to come and could do nothing to stop it or even slow it down. She left her bedchamber with her head held high. Surely this was how walking to the gallows felt.

❧

"Dear, you've barely touched your dinner. You'll waste away to nothing if you don't eat." The Duchess of Thornwood laid down her own fork to further investigate her son. Her eyes narrowed as she looked him over in the candlelight of his Mayfair dining room.

"Mother, last I checked, I was fourteen stone of solid muscle. I am hardly at risk of wasting away." Devon flexed inside his coat, testing his statement's truth with a pat of his arm before looking back down the dining table at his mother. "Yes, quite fit. No reason for you to be alarmed."

He'd chosen to begin the evening with his family in the smaller of the two dining rooms since there were only the three of them. He was regretting that decision somewhat because it put his mother within easy reach for conversation. Having recently arrived from the country, she'd been taking the opportunity to be motherly. And of all mothers, he believed his to be the most motherly.

She spent most of her waking hours being motherly to his sister Roselyn. But since his mother's arrival only three days ago to stay with him in the city and enjoy the season, she had deemed it his turn to be mothered. He was hardly in need of her skills. He was two and thirty, after all. But from all appearances, that mattered little to her.

"It's the new cook I arranged for, isn't it?" she asked in a loud whisper.

"Hmm. No, this beef is interesting. The sauce is certainly different. I'm not sure what was wrong with my old cook, but that's a discussion for another day." Devon sawed another piece of the beef off to reassure her that he would not starve. He almost choked on it but managed to swallow it with the help of a large gulp of wine.

"She came with the best of recommendations. Lady Cale positively raved about her."

"Perhaps Lady Cale was simply happy to be rid of her," Devon quipped.

"Devon! You shouldn't say such things of society matrons who are held in high esteem by all of London. You know your reputation would be improved by playing by the rules occasionally, dear."

"Nothing can change my reputation, Mother. That fate was sealed quite a while ago. And at any rate, I find rules less palatable than these carrots, if that is possible," Devon returned, pulling a face of disgust.

A bubble of suppressed laughter down the table drew Devon's attention to his little sister, who was trying to hide her smile behind a water glass. He was glad to have an ally in the family on occasions such as this. Too bad that ally was a girl barely out of the schoolroom. She couldn't stand up to their formidable mother as effectively as he could.

"Now, Roselyn, you too would benefit from Devon watching his step in society. Your come-out is only a year away! As the daughter of a duke, your chances of making a good match should be excellent. If the current duke would toe the line, that is." She shot Devon a look down the table, the stormy gray eyes he'd inherited from her slicing through him.

Her dark hair had silvered with age, yet she was still the statuesque woman she had always been. He secretly enjoyed their dinnertime battles when she came to town, although he feigned boredom and annoyance. It was nice to have someone to talk to over dinner who truly knew him, although he would never admit that to the scowling woman.

"My actions don't matter to these people, Mother. They tossed me in with Father the moment I set foot on a ship. I might as well enjoy being 'mad.'" He lifted his wineglass in the name of madness and tossed back the contents.

"Your father was a brilliant man," his mother countered.

"Your precious society sees that a bit differently." Devon shrugged. "Since my return to England, I will have you know, I've taken madness to new heights.

I'm not about to sell my soul to the ton for the likes of Roselyn." He gave his sister a warm smile and a wink.

"I wouldn't hear of it, Brother," she returned with a charming smile that would surely melt a thousand hearts come next season.

He didn't want to think about it. This year he was still free of ballroom responsibilities. This year he could do as he pleased. He turned his attention back to his mother. "There is an entire year before I will be forced to attend garden parties." He shuddered for effect over the last words before continuing. "I may not even stay in town the entire season this year. Parliament existed before I arrived, so I hardly see where my daily presence is needed. It does nothing to increase our family's coffers. Ships, on the other hand…"

"After all that your father did for this country?"

"And what did this country do for him in return?" Devon asked, arching one brow in his mother's direction. "Drove him to an early grave with their taunts, took him from his family… English society be damned."

"Devon, don't say such things. Geoffrey—God rest his soul—will be turning in his grave with talk like that."

"Rest assured, Mother, Father was much too preoccupied with gaining the favor of the *ton* to ever turn in his grave for the likes of me."

"He was a wonderful duke, dear. You should really try to be more like him."

"I'm too much like him. That is why none of this suits me." He waved his hand around to encompass the dining room of his Mayfair home and the town it sat within. "I belong on foreign soil—exploring, mountain climbing, and investigating for scientific research. Not here arguing with a room of fifty men over inconsequential tax laws by day and enduring their ridicule by night."

"Traipsing about foreign lands is not doing your duty for your family."

"I never asked for this. I returned for a reason, and that reason is now buried on Thornwood grounds."

His mother dabbed at the corners of her eyes. "You are the duke now. And you must settle yourself and fulfill your duty to your title. Attend Parliament sessions. Find a suitable wife. Have a child. Your place is here, Devon. You had years of walking on mountains to fill your time. Now, this is your life. And you have those little boats of yours to occupy your time, which should be enough for you."

"It's mountain climbing, not walking on mountains, Mother. And those *little boats* are a fleet of three-masted frigates."

"Why should it matter to me how many masts are on your boats? You know I know nothing of the details of your work, dear."

If all went according to plan, she had no need to know the details of the shipping business, either. He took a steadying breath. The additional ships would make his venture profitable—they had to. Lord Harrow had undercut him for far too long with his corrupt contracts. Devon would set things to rights for his family by honest means—a sentiment Harrow had never understood or abided by. Devon shook off the thought of his rival at sea.

"We will be ready to set sail not six months from now. I know what is asked of me here, but I plan to be on board when they cast off. I must oversee—" He was cut off by his mother's quick change of subject.

"Come with me to the Dillsworth ball. It is rumored to be the event of the season. Quite the crush! All the matrons will be there showing off this year's crop of young ladies."

"Absolutely not, Mother."

"You will force me to attend the first large ball of the season with no escort at all?"

"When you've described it in such appealing terms? Yes. There is no possibility I will attend."

From down the table, Devon heard a small "I wish I could attend."

His mother answered Roselyn with a quick "Next year, dear." She then settled her glare back on him. "It is time you showed some interest in marriage, Devon."

"Yet I have none. I am mad. Not to mention a confirmed bachelor. Or have you not heard what they say about me?"

"That is neither here nor there, dear. I only wish that, before I depart from this world, I will be able to hold a grandchild in my arms and know that your father's legacy will live on. Then I might pass on in peace."

"Oh God."

"Yes, that is certainly who I will meet in the end, dear. I am glad we are in agreement on that point at least."

"Mother, you are nowhere close to dying. I am not going to that ball with you. And I am certainly not selecting one of the virgins on parade in the Dillsworth ballroom with whom to sire an heir. Have you ever been forced to converse with one of them? Egad! Dreadful stuff."

"Suit yourself. You always do anyway. I will attend alone. I do hope ruffians do not overtake my carriage on the way there." She cut a sidelong glance at Devon to see if her remarks were denting his resolve.

"If they do, make sure you hide the good jewels," he returned with a smile.

"Really, Devon. What am I to do with you?"

"Rap the backs of my knuckles?" he asked, flexing his large hand over the white tablecloth for her inspection. "No? Well, then perhaps I am a lost cause," he offered with a smile.

"Never." The duchess rose from her chair and motioned for Roselyn to join her. "Good night, dear," she said, lifting her cheek to Devon as he rounded the table. He kissed her good night and watched as her dark gown sailed around the corner and out of his dining room.

"Never" was right. But she would never leave him alone about his life choices. Wife, heir, and duty to his country had been drilled into his mind for as long as he could remember. It was too bad that those prospects did not sound the least bit appealing. He wanted more from his life—to see and experience it, not have it dictated to him. He sighed. Perhaps he was fighting a losing battle.

He was a duke and there was no changing that fact. Certain behaviors and standards were expected of him. Yet it all seemed so vapid and meaningless. The same words could be applied to the ladies he was supposed to court and marry. He ran a hand through his hair in exasperation.

He would not change who he was. Nor would he attend some silly ball. With a smile of self-satisfaction on that score, he left the dining room to return to his library for the evening.

❧

His lips were sweet from the fruit liqueur that had flavored their lagers. Her hands slid over his shoulders and into his silky dark hair just as he pulled her onto his lap. The carriage jostled down the street, his thighs flexing beneath her to hold them steady. She could feel the solid wall of his chest against her as she murmured his name. *Devon.*

Then, as dreams often do, he melted away just when she wanted him to stay.

"Lillian, we will be to the city within the next hour. Wake up now, and do try to make yourself presentable." Solomon's voice carved through her dream like a knife taken to her warm thoughts.

She blinked at the afternoon sun that filtered into the carriage through the window, hoping she had not said Devon's name aloud as she had in her dream. The carriage ride must have brought that particular memory to mind, or perhaps it was her return to London where they had met. She was not sure which, but she shook the last of his hold on her mind free with a quick toss of her head.

Glancing out the window, she noticed that the homes and buildings had become denser, indicating they were nearing the city. Devon was most likely somewhere in this city at this very moment. Although she was extremely unlikely to run into him since he haunted seedy pubs while she would be spending all of her time in parlors and ballrooms. She worried for a moment about what she would do if she did see him again.

Gazing down at her gray traveling dress, she smoothed a wrinkle from its surface. If she did see him again, would he recognize her? Most likely not. He wouldn't even glance her way if they saw one another in the park, say, or on the street. She'd dressed in clothing she would never again wear and had acted as she never would again. She took a steadying breath. That day was long in the past and buried there.

Now she was in town on a different mission, a survival mission. Could she escape the trap of marriage this season long enough to reach her majority next spring and be free to make her own decisions?

"Lillian, did you not hear me? Where is your head today?" Solomon slanted a dark-eyed glare at her from across the carriage.

"Solomon, it hardly takes me an hour to ensure that my hair is in place. However, I am awake now, so you may go back to..." She paused, trying to think of something he appeared to be doing. However, he sat completely still, staring ahead without a paper or a book to read in sight. "I'm not sure how you were entertaining yourself on the journey, but rest assured you may return to it now."

"I would rest assured if you were not insisting on staying with that Mary of a brother of ours. How will that look to your suitors?"

"Do *not* call him that! Nathaniel has chosen his path in life, and I find no fault in it. If you want my participation in any of this despicable marriage business, you will cease this line of conversation."

"You do not make the rules in this family, Lillian."

"Neither do you, Solomon." She spat the words back at him as she reached up to refasten a loose pin in her hair.

"Lillian, you must see the prudence of staying in our family's home while in London. Nathaniel is a bachelor of sorts. It's not appropriate for him to host you while you're in town."

"I will move to a brothel before I stay one night under your roof." She paused for a moment, allowing that barb to sink in before adding, "I cannot see how staying with you would improve my situation. After all, *you* are in trade, dear brother."

A moment of silence passed, the wheels rolling over stone and the distant clip-clop of the horses' hooves the only sounds as they progressed into town. Then Solomon's dark eyes found hers and he attempted a smile. "Lillian, dear Lillian, how did things become so heated between us? We are blood relations, after all. Surely it is not this nudge toward a better life in marriage that upsets you."

"A better life. Is that what you believe you're accomplishing by selling me to the highest bidder to further line your pockets?"

"Lillian, if any peer is going to offer for you, you must learn to watch your tongue. And I *am* seeking a better life for you. Surely, you don't wish to grow old with Josiah as company."

"His company has nothing to do with the matter. Our family's lands will suffer in my absence. Josiah is not the one who manages the estate. I wish you could get that through your head."

"Don't fret on that score. I will assist Josiah in the estate business. You need not trouble yourself over such things. You should be focused on presenting yourself well at balls and such." His eyes narrowed on her. "You may want to practice some light banter that does not challenge the listener so."

"I will present myself as I always do—with dignity and grace. And while we are discussing my presentation in town, I will need a ball gown or two to wear while here."

"I'm sure Nathaniel can point you in the direction of the appropriate shops. That is hardly something I need to be involved in." He shifted his weight to cross his ankles and look down at his hand, assessing the ring he wore on his little finger.

"Yes, however the bills for those gowns will have to be paid. Did Josiah draft the appropriate account to cover the costs before we left?"

"Certainly not. You have dresses you can wear." He waved a hand toward her in dismissal. "You have one on now."

"This is a traveling dress. The fanciest thing I own is only appropriate for a small country dinner party. I can't wear that to a London ball."

"Must we discuss London fashions? You have pin money. If you would like something new, use your own funds."

"The pin money I receive is only enough to bet

while playing a round of whist or to purchase a new fan. It's not enough to cover the cost of a gown worthy of a London ballroom."

"That is too bad. Perhaps if you had been more agreeable with the family over the last year, I might see fit to spend precious funds on your wardrobe, but that ship has sailed, hasn't it?"

He straightened his cuff and looked back at her. "And yet, it matters not what you wear. I will find a suitable husband for you without spending a fortune on fancy dresses and such. All you need to do is be available for the gentlemen I see fit as potential husbands to view you and see that your looks are acceptable.

"So you see, frills and lace are quite an unnecessary expense. Men truly don't care about a lady's ball gown, only that she is well-proportioned within it. That points to healthy heirs in the future, you know. By the way, you could stand to eat a bit more while we are in town. You're a little on the thin side as of late."

"You make it sound as if I will go up for auction just like Mama's writing desk or Papa's horse."

"Don't be so dramatic, Lillian. Being married is what every woman desires. How that end is achieved matters not."

"I don't! I don't desire to be married!"

He looked at her in astonishment as if he were seeing her for the first time. "Truly? How odd. Nevertheless, it's what is best for you. I only push this issue with you because I care."

"You don't care for me. You only care for the monetary gain or influence you could achieve through my marriage. Will it help you build more ships,

Solomon? I know the profits from your ship-building business are all you really care about."

"Again with that sharp tongue of yours. Do try to work on that, or we will have difficulties in this little endeavor of ours."

"I want no part of our little endeavor!"

"As I pointed out to you back at Bixley Manor, you have no choice in this matter. Please, do not make me the villain in all of this. I am only doing what the family requires."

"And you cannot see fit to even purchase one ball gown for me to wear while I endure this catastrophe?"

"All funds are allotted, Lillian. I have expenses, too, you know."

"Yes, I can see that by the new cravat pin you're wearing." Lillian gripped the seat cushion to keep from hitting him in the face.

"Let's not begin this adventure on the wrong footing, Lillian. I do not wish for my decisions to be questioned. It upsets me greatly to be contradicted, and I know you do not wish to upset me. We are family, and we should stand together and act accordingly."

"I will be standing with Nathaniel, as he is my family."

"Lillian, I do not wish to quarrel with you, so I will allow you to stay with Nathaniel if that is your choice. But I insist that, in return, you honor my choices."

She would agree to almost anything to end this conversation and get out of this carriage. "I will not disagree with you in public, if that is your worry. My beliefs, however, will not change for you or any other man."

"That is very well…for now. I believe we are there."

"Good."

"I expect you to be at the Dillsworth ball in three days' time."

"I'll fulfill my family obligation and make an appearance, although I will be in rags, thanks to you."

"You need only be in attendance."

She nodded, gathering her skirts and stepping down before assistance could be offered to her. She did not want to spend even one second more in Solomon's company, and she certainly did not want help from any man just now. Thankfully, she found her footing on her own as her half boots met the brick pathway leading to the front steps.

Gulping large breaths of fresh air, she tried to push her anger at Solomon down before it suffocated her. Her hatred of him had increased over the past hour, if that were possible. How was she related to such a horrible man? His selfishness knew no bounds. No ball gowns? And he made her feel more than ever before like a cow up for auction. This experience was going to be just awful! However, now she was at Nathaniel's home. Friendly territory, as it were. And she would not allow Solomon's vileness to cling to her hem as she entered.

"Your trunks, m'lady," the driver offered as the second trunk dropped at her feet with a thud.

"Thank you. I will see to my things from here." She shook out her skirts and gazed up at the facade of Nathaniel's home. It was not as large as a few homes she had seen out the window of the carriage, yet it was quite elegant for its size. The white trim surrounding the bricks almost still held the smell of fresh paint where it nestled with ivy that was allowed to grow artfully on the corners. Lillian smiled at the sight of yellow roses lining the small garden, because Nathaniel had always been partial to yellow roses.

Striding up the front steps, she glanced around to see that the carriage was already gone. Solomon had not even waited to ensure she made it inside safely. A small part of her was offended, while the sane majority of her mind was relieved that he was no longer there. It was just as well. He and Nathaniel had not carried on a civilized conversation in years. Even when Papa passed, they could not manage to get on for the sake of appearances while the family gathered to grieve.

"Lillian! You made it safely!" Nathaniel's voice called over her shoulder.

She turned back to the house to see his tall, fashionably clad frame filling the doorway. She was tugged inside, and orders were being given for her trunks to be brought in and a bath made ready before she could even respond.

"Nathaniel, I'm glad you received my letter. You are willing to let me stay with you?"

"You're always welcome here, darling. I could never leave you to the wrath of our brother. How did you fare on the journey here with him?"

"It was so terrible that I cannot even think about it now that I'm here. I will just say that I did in fact survive. Let's discuss a more pleasant subject."

"Of course. We'll leave the ugliness of our family relations out in the streets where they belong." He finished with a dramatic slam of his door that rattled a crystal vase filled with flowers on a nearby table.

Lillian jumped, chuckling at her brother's outlandish actions. His own butler appeared outraged but did not say a word. She looked up, taking in the ornate chandelier filled with candles and the polished staircase that wound its way to the upper floors. "Your home is lovely."

"Oh, this? It is a work in progress, you know, but it does serve to keep the rain from my head."

"I didn't interrupt your daily routine, did I? I don't wish to be a burden while I'm here."

"You? A burden? Don't even think it. Now, let me show you the suite I have had readied for you. I think it will suit you." With that, he turned and led her up the stairs with an endless string of chatter over this vase and that painting.

She could feel the tension of her journey fading from her limbs. Perhaps she did not like the reason for her trip to London, but at least her stay with Nathaniel would be enjoyable. He had the ability to put her at ease and make her laugh even in the worst of situations. And this situation certainly qualified as the worst she had endured so far.

Four

"THORNWOOD? THORNWOOD! ARE YOU STILL IN THE game? Did you hear me? I said I hate to steal from you. Next thing you know, I'll walk out of here with your pocket watch and cravat pin, the way you're playing."

There was an answering round of laughter and someone hit Devon on the shoulder in jest. It was true. His mind was not on his play this afternoon. He smiled, hiding the turmoil that stirred within him at the mention of someone stealing his belongings.

"Gentlemen, this game has become too rich for my shallow pockets. I wish you the best of luck in squandering your collective inheritances. Enjoy your future of poverty," Devon stated as he rose from the card table at the back of White's gentlemen's club.

There were one chuckle and a few intakes of breath at the insult. Yet Devon was no longer entertained by the cards in his hand or the conversation at the table, especially after the mention of stolen pocket watches.

He'd been sitting there all afternoon, partly in search of some diversion on an unseasonably warm day, but mostly hiding from his mother. She had been in fine form over luncheon, pressing him further about tonight's ball and fussing over his clothing, the food on his plate, and how his hair desperately needed to be cut.

Escape could not have happened fast enough. So he was greatly relieved when he spotted an old friend arriving at the club as he was preparing to leave. "Steelings, I thought you were set to be in the country for a few weeks. Back so soon?"

"My trip was cut short. It's a rather long tale as to why." His blond brows drew together into a grim expression rarely seen on his jovial face. "I will just say I've returned. It's good to see you, Thornwood. Care to have a drink?"

Devon had been friends with Holden Ellis, Viscount Steelings, ever since he had shared the answers on an exam with Holden during their school days. From that day forward, they had been finding trouble together. Months—or once even years, while Devon was in Africa—would elapse between their visits. Yet they always picked up the conversation where they had laid it down at the last meeting, as if no time had passed.

"Certainly," Devon returned. "I'm looking for any excuse to avoid my home at the moment."

"Her Grace is in town?" Steelings asked, pulling out a chair from a nearby table to sit.

"And wreaking havoc on my sanity. She has it in her head that this is the year she will convince me to bend to her will and marry. She believes my being settled will be to Roselyn's benefit next season. I keep telling her it won't happen, but does she listen?"

"Does anyone of the female persuasion listen when we proclaim what is truth?"

They paused in their conversation to signal for drinks to be brought to their table. That was one of the benefits to White's over dark taverns on the other end of town: They knew his preferences here and kept a bottle of his preferred whiskey in the back room. It was a small benefit in the face of being known and watched by everyone, but a benefit nonetheless.

"What are your evening plans?" Devon asked idly as he leaned back in his chair, settling in for an afternoon of chatting with his old schoolmate.

"I'm escorting my cousins to the Dillsworth ball. Will you be there as well?"

"Hell no." Devon recoiled, his brows drawing together in concern for his friend's sanity. Why would he go there of all places? And why was Steelings subjecting himself to such torture? "That's the same ball my mother is harping on me to attend. Cry off from your cousins, and we'll drink ourselves senseless."

"Not a chance." A guilty look crossed Steelings' face and he attempted to cover it with a shrug of his shoulders.

Devon had seen that look on his friend's face quite a few times, and it usually indicated a distinct lack of honesty. His eyes narrowed on Steelings as he waited for him to confess whatever agenda he had for attending the ball this evening.

Steelings dropped his voice so as not to be overheard before continuing. "You see, there is this extremely vexing female."

"There always is." With Steelings' charm, he had

never been in short supply of female companionship, however short-lived that companionship might be.

"Yes, well, this particular vexing female is said to be attending the ball this evening. She's actually the reason I'm back in town so soon."

"I do believe there's a story here," Devon teased, wondering why in the world Steelings would change his travel plans for a woman. Even for him, that was rather extreme.

His friend then set into the telling of his rather long-winded story of a vanishing lady and his subsequent chase across half the country. Steelings always did have a flair for the dramatic. Yet there was a look about him as he spoke of this woman... "My God, you're smitten! I can hardly believe it! Who is this temptress who's lured you in?"

"Her name is Suzanna. Lovely, isn't it?" There was a dreamy look in Steelings' eyes that Devon had not seen there since Miss Fountaine when they were seventeen. This was serious indeed.

"And this is all you know of her?"

"Well, yes. She disappeared, you see. You have no idea how infuriating it is to have a chit vanish in such a manner. I only want to see her once more. Perhaps it is only a proper ending to things that I am looking for tonight." His brows drew together as he became lost in thought, taking another sip of his drink.

"Disappearing ladies are annoying, to say the least." Why did Lily's memory keep coming to mind today? Devon had lost a month of productivity in organizing shipping routes last year in a fruitless search for her. Now, just when he thought he had permanently banished her from his head, he was thinking of her twice in one day? He ran a hand through his hair. It had all been a game to her.

Her cruelty still rankled to this day, but he didn't allow himself time to think about her. He had, therefore, spent the last year focused on profitability in his business, attempting to make up lost ground. Yet today her memory kept creeping back into his thoughts. Only he knew now that he would never see her again.

What he *could* do, however, was stop his friend from becoming entangled with a devious lady such as this Suzanna. "She disappeared on you. She could be running from any sort of thing. She could be a thief. Did you check your pockets after that dance?"

"A thief? Why in the devil would you think that?"

"It's a possibility to be considered. I'm sure it happens occasionally."

"I hardly think a lady would steal from me while at my cousin's home. What's gotten into you?"

Devon released the tense knot that had grown in his stomach and was etching lines of concern on his face, instead relaxing into an easy smile. "It's nothing. And I've changed my mind. I believe I will attend the Dillsworth event this evening. I must meet this mystery lady that has you chasing her all about the countryside."

"Spectacular! I really wasn't looking forward to keeping the company of my cousins for the whole evening. They tend to squeal. It's quite annoying, really. But with you there, I can slip away easily."

Devon attempted a smile. "I suppose if it keeps you

free of unwanted relations, you can use my notorious nature for good this evening."

"It should go to some good use. You certainly haven't used it recently, staying holed up in your library working, with no time for any ladies or entertainment. Yes indeed, this will work perfectly. My cousins are terrified of you as it is. I'll have the whole evening free of them to find Suzanna. And you will finally leave your home to socialize with me. Who knows, perhaps you'll even dance."

"Ah, but now you will have me taunting you as you make a fool of yourself for a lady. Yes, this evening's entertainment is sounding more enticing by the second. But there will be no dancing," Devon warned as he rose from his chair. He clapped his friend on the back and headed for the door. "I'll see you there. I have a few things to attend to first." With a nod he was striding down the street toward home.

❧

After a morning spent stalking aimlessly through the well-appointed town home, Lillian sat in her bedchamber with her nerves jangling. The day of the Dillsworth ball had arrived. The four hours until she must leave had turned slowly into three and three-quarter hours.

The trouble was that there did not seem to be a single useful activity she could sink into. Some task about the house would at least give her something else to focus on for the afternoon, rather than sitting in dread. Much to her chagrin, however, Nathaniel ran an immaculate home.

Her room was lovely. Perfectly arranged flowers sat on the writing desk by the window. All of her dresses were already hanging in the wardrobe. Her books were stacked neatly on a table. And the clock on the mantel opposite the bed kept perfect time. She knew, for she heard every tick, tick, tick.

Taking a deep breath that did nothing to calm her nerves, she took down her tightly knotted hair and brushed through it once, then twice, before replacing it at the back of her neck. Was this the worst day of her life? Surely, it had many rivals. But this would certainly go down in the history books as the most humiliating.

Her eyes darted over to the dove gray dress lying across the bed. It was the nicest gown she owned and certainly suitable for a dinner. However, a ball gown it was not. She would surely be the worst-dressed, not to mention the oldest, lady in attendance this evening.

The dress would serve the purpose of keeping any marriage-minded men away, if Solomon wasn't planning on forcing someone upon her anyway. Therefore, it only served to humiliate her in front of London society. The mended seam that had split when she tried it on yesterday stood out under her gaze. No one would notice, but she knew. She was going to look like the most ridiculous spinster that ever lived.

Worse still was the knowledge that all of this humiliating production was to find a husband she didn't desire. The last thing she needed in her life was another man who would bully her into following his will.

Why must all men insist that they knew best?

She slammed her silver-backed brush down on

the vanity table a little harder than she had intended. Taking an unsteady breath, she looked into the abyss of the mirror until she saw only a grouping of shapes and colors swirled together. She was not sure how long she had been sitting there, mourning her short-lived freedom, when there was a knock at the door.

"Lillian?" Nathaniel's voice called through the door. "You haven't jumped from the window to end your misery yet, have you?"

"Come in," Lillian called, blinking her eyes back into focus and straightening her high collar with a gentle tug of her dress. As she heard the door open and footsteps cross the floor, she mused, "As I am only on the second floor, I would likely just break both legs. And Solomon would carry me into that ballroom in full bandages if he had to."

"It seems you've already thought that option through," Nathaniel returned with a chuckle.

Lillian attempted to smile but knew she had not achieved it.

Nathaniel took a few steps closer to her, appearing behind her in the mirror. "I shudder at the thought of being presented to the *ton* while completely wrapped in bandages. That would certainly be the talk over tea tomorrow. As compelling as it may be to make such an immediate impression on London, might I offer another option?"

Lillian turned abruptly to regard her brother with narrowed eyes. "There's another option?"

"Yes, although it does involve attending tonight's ball."

"Oh. I don't believe I like your option after all."

"You have yet to hear it, but I do understand if you still desire to jump."

"Very well. What is this brilliant idea?"

"We make you over into a ravishing beauty for the ball. You will make a grand entrance and turn every head in the room. Then you will meet your one true love and dance the night away, and Solomon will be out of your life forever."

"Have you been reading gothic novels again, Nathaniel? Such romantic notions. I hate to disappoint, but I hardly think I could be made into anything more than a poor relation who is also a little long in the tooth."

"Oh, Lillian. I wish I could change this for you somehow." He walked over to the gray dress and lifted the edge, inspecting it with disgust. "Dreadful," he muttered to himself.

"I know. But none of this is your fault, Nathaniel." She took a deep breath, forcing the usual calm back into her limbs as her spine straightened at the challenge before her. "You are helping by allowing me to stay in your home. If I had to spend all of my free time with Solomon, I might just leap from a window."

"Pleased to be of assistance. And I did do a little something for you." Nathaniel's smile could be heard in his voice as he walked back to the door and reached into the hallway to pick up something he'd left there. When he returned, he was holding a teetering stack of parcels, a broad grin covering his lean face as he peered around the tower in his arms.

"What did you do?" Her eyes were wide as she rose from the chair at the vanity table. It looked as if he had bought the entire selection from every window on Bond Street!

"It doesn't take much twisting of arms to convince me to do a little shopping, darling," he replied, dumping the stack of boxes on the top of her bed and covering the old gray dress in the process.

"Oh, Nathaniel. I can't believe you did this! What have you purchased?"

"Only a few necessities for my dear sister. I couldn't have you traipsing about fashionable London in those horrid country rags you brought with you. I have a reputation to uphold, you know." He gave her a friendly shove on the arm.

"But Solomon and Josiah refused to pay for a new wardrobe for me." She ripped her eyes away from the packages and parcels to peer into his face. "How can you afford this, Nathaniel?"

"Never mind the finances of it all. Your only concern should be which slippers to wear this evening."

Lillian was once again skeptical of Nathaniel's apparent wealth. Not only did he have this lovely home in a fashionable part of town, but now he was buying her lavish gifts? How did he afford all of this without the benefit of their family connections? How long had it been since Father disowned him? Ten years, perhaps? He didn't appear to have gone into trade. But the thoughts slipped away into silken dreams as he lifted the lid to the first box in the pile on top of her bed.

"You must try this on, darling. It was made for a French lady with obviously exquisite tastes. I talked the seamstress out of it with my English powers of persuasion." He paused to laugh over the memory. "It was a bit of a job. If only you could have seen the way she tried to shoo me from her store. I believe I still have a few holes where she tried to make use of me as a pin cushion."

"Oh, surely not. You hardly look holey to me." She chuckled and gave him a shove on the arm. For a moment they were children again. Laughing. Talking. She was not being forced to marry and he was not consoling her. Then the moment came crashing down as she traced a finger over the seed pearls that ran in a band around the high waist of the blue gown. She would be wearing this dress to the commencement of her horrible fate this evening.

"When I saw it I knew you must have it for your first ball. Isn't it glorious? Pull it out. Wait until you see the pearls along the hem and dotting the puffed sleeves. Exquisite!"

"Nathaniel, this is too much. It's beautiful." She pulled it from the box, holding it up in the afternoon light. "My, but it's cut low. I couldn't possibly wear this. It's unseemly, is it not?"

"Posh, try it on. That is the style of all of the gowns now, darling."

"Well, you do know the fashions more than I do. You always have. And I've hardly had the need to keep up with such things, living in Whitby and all." Her voice trailed off as she gazed down at the ice-blue silk dress she held in her hands. What would it feel like to wear something so fine? She almost cried in relief that she would not have to wear her old clothes.

"You will look the picture of youth and beauty

tonight," he said quietly, somehow reading her fears of looking the old maid.

"You are the best brother I could ever ask for." She leaned her head against his arm, unable to take her eyes from her first ball gown.

With a grim smile, she knew there would be no jumping from windows. She would meet this challenge head on as she did all others. She would wear her ball gown as if it were her armor in battle. She reached up and grabbed her mother's pearls from around her neck, trying to pull some strength from their bumpy surface. She was lost in a distant thought of her mother when she heard Nathaniel's voice calling her back to the present.

"Those aren't Mother's pearls, are they? I hadn't noticed them until you began fiddling with them. How did you get them back?"

"I bought them back," she said defiantly. The memory of that fateful day last spring was coming to mind far too frequently now that she was in London. However, it served to further steel her nerves for the oncoming war. For if she had survived that incident unscathed and truly as if it had never happened, then she would survive this, too. There was only a tiny note of trepidation left within her as she dropped the pearls back to rest around her throat and smiled at her brother.

Nathaniel looked dumbfounded. "How? You've been at Bixley for the past year."

"Oh, I managed to accomplish it," she replied evasively. "Now, I do need to begin getting ready for the evening, if you don't mind."

"Of course. I need to do the same. I'll see you downstairs in an hour."

"Yes, and thank you many times over for the clothes."

"Don't even think of it. The daughter of a peer does not appear in a ballroom in an old country dress. Our brothers should know better."

"Indeed." A silence fell between them with nothing more to say on the subject of their brothers. With a final nod, he turned and left the room.

Lillian lifted the gown off the bed. Pulling it up in front of her, she gazed into the mirror across the room. She may not be ready for tonight's events, but at least she would be walking in to greet her future in a lovely new gown.

⸙

She had barely been able to string two words together on the ride through town. Lillian was simply too nervous to discuss what fashions would be seen this season or anything else Nathaniel attempted to inject into the silence of the carriage. However, now that they were here and the threat of the evening looming in the distance came into sight, she finally found her voice.

"About the dresses and such you bought for me... Nathaniel, how can you afford it all? Not to put too fine a point on it, but you have no inheritance and no employment."

"That is a rather fine point, darling. I assure you I do just fine." His gaze shifted to the window with a smile. "Oh look, we're here. I simply adore the Dillsworth home. With all the white stone and the columns, I half expect Roman gods to walk out the door." His eyes flashed with anticipation as he clasped his hands together. "It's simply fabulous."

All of Lillian's questions and wonderings about her brother's life situation fell into silence as the door to the carriage opened and a liveried footman held out a white-gloved hand to assist her to the ground. She stepped down, watching as groups of ladies and gentlemen made their way toward the door of the Dillsworth home.

She was so in awe at the sight of the elaborate evening wear donned by the other partygoers that Nathaniel had to cough to get her attention so he could escort her inside. Light shown in the windows of the grand home, beckoning her feet to move forward toward its ethereal glow.

As she reached the front steps and merged into the forming crowd waiting to greet the hosts and be presented inside, Lillian didn't feel there was enough air to breathe or room for her heart to beat inside her gown.

This was it, her come-out, and she was only experiencing it five years too late.

When she looked back toward their carriage, ready to surrender and flee, Nathaniel nudged her forward. Looking up into his face, she took a breath, lifted her chin to the oncoming battle, and relaxed her face into a serene expression just in time to be escorted over the threshold to meet her fate.

The glow of a thousand candles glinted off jewels of every shape and size. Lillian could not believe the elegance of the Dillsworth home, the starkness of so many intricately tied cravats, the almost overwhelming scent of roses, or the fact that she was standing amid it all. She and Nathaniel made their way into the ballroom.

Everyone here seemed to know one another, yet she knew not a soul. A single friendly face would be most welcome at the moment. What if she was forced to stand alone all evening? The sound of music became louder as they reached their destination. Looking up, Lillian could see a balcony wrapping around the dance floor, which was covered by a roof of glass.

"I believe you could use a drink. I'll run and get you champagne, darling. Wait here for me by this column. And do stop fidgeting with your pearls." With that, he was gone and she was alone. Somewhere at the ball, Solomon lurked, but she didn't see him at the moment. However, her eyes were trained on the swirling movements on the dance floor and she could not in a million years imagine Solomon dancing.

"Lillian?"

She turned at the sound of her name uttered by an exuberant female voice. Who here would even remember her when she had been so removed from society for so long?

"Lillian! I knew that must be you! It's been ages!"

Relief flooded through her at the sight of Sue Green, spritely and rosy-cheeked, standing there in a rose gown. Her hair was the same light brown color it had been years ago at school and her face had not aged a day.

"Sue! You have no idea how happy I am to see a friendly face here tonight. It's been ages, has it not? We must catch up!"

"Yes, we certainly must! Isn't this ball exquisite? I

always love attending the Dillsworth affairs. Have you tried the cakes in the parlor yet? They never last very long, especially the ones filled with strawberry jam. You would think from year to year they would realize the popularity of the cakes and prepare more. But alas, we are forced to clamor over a single table of sweets as soon as we arrive to get one. Who are you here with?"

Sue beamed up at Lillian, awaiting answers to her questions. It was nice to see some things in life were consistent, such as Sue's ability to fill both sides of a conversation.

"Two of my brothers are here as my chaperones. One is getting me a drink and the other I choose not to think about. Who is with you this evening?" Lillian assumed that Sue, like everyone else their age, was married, but didn't want to ask the wrong question so as not to offend.

"My family. You remember my sister Evangeline. It is her come-out this year. She is preening in the upstairs ladies' retiring room at the moment. You remember how she is, unable to take more than two steps away from a mirror to this day. It's rather annoying, if I can be honest," Sue finished with a laugh.

"I believe she must have been ten years old the last time I saw her. I don't want to think about how young we were. Does this mean you're not yet married?"

"This is my fifth season, if you can believe that. If I have to return home with my mother at the end of yet another year, I may die. And with all of the focus on Evangeline's come-out, it's very likely I'll meet that doom in a few months' time." Sue made a slicing motion across her throat and pulled a face of pure horror.

"You mustn't end it all when we've only just met up again after all these years. If it eases your mind, consider this is my first season and I'm a year older than you."

"What happened to keep you away so long? I've thought to see you in London for years now. Every year I've kept my eye out for you, as well as some of the other girls from school, but I had lost hope that I would see you again."

"Papa became ill. Family matters kept me in Whitby until now. I'd thought to become an old maid and live out my days in peace, but it seems my brothers have other ideas."

"Whitby's loss is my gain this evening, Lillian. I'm thrilled to have someone to converse with, other than Evangeline and my twin cousins. Oh, here they all are now."

As introductions were made to Sue's sister and cousins, Lillian couldn't help but notice how beautiful Sue's family was. It was as if she came from a family of exotic wood nymphs, with their hair all hanging in perfect ringlets around rose-colored lips and large eyes. Lillian felt a pang of sympathy for Sue who clearly took after some lesser-being side of the family. Sue was lovely, yet surrounded by the radiance of her family, she appeared rather plain. They had settled into companionable discussion of the evening's fashions when Nathaniel returned carrying two champagne flutes.

"Here's your champagne, darling. It seems you have found friends already. That's splendid."

"We've just been becoming reacquainted. My

brother, Mr. Phillips, this is Miss Green, her sister Miss Evangeline Green, and her cousins, the Misses Fairlyn."

"Good evening." Nathaniel offered a slight bow as the ladies dipped a quick curtsy, before turning his attention back to Lillian. "Since you have found friends, do you mind if I find a few of my mates?"

"Of course not. Don't let me keep you from having an enjoyable time here."

"Thank you. I'll check on you after I've won a few hands of cards." Nathaniel disappeared into the growing crowd surrounding the dance floor. Lillian stood watching the swirl and swish of skirts as the ladies moved around the floor. It was quite lovely to watch.

She turned her attention back to Sue in time to see Evangeline being led to the floor by a young man with dark hair. As the crowd around them thinned to join the couples on the dance floor where they participated in a country dance, she watched the color drain from Sue's face in an instant.

"Sue? Are you well?" Lillian asked.

"Oh, yes. Quite."

"You look as if you've seen a ghost."

"In a manner, I believe I have."

Lillian followed Sue's gaze across the crowded dance floor but saw nothing alarming. She looked back at Sue. "Clearly something has you distressed. Is there something I can do? Do you need a drink? The champagne has helped my nerves considerably." She took another sip as if to prove her point.

"No, thank you. Although perhaps I could use some air. Will you excuse me?"

"Certainly," Lillian replied.

Yet Sue had only taken one step away when she halted. Her complexion turned from white to a dark pink that rivaled the color of her gown. What—or who—had Sue behaving in such a way? Lillian turned her confused gaze from Sue to the faces of two men moving their way through the crowd, just in time for her own heart to stop.

Five

"THORNWOOD, GOOD TO SEE YOU OUT IN SOCIETY," the Marquess of Elandor offered as Devon paused in the main hallway of the Dillsworth home to procure a drink from a passing footman.

"I've come for the sole purpose of tormenting a friend. After surviving this crowd, I'll surely go back into hiding for some time to recover."

Elandor stepped out of the path of a lady with a nod of his head in her direction before turning his attention back to Devon. "It is good to see you here, at any rate. I've been meaning to speak with you."

"Oh? With regard to the House of Lords, I suppose." Devon knew Elandor more by sight from Parliament than he did personally. Elandor was rumored to be so consumed with law-making and his position in society that he had no time for or interest in ladies or sport. He had a dusting of gray at his temples, but still every lady passing in the hallway batted her lashes at him. Devon drained the champagne in his hand and asked the footman for something stronger, settling in for a long talk about the laws of their fair country.

Elandor spoke in an all-business tone as he answered. "In a manner, yes. It is about the House of Lords. You see, I'm head of His Majesty's Treasury and, as such, of any advancement the Crown oversees. I would like someone with your experience to serve alongside me."

"My experience? Truly, you must have me confused with someone else. I have no background in finance."

"You have an interest in shipping and you've spent a great deal of time on expeditions, have you not?" Elandor's eyes narrowed.

"I have." Devon couldn't see the connection between funding for the Crown and his interest in shipping or exploration. He needed to find Steelings. He hadn't come here to get more involved in society or Parliament.

"We supply funding for ventures deemed worthy by the Crown."

Devon poured two glasses of whiskey from a decanter the footman brought back on a tray and nodded toward Elandor as if he was interested in their conversation. He took a drink from one glass, wincing over the wretched quality of the liquor. "I'll give your suggestion some thought, though I would much prefer to be the one aboard the ship instead of signing papers to send others."

"Very well, think about it. I think you'll find there is more to it than signing papers."

"I'm sure. Very involved. Nice to see you, Elandor."

"Yes, I must be on my way, as well. I am to meet someone in the card room. Think about what I have said, Thornwood."

"I will indeed," Devon called out to his retreating form.

Not wishing to get involved in any more pleasantries, he made his way down the hallway to the less populated refreshment room. Steelings could usually be found near any table of sweets, so that was where Devon would wait. He leaned against a window enclosure, allowing the fire of the whiskey to slip down his throat, numbing him to its taste and soothing his growing agitation over attending this damned ball. Setting one empty glass on a side table and beginning on the next, he glanced once more at the door just in time to see Steelings striding in. His friend appeared harried but had a look of determination in his eyes.

"Steelings, there you are. I was afraid I would have to find someone else to torment for the evening," Devon said, clapping his friend on the back as he approached.

"I'd hate to disappoint you, Thornwood. I was delayed by some devastating emergency involving my cousin's gown. You would have thought the world was coming to an end, all for a missing bead of some sort. There were tears and wailing." Steelings shuddered.

"That does sound like quite the dramatic beginning to the evening. I do hate it when they wail, though. How are we to deal with that? Where did you leave them?" Devon looked around but only saw a few gentlemen fetching drinks from the refreshment table against the far wall.

"I made my excuses in the hallway. Now that you're here, I must begin my search for Suzanna."

"Ah yes, the mysterious Suzanna. What does this vixen look like?"

A dreamy haze filled Steelings' eyes as he said, "I would know her anywhere. She was just over five feet, hair the color of burnished gold…"

"*Burnished gold?*" Devon chuckled at the description. His friend must be far worse off than he had originally believed.

"Very well, blondish-brown if that's more to your liking."

"No, I believe I prefer 'burnished gold,' although I don't see that color in this side parlor. Perhaps we should look in the main ballroom?"

"Yes. Isn't there a door that adjoins the rooms over there behind that potted palm?"

"Indeed. I recall making use of it once when Miss Rashings had me in her sights years ago. It made for a timely retreat."

"The face of a horse, that one, and the hindquarters to match," Steelings mused as they made their way to the door.

"That is actually a bit kind where that particular lady is concerned." Devon's chuckle was lost to the sounds of the orchestra striking up a country dance from the balcony far above the chatter of the room.

They arrived in the ballroom from the far side of the main entrance, thus avoiding the crush of people now flowing through the entrance. Devon never ceased to be amazed by the glass roof above the Dillsworth ballroom, half expecting it to fall in shards on his head, half entranced by the view of the stars it provided.

The crowd had grown thick under the starry sky,

with couples dancing the night away while society matrons looked on in appreciation. Somewhere in this room his mother sat ensconced with her friends. With any luck, she would not become aware of his presence and he could avoid her altogether. Although it was highly unlikely that Devon's name would not be mentioned. After all, this was the first public event he'd been coerced into attending in over a year.

"There are well over a hundred ladies here, and most of them are moving around. This could take all evening," Devon complained as a group of them passed by.

"You act as if a moment spent in a ballroom will poison you for life. This will be simple. I'll find her within a matter of minutes. Before you know it, you'll be back drinking in one of those lovely hovels you so enjoy," Steelings returned, his eyes scanning the crowd without blinking.

"Very well. Just over five feet, you said? You couldn't be searching for a tall chit. No, it would have to be a tiny, hard-to-find one." Devon had spent only a few minutes looking through the dancers on the floor in search of *burnished gold* when Steelings jabbed him in the ribs.

"I've spotted her friends over there by the first column near the main door. She must be nearby. Let's make our way in that direction."

"By the first column, you say?" Devon abandoned his drink to a pedestal holding a large vase of roses and moved to follow his friend, who was already slipping between conversations and gathered matrons. He caught up to Steelings as they rounded the corner of the dance floor. It was slow progress to walk in such a crowd.

As he passed, he mused to one lady, "What a lovely example of the Java peafowl."

She blinked, the feathers on her head quivering at him. "What did you just call me?" she asked in outrage as Devon continued to weave through the throng after Steelings.

Ladies all seemed to duck behind fans to chat at the moment he walked by. The whisper of madness floated in the air around him. Was that truly all anyone cared about? How dull their lives must be for his existence in a ballroom to start their chatter.

He could suggest hobbies or contributions to the betterment of mankind to them, but such talk was not done at a ball. No, he had been swatted with too many fans by too many ladies over the years for discussing foreign soil at just such an event as this to try it again. God, how he hated balls! Why must being accepted in society require one to be so dull?

He only narrowly missed being detained by Lord Fanning, who stepped forward to speak to him. His wife pulled the man away with a hiss of disapproval. Devon offered to her in passing, "Lady Fanning, I remember you having many more wrinkles last I saw you. Your face creams must be working." He continued to trail behind Steelings, not hearing her response.

Just then the crowd shifted enough so that he could see the group of people they were walking toward. An older couple was deep in conversation near the wall, and standing just before them were two ladies. The petite one in the rose gown seemed to be staring straight at Steelings. Perhaps this was his Suzanna. She was attractive, but not the exotic beauty Devon had imagined would catch his friend's attention. How odd.

Devon's eyes slid to her right where another lady stood taller than her companion, dressed in faint blue and with golden blond hair that swept away from her face to reveal pink cheeks and full lips that were currently pursed in concern.

"Bloody hell," he heard himself say.

Her gaze had just shifted to his, and for the first time since their night together a year ago, he looked into Lily's clear blue eyes.

Was it truly her or a trick of the light in the ballroom? He watched as her hand moved to fidget with the pearl necklace at her throat. Lily had made the same motion with the same necklace. Her hair was arranged in a knot on the back of her head, not like the loose curls of a year ago, but it was the same hair. Her gown was not the out-of-date fashion that she had been wearing when he saw her last, but her slim curves were the same.

What was she doing here? How had she gained entrance to such an event? Had she convinced someone she had ties to the peerage? Why here? Why now?

She'd vanished into the night, only to turn up by way of a chance meeting in a ballroom a year later? He tamped down the disbelief swirling through his head as they neared the two ladies in question.

He heard Steelings at his side offer a cordial greeting. His eyes only narrowed a fraction as he nodded in Lily's direction.

"I don't believe we've been formally introduced. I'm

Lord Steelings, and this is the Duke of Thornwood," Steelings stated.

"I'm Miss Green," the other lady said.

"Pleasure to make your acquaintance, my lady." Devon's eyes only darted to the smaller woman for the briefest of seconds before landing back on Lily. He did not want her to slip away as she had a year ago. He had wasted a month looking for her!

"Your Grace, my lord, may I introduce my childhood friend, Miss Phillips. She's from Whitby and only arrived in town recently for the first time. Isn't that right, Miss Phillips?"

"Miss Phillips from Whitby." Devon allowed the words to drop like anvils from his mouth as he looked into her stunned face. "This is your first time in our fair city?"

She cleared her throat before stammering a quiet, "Yes, yes it is."

"I should like to show you the sights, then. Although, with the season now in full swing, I don't know if there will be *time*. Speaking of, I don't suppose you *have* the time? Do you…have the time?" It was a subtle statement that no one but the thief of his pocket watch would catch. He watched in satisfaction as her bright blue eyes widened.

"No, I don't, Your Grace. I…I was about to leave when you arrived. Please do excuse me."

"It would hardly be gentlemanly of me to allow you to *vanish* without an escort. Please, allow me."

"Oh, um, perhaps I can stay for a moment," she uttered in a breathless voice.

"I'm pleased to hear it," Devon stated. His anger

from a year ago flowed back into his veins, simmering just below the surface.

Steelings didn't seem to have noticed anything amiss because the next words out of his mouth were, "Miss Green, would you care to dance, if there is room on your card this evening? I am interested to hear about your family's well-being since I saw you last in the country."

The rosy-cheeked lady replied, "Certainly." She then turned to Lily with a tight smile. "I trust you will survive the duke's company for a few minutes."

"I'm sure I'll be fine," Miss Phillips said confidently, although her eyes told a different story as she fiddled with her pearl necklace.

"Yes, I have a feeling she can fend for herself quite well," Devon said with something between charm and a snarl.

Once the other couple left for the dance floor, Lily said, "I am not sure what interest you have in me, Your Grace, but I really must be leaving."

"You've developed quite the habit of leaving abruptly, haven't you, *Lily*?"

"My given name is Lillian. Although I do not recall giving you leave to use it." Her chin rose in defiance in the same way it had when he'd first laid eyes on her outside the Stag and Doe.

"That matters not. 'Lily' suits you better anyway. I have no use for calling you Lillian."

"You must have me confused with someone else," she blustered, taking a step away from him to create a gap he instantly closed.

Did she truly think to pretend to be someone else

and deny her actions of a year ago? He simply could not allow that. With a smirk creasing the corners of his eyes, he leaned toward her to say, "Do I, Lily? So you don't have an affinity for drinking sangarees and a weakness for being kissed here..." He reached out to run one gloved finger across her collarbone before she could react. "Just where your pearls lie at your throat?"

"Do *not* touch me with such familiarity," she hissed through gritted teeth as she took a step away from him. "How dare you say such things in the middle of a ballroom? Passersby may get the wrong idea entirely by the tone of your banter." Lily's hand moved to touch her lips as she glanced around to ensure no one was listening.

If he did not know otherwise, he would think her the primmest of all the misses at the ball this evening. Who was she trying to fool, and to what end? After the way she'd deceived him, he had to know of her plots of thievery now. If not for his sense of satisfaction, then to protect the poor sod she had targeted tonight.

"If what you say is true and we do not know one another, then why are you blushing so? Why did you touch your lips at the mention of my kisses? Are you going to say it never happened? After all that passed between us...after you stole from me?"

Her eyes flared in outrage. "I did not steal from you. I only took back..."

"Ah, so you do remember our little night together. Let me ask you, Lily, what is your game here tonight? Who are you swindling this time?"

"I…" Her words evaporated into the rose-infused air as another lady approached, having just returned from the dance floor.

"Shall we have that dance now, my lady?" he asked Lily.

"I'm not available this evening," she replied in a shaky voice.

He grabbed the card on her wrist and lifted it up for inspection before she could react. Empty. "As it happens, it seems your next dance is free. How fortuitous."

After a slight hesitation, she lifted her chin and replied with a tight smile, "Oh, I must have been mistaken. That would be lovely then. A dance…with you."

Of all of the disasters Lillian imagined befalling her this evening, seeing Devon again was not one of them. He had completely taken her unawares and made sport of her in the middle of her first ball. If Evangeline had not chosen that exact moment to return from dancing, Lillian would have never agreed to dance with the man—nay, the duke! He had hardly been the epitome of honest behavior that night himself.

Mr. Grey. You may call me Devon. Ha! And now she would be forced to dance with the arrogant man.

He did look dashing in black evening wear. If he were anyone other than a lying duke, she might actually enjoy her very first dance with a gentleman. He, however, was no gentleman. She pasted on a superior smile and glided to the floor, trying not to think about the flinching male muscles under her hand.

They stood together waiting for the quadrille to

begin. He grasped her hand in his as he asked, "So, Lily, whose jewels are you after this time?"

"I am not a thief," she whispered through clenched teeth. She tried not to think of the warm hand wrapped around hers and looked over his right shoulder as she said, "I am here for the same reason as all of these other ladies tonight."

"I would believe you if I had not experienced first-hand your light fingers when it comes to valuables."

"I do not have light fingers."

"No, your fingers do appear to be the correct weight. Your skirt, on the other hand..."

Her eyes flew up to meet his dark gray gaze. "What are you implying? I am not that sort of lady!"

"Oh? You could have fooled me. Or was that all a ruse just to steal from me? Should I lock away the pin on my cravat? It's a ruby, you know."

At that moment the music began to play from the balcony overhead and the dance began. Lillian arranged her face in a semblance of pleasantness as they crossed the floor together and she curtsied. Her hand fell from his as she moved away to dance a turn with an older gentleman before returning to the duke.

"I don't want your cravat pin!" she said through clenched teeth. "How dare you talk to me that way? You were hardly honest last year, *Your Grace*." She threw his title at him as if it was the worst insult before gliding away again to circle a lady squeezed into a froth of dark pink frills.

When the dance brought her back to the duke, he leaned toward her to say, "My leaving off my title is not the same as you leaving with my belongings.

Perhaps Lady Dillsworth should put away the good silver. I shall go advise her to do so, shall I?" He made to pull away, leaving her on the floor dancing the quadrille alone.

She held his hand a bit too tightly as she moved across the floor with him once more. "Don't you dare! You could ruin me."

"Ah yes, I could, couldn't I?" He seemed far too comfortable with the prospect of destroying her reputation.

"You would do that to me? You don't even know me." She didn't wish to marry, yet she also didn't wish to be banished from society. She'd been shut away for too many years already. She wanted to live, and this arrogant arse was not going to ruin her chances of enjoying what little freedom life had to offer. She moved away again, turning once more with the older gentleman. Her smile felt etched onto her face, as if she might never be able to remove its false cheerfulness when she returned to the duke.

He glowered down at her as he said, "I know you're here in an attempt to pass yourself off as a virgin to suitors, and we both know how false that is."

She gasped. "You wouldn't." The last thing she wanted to do just now was to finish this dance with him. She wanted to hit him. And yet she glided away to circle the lady with the pink dress. The blasted quadrille! She wanted to rail at him, yet here she was prancing about the floor like a ninny! She was having trouble keeping the harsh thoughts from showing in her eyes by the time she returned to him.

"I could be persuaded to keep my mouth closed, for a price," he offered with a smile.

He was smiling at her! Was he enjoying this torment of his? "I don't think I would be willing to pay *that* price, sir." She could not believe her ears. Duke or not, no man could suggest what he was suggesting. She would rather die a thousand deaths than to ever allow him such liberties again.

"Oh, I'm not as horrible as that. I only wish to have some entertainment this season. Innocent entertainment," he clarified as he turned her to a halt before him. "And thanks to you, I'll get it."

"How do you know I'll agree to your terms of…of blackmail?" The music died and the couples around them began to move away. Lillian seemed to be rooted to the parquet floor as she stared up at His Grace in disbelief.

"Because, Lily, you cannot afford to lose your reputation. Not if you are, in fact, husband hunting, as you claimed earlier. And if you are here on less than honorable terms, as I suspect, then you cannot afford to lose this cover as a proper miss that you've created for your crimes."

She truly did not care about her chances at a good marriage, but she did not want her family's name dragged through the dirty streets of London. She often criticized her brothers for not upholding the notion of family honor.

How would it look if she did the same? No. She could not allow this vile man to spread the tale of her one night of rebelliousness to every listening ear within the *ton*. "Perhaps I will agree to your proposal. You must allow me time to think on it."

He smiled, the light that gleamed behind his gray-blue eyes holding her still in spite of her desire to blacken those eyes until they were narrow gray slits. Her nerves frayed further at the thought of what he was planning. No good could come of that devious look.

"Who knows? You may just enjoy the game by the end of it all."

"Somehow I doubt that. I would have to be mad to enjoy any activity that involved you." She turned and began to walk away, only to have him catch up with her within a few paces and place her hand on his arm.

"Oh, you wound me, Lily. Although I must admit it's rather nice being mad. You would do well to try it." He chuckled and patted the hand on his arm.

"You're admitting that you're mad? Clearly, I've known so for the past half hour, but to hear it from your own lips is astonishing." She looked up into his face, her gaze landing on the lips she had just referred to. That was a mistake because it only brought to mind how those lips felt pressed against hers. Thankfully his next statement jarred her back to their present situation.

"Have you not heard? I'm the Mad Duke of Thornwood. Although I believe we moved past formalities when you screamed my given name in a moment of passion while naked in my bed."

Her hand clenched on his arm as she urged in a hushed whisper, "Please stop saying such things!"

"Agree to my terms and I'll be happy to oblige," he countered with a grin.

"Very well."

"There. That wasn't so terribly difficult, was it?"

"I hate you," she huffed as they wound their way

through the crowd back to her friend and their spot near the column.

"Ah, the passionate Lily of a year past may reemerge from her confinement still," he murmured close to her ear.

"Perhaps, but never for you."

"Never? Hmm, that sounds like a challenge. We won't think about that for now, though. I must leave you to your friends, or people will indeed begin to talk about us. Now that you've agreed to my terms, I would hate to tarnish your reputation by mere association with me."

"You did not directly state the terms of your hideous blackmail, *Your Grace*." She chanced a look back up at him, trying to read his expression, to no avail.

"That I did not, did I?"

"No, you did not," she pressed.

"And here you are back safely with Miss Green. As I promised, Miss Phillips remains in one piece. Now, if you will excuse me, ladies, I must go." With a charming smile and a nod of his dark head, he was gone.

Lillian turned to Sue and noticed she was biting her lip, her brows drawn together in concern. Was everyone distressed by the Mad Duke's presence? *She* certainly found him most distressing.

Sue's voice shook slightly as she said, "Lillian, I have a feeling this season is going to bring some interesting developments for us."

"Yes. I fear the same."

Sue turned to her with wide brown eyes. "You danced with the Mad Duke. He never attends balls, let alone dances with anyone."

This made Lillian remember that Sue had spent many years mingling with the *ton* and therefore knew much more of the people there than she did. Perhaps she could learn something more about her adversary that would help her fight back against him. With that in mind, she asked, "Why is he called the Mad Duke?"

"All I know is that people say his father was mad and passed the condition to his son. Positively everyone talks about him. I'm sure his presence here will be discussed in every salon across town tomorrow. And he only danced with you. That makes you rather scandalous, too. How exciting."

"I have done nothing scandalous!"

"I meant nothing by it, Lillian. This will only serve to make you more popular. You're sure to be betrothed this season now, thanks to the Mad Duke's attentions."

"That insufferable man's presence is going to destroy all of my plans. I wish I had never met him. If I could only go back and change it all…"

"You talk as if you were acquainted before tonight. It was only one dance, Lillian. How is he destroying your plans?"

"Oh, Sue, it's already far too jumbled a mess to explain."

"That I completely understand," Sue replied with a kind smile. "Like I said, this season is going to be interesting. That much I believe we can count on."

Six

DEVON SHRUGGED INTO HIS COAT, GAZING AT HIS reflection in the mirror. "Ah, yes, you were right. The light gray does look better with this coat. I would hate to be unfashionable while inside my home with no one to take notice." He turned a wry grin on his fastidious valet.

Heston had served him for eight years. They'd traveled together to foreign lands, making scientific discoveries along the way. The man had been at Devon's side as he sailed to unknown worlds mapping shipping routes. And now they were finding a path through London's society together. He was older than Devon by quite a few years, although he had never asked Heston's age. Wherever Devon's adventures had taken him, Heston had always gone along without a complaint, although Devon knew he was pleased to be back on English soil.

He was glad of the man's assistance, for Devon could dress well enough for a Himalayan mountain-climbing expedition or an African excursion, but the wilds of London could never be tamed if not for his trusted valet's influence. Devon's mind was always elsewhere—in a book or a scientific journal, perhaps thinking over cargo holds or new destinations and profitability—but never on what cravat he wore. And a crime of fashion, like madness, was a sin the *ton* would not forgive.

"I am glad you approve of the waistcoat, Your Grace. Do you require any clothing be made ready for this evening?"

"No, I plan on spending the night at home. One ball a week is quite enough for me, thank you."

"Yes, when she cornered me in the hallway this morning, Her Grace was quite curious about your appearance at the ball last night."

"You didn't tell her anything, did you?"

"Of course not, Your Grace. I said I could only comment on the cut of your coat, which was quite fine."

"Very good, Heston. I'm sure I'll have to speak with her eventually. It seems she has taken to lurking around the library when I am attempting to work. However, I hope to delay that conversation as long as possible. I'm sure she is none too thrilled that I attended last night yet didn't escort her." He sighed. "It couldn't be helped. I hadn't planned on attending, you know. It was all quite last minute."

"Yes. I recall. You wouldn't even allow me time to properly prepare your evening wear."

Devon waved the comment away as if it were a pesky bug. "I looked fine. You're such a worrier, Heston. Not everything in life can be planned."

"No, yet we must endeavor to be starched for the occasion when possible."

"Quite right, Heston." It was true. When possible, it did pay to be prepared. The image of Lily drifted into his mind. His hands curled into fists at his sides, and a menacing look clouded his eyes as he gazed at his image in the mirror. The very idea of her got under his skin. His wounded pride from last year must be mended. And now he had his chance.

Only, what to do with her now? What was the appropriate sentencing for a lady who seduced, stole, lied, and disappeared? He would have to think about it. There was no rush in the matter. No, he would take his time. As Heston said, he should be prepared. He would wager that right now she was fretting over what he might do to her or if he would change his mind and tell everyone of her past escapades.

A smile creased his face. The thought of her worrying over him was rather satisfying. Finally, the shoe was on the proper foot. Perhaps he would let her stew for a day before he took advantage of her situation and forced her to do something for him. Now, that would take some preparation. What would hurt her the most while here in London...for the season...the blasted season of the *ton*...while she husband hunted?

"Heston, I need you to assist me in my research today."

"Research for shipping routes or the construction of the new ships? I would be honored to aid in your work. What do you need?"

"No, this research is of a personal nature."

"Of course, Your Grace."

"There is a lady..."

"A lady?" Heston raised a brow.

"Yes, a lady. You know those reasonless beings you see on the streets wearing dresses."

"Of course. My apologies. Please continue."

"There's a lady who is new in town, a Miss Lillian Phillips. I believe she may be of some relation to Lord Bixley. She must be an unknown cousin or some such, because I only recently heard of her existence. I need you to gather some information. Where she is staying while in town. What balls she will be attending. If she has been seen with anyone around town or if her name is attached to any gentleman's name…"

He broke off as he pulled open a drawer in the table beside his bed. His fingers trailed over the silk stocking Lily had left behind last year. Clearing his throat, he slammed the drawer, resolve steeling his voice as he turned back to Heston. "I want to know anything you can discover about her. Every detail."

"Yes, Your Grace. May I be so bold as to ask if this lady is of a particular interest to you as your future duchess?"

"God no! I merely have some business dealings that involve her to a degree. At present, I would expect her to steal my silver at a dinner party."

"Quite."

"So you see why I need much more information here. She will not get away with anything this time. That is a fact."

"This time?"

"Oh, just retrieve the information I seek and do be stealthy about it."

"Always."

"Oh, good morning, Nathaniel. I was just having some tea. Won't you join me?" Lillian lifted the teapot and began to pour before he could reply. With those circles under his eyes, he looked as if he could use the entire pot of tea.

"If that is the strongest beverage you're offering this morning, then yes. Tea it is. Apologies, darling. It was a long night."

"Anything of import, or simply long?"

"I had a bit too much to drink at my club and lost horribly at cards. I shall have to live that loss down with my mates for quite some time. And then, as if that were not atrocious enough, I ran into Solomon." Nathaniel slumped into the dining-room chair nearest Lillian and lifted the tea to his mouth, draining the entire cup. "Ah, that does knock a few of the cobwebs off."

Lillian refilled his cup, dreading the conversation about their brother that seemed destined to occur this morning. Her fingers curled into fists around the napkin in her lap, and her spine went rigid. She had managed an entire evening without thinking once of Solomon. Granted, it had been an evening spent at home. Her mind had been inexplicably filled with a certain obnoxious duke, but she'd had no thoughts of Solomon. And Lillian had only caught a distant glimpse of Solomon at the Dillsworth ball. She should have known her reprieve would not last.

"What did our brother have to say for himself?"

"He gave me this." Nathaniel pulled a folded piece of parchment from his pocket and tossed it onto the table in front of Lillian. She looked at it for a moment, hoping it would burst into flames and she wouldn't have to learn what it contained. She reached out and placed one finger on the paper, sliding it closer across the dark cherry tabletop. "Do you know what it's about?"

"It seems to be in reference to your potential suitors."

"I don't have any potential suitors."

Nathaniel heaved a sigh as his eyes met hers. "You do now. Read it."

"What do you mean, I do now?"

"I know you said that you didn't dance with a soul at the ball night before last, but you only arrived in town a few days ago. What does he expect?"

Lillian ignored the lack of truth in his statement, for she would not consider His Grace a suitor—ever. No, she had no suitors, and that was the way she wished it to remain. What had Solomon done? Her mind came back to the present when she realized Nathaniel was still speaking.

"I told him as much last night. Selecting suitors for you without your consent—it's horribly out of fashion."

She ripped open the missive and saw a list of names swimming before her eyes.

Viscount Amberstall
Earl of Harrow
Marquess of Elandor
Viscount Hingsworth
Earl of Erdway

Who were these men? They certainly didn't know her. Why would they be interested in marriage? Her dowry was not large. And what could Solomon possibly have to gain from an arrangement with one of these men? She truly was going to be auctioned off like an old plow mule. The idea was appalling.

Her hand shook with anger, making the parchment tremble before her eyes. She carefully refolded the letter and laid it back down on the table. "Yes, well, I believe I am in need of some air, if you will excuse me." Sliding her chair back, she rose, turning for the door.

"Lillian, we'll find a way to stop him. There must be a more suitable husband for you than these gentlemen. Surely you'll catch someone's eye who is not a friend of Solomon's." Nathaniel's words stopped her progress for the door.

"Yes. All will be fine. I'm going for a walk in the park now." Her voice was a bit too chipper as she spoke. She could hear the suppressed anger but could do nothing to stop it. Her throat was closing, her world was closing, and she needed air now.

"At least take a maid for your safety and propriety," Nathaniel called out.

She ignored his plea. If only she believed her own words when she said that all would be fine. Solomon was set on choosing a husband for her in the most barbaric fashion possible. It sounded as if she had no choice but to marry. She could choose from his list or run away with no money and no place to go.

Where was the third door? She wanted a peaceful life of freedom. Freedom could never be found within the confines of marriage. She had been bullied by enough men in her family to know the truth of that. A gentleman would never allow his wife as much as a free thought. She grabbed her hat from a side table in the foyer, stuffing it on top of her head. Without a glance in the mirror, she was racing down the front steps.

The morning air was cool and crisp against her face. It did not, however, serve to cool her heated thoughts. Was there no option for her in which she could grow old without a man telling her what she could and could not do?

It didn't seem like Solomon was going to allow her room to dissuade any gentlemen from courting her. She didn't know any of the gentlemen on that list. A few of the names she recognized, but they didn't know her. They didn't care for her. She was expected to spend her life looking across a dining table at a man she felt nothing for. At that moment, for some unknown reason, a vision of storm-cloud blue eyes gazing at her from across a table filled her mind. She blinked away the thought.

Where had that infuriating man's face come from when she was thinking of her future? She would sooner choose from Solomon's list than spend her days with His Grace. She rounded the corner into Hyde Park, so angry she paid little attention to where she was going. The trees around her grew dense as she walked, forcing her to duck under occasional limbs and step over fallen logs. If she could keep walking forever she would, never looking back. Lillian came to a small clearing, relishing the feel of the cool breeze that the trees had been blocking. It brushed against her cheeks and pulled at the ties of her hat under her chin.

With no one here to see, she removed her hat, allowing the sun to warm her head. Escaped strands of her hair danced across her face in unison with the wind. She felt peace for the first time since arriving in the city. Her problems were behind her, caught in the brambles of the woods at her back. Here, she was alone with the weak morning sun and the tall grass at her feet.

She sat at the base of a tree, taking a moment to arrange her skirts. Brushing a bit of dust off here and flicking a leaf to the ground there, she had only just looked up from her mindless task when a rider entered the clearing on a magnificent gray horse.

Hidden at the edge of the woods, she stilled, watching him as one would a duck on a pond or a bee on a flower. He cantered around, then dismounted near the center of the clearing. The man seemed to be enjoying the same sunshine she had been soaking in, for he turned around in a circle with his face lifted toward the sun.

She was not close enough to see his features, but he looked to be talking to his horse now. He laughed loud enough for her to hear as the horse nipped at his pockets. It was a deep laugh, the laugh of someone who enjoyed every drop of sunshine in a day. She felt a smile tug at the corners of her stubborn lips.

He pulled something out and offered it in the palm of his hand. The horse took the treat greedily, and then the man patted his mount on the shoulder in an affectionate manner. What a kind man. She had seen many men whip their animals to inspire speed or good behavior, yet with these two, there seemed to be a kinship. It was refreshing to see that there might be one decent gentleman left in the world.

He pulled the reins down and began to walk toward her corner of the clearing, leading his horse behind him. Oh dear. Should she move? But perhaps he still would not see her, and she did not want to leave just yet.

Her eyes were busy idly exploring the cling of his breeches to his muscular thighs and the hang of his jacket across his broad shoulders. She was reminded of Devon's muscular build when she had seen him unclothed a year ago. It was no surprise, for she compared every man to him. His was the only male body she had seen—or felt. She grinned.

It really was too bad he'd turned out to be such a tyrant when they met again. His behavior at the ball did not match the man of her memory. That was the way of memories, though, wasn't it? Only remembering the good or the bad, depending on one's perception at the time, went with the territory. In this case, her memories must be deceiving her, for he was clearly a horrible man at heart.

What would he force her to do for him to keep his silence? He had not given her any hint. He thought her a thief. What if he made her steal for him? That was a terrible notion. The gentleman in the clearing was walking steadily closer. She now wondered if she should have moved away. He would surely tread on her if he kept on his current path. His features were now close enough to see.

Storm-cloud blue eyes regarded her with a look of surprise from beneath unruly black hair. She would have laughed if it were not so horribly mortifying. How had he found her? Had he known she was sitting there? And now it was too late to move, too late to hide, because he was approaching.

"Good morning, Your Grace," Lillian chirped, completely annoyed by his presence.

"Lily? What are you doing here in the least inhabited area of the park?" He glanced around before adding, "Alone?"

"I took a stroll, not that it's any of your business."

"A stroll that brought you to the only wild area of a five-thousand-acre park?"

"Yes."

"Without so much as a maid?"

"Yes," she returned with defiance.

He shrugged. "Very well. Should we call this fate?"

"I hope this is not what fate would favor me with this morning, although I should not doubt it."

He sat beside her on the ground, propping one elbow on his knee in a relaxed manner while his horse wandered away, grazing on grass. "You are a difficult lady to find, Lily."

"You *did* have me followed here. I knew it!" Her spine straightened even further as she turned accusing eyes on him.

"You knew no such thing. I was out for my morning ride, the ride I take every morning. I could accuse you of following me," he said, breaking into a slight smile.

"I would never—" She broke off when he continued speaking.

"I was referring to your stay with the younger Mr. Phillips when there is a Bixley residence in town used by the Phillips family. I found it curious. Lord Bixley is ashamed of having you as a poor cousin, is he?"

She bristled at the thought of Josiah being in a position to look down on her presence. Her temper flared in an instant. "Lord Bixley is my brother, you arse! And I would not stay under that roof if it were the last dwelling in England."

He looked taken aback by her outburst. Silence fell for only a second before he recovered. "That makes Solomon Phillips your brother as well."

"That is generally the way that family trees are arranged."

"Hmm, well, it matters not. I've made arrangements to attend the Geddings' ball. You will be attending as well, I've heard."

"How did you know that?"

"A lady's schedule while in London is hardly secret. I asked a few questions and discovered answers to those questions. It was surprisingly simple once I learned where you were residing."

"You've been spying on me?"

"When phrased that way, it sounds rather distasteful. I prefer inquiring after you. Much more pleasant, don't you think?"

"No, I don't think. I don't find any of this pleasant. Why must you put me through this? You can control whether you tell of our past or not. Surely my transgressions don't warrant such behavior. It was nothing really."

"Nothing," he grated back at her. "You lied about your identity and then stole from me. That is more than nothing, Lily."

"I only took my…rather, *your* pocket watch. A watch that you only owned for one afternoon. I don't see why it upset you so."

"It's not about the watch!" He looked away and took a deep breath. "See that you are at the ball tonight," he demanded. "I trust that you will save me a dance between those of all your suitors."

She blinked up at him. "You know, then?"

There was a moment of pity mixed with some more intense emotion that she could not decipher in his eyes as he gazed at her. "Lily, when wagers are entered on the books at White's gentlemen's club over the outcome of a lady's London season, everyone knows." With that, he turned on his heel, strode to his horse, and mounted in one fluid motion.

He left her there swallowing those last words like bitter medicine. She had become the subject of gambling now? It was mortifying. How far was Solomon going to take her torture? Tonight she would have to put on a smile and arrive at a ball where everyone knew she was being gambled upon and auctioned off. If that was not enough, now she would also be doing the bidding of the Mad Duke.

Had he just demanded another dance? Did life get worse than this? If it did, she was going to set off across this clearing and keep walking until she was well away from everything she knew. She leaned her head back on the tree and stared at the hazy blue sky, listening to the clopping sound of the duke's horse as he rode away.

If she had the ability to turn back time and choose a different path, would she? Would she still walk into that Bond Street shop, knowing what she knew now? Her hand drifted over the pearl necklace at her throat.

It had all begun so innocently, with the toe of her black half boot sinking into the mud of a soggy Bond Street while she was on a quest to retrieve a few family heirlooms. If Lillian had known what disasters that man would bring into her life, would she have still run after him? She shook her head in wonder.

However, the answer to that question made no difference today. The past was in the past and could not be changed. Sighing, she rose to her feet, picked up her hat, and set off back to Nathaniel's house.

Seven

THAT EVENING, LILLIAN FOUND HERSELF DRESSED IN a gown of creamy yellow and standing in the middle of the Geddings' ball. The day had passed in a haze of anxiety that she had escaped mostly by hiding in a book. Nathaniel had led her to the ballroom and disappeared into a card room, as was apparently his custom.

In the crush of people, Lillian did not see any of the ladies she had befriended a few nights prior. Therefore, she busied herself by walking the perimeter of the room and admiring the large tapestries that adorned the walls. She stepped around a tree that had been brought inside for decoration and was passing a group of giggling young ladies when she saw Sue.

"Lillian, I am so happy you've arrived. I thought I would have to chat with my mother all evening. You know I love chats with my mother. But at a ball, who wants to endure that humiliation?" Sue beamed as she grabbed Lillian's gloved hand, dragging her across the floor toward the refreshment table. "Not I," Sue said over her shoulder.

Lillian stumbled after Sue, attempting an air of decorum while being pulled through the crowd. "I am always pleased to be of assistance. May I ask where we're going?"

"I spotted Lord Steelings entering the ballroom, so we are leaving it. Shall we escape to the terrace or the corridor, or perhaps the ladies' retiring room? Yes, that will be just the place. Don't you think so? He couldn't possibly find us there. Can you imagine the look on the ladies' faces if a gentleman entered the ladies' retiring room?"

Lillian was struggling to keep up with Sue's spritely pace, along with her trail of thoughts. "Or we could slip into this parlor. Why don't you wish to see Lord Steelings?"

"His incessant questions, his annoying sense of humor, his looks…" Sue ticked off reasons on her fingers as they entered a side parlor where older matrons were gathered to hold court and sip lemonade.

Lillian was confused by Sue's chatter about Lord Steelings and tried to get some clarification. "Does he have a poor sense of humor?"

"No, but that has nothing to do with it."

"Oh." Lillian was unsure what her friend was talking about but decided to drop the conversation as the subject of Lord Steelings seemed to anger Sue.

Lillian followed Sue into the room, where they tried in vain to blend in with their surroundings. Finding two chairs near a corner, they sat together, ignoring the stares they received for daring to be young and present in this particular side parlor. Lillian gave a slight smile to the elegant older woman to her left. She was dressed in deep blue and had kind, gray-blue eyes that fell across Lillian with the not-quite-masked look of someone who was just given an unexpected gift.

Lillian hoped this would not lead to an entire evening trapped in conversation with a lady who only spoke of her grandchildren and her bunions. She put on a smile and did as she must, offering a polite greeting. At her side, she could hear Sue doing the same for the lady at her right.

"Good evening. I do hope we haven't taken the seats of any friends of yours."

"You, my dear, may sit anywhere you wish. However, I wonder that you are not in the ballroom catching the eye of some gentleman, perhaps even a duke?" The woman's eyes twinkled with delight at her new company.

Lillian's eyes slid to Sue at her side. "We are rather trying to avoid the ballroom at the moment. I hope you don't mind our company."

"Not at all, my dear. Not at all. I have discussed Lady Autright's ailing feet and Lady Milford's hurt back until I feared I might never hear proper conversation again. Tell me about yourself." She patted Lillian's arm in a motherly way that Lillian had not experienced since she was a girl.

"I'm Miss Phillips and this is my friend Miss Green. You may call me Lillian. This is my first season. I'm in town from Whitby where my family resides. Miss Green is…"

"Phillips, you say? Are you Lord Bixley's daughter? But of course you are. You have your mother's eyes. I was so sorry to hear of your father's passing last year."

"You knew my mother?"

"Of course, dear. Everyone knew Honoria. Quite popular, you know. How fortunate that you are the one who has…" She paused with a smile. "That you are the one who has chosen to sit with me this evening."

Somehow Lillian didn't think that was what the woman was originally going to say, but she smiled in return. With Mama gone for so many years now, it was refreshing to find someone who had known her. Lillian's own memories had begun to fade with time.

"I can remember back in our day when Honoria would sweep into a room and every head would turn, much like with you this evening in that lovely yellow gown. It serves to bring out the gold of your hair. Although you have no need of that fichu at your neck. Styles are quite low this year. Your mother would not have bothered with such. She liked to be fashionable. Between us, dear, she dressed to hide her bookish nature. Not many people in the *ton* knew how intelligent your mother was beneath her loveliness. Tell me, are you as well read as she?"

"I do love to read, mostly novels and travel journals. I know it's not particularly appropriate for a lady to admit to such bluestocking tendencies, but I trust that you will not spread my secret."

"Oh, certainly not, dear." The woman tittered and patted her hand again, making Lillian smile. "I can see that we will get on just fine. You must come and take tea with me."

"I would be honored to do so. I am sorry, but I don't believe I heard your name."

"I'll tell you stories of your mother. I have a feeling

you'll find my current residence most interesting. There are quite a few collections of foreign artifacts and plantings, as well as an extensive library of travel journals. I did forget to introduce myself in all the hubbub of getting acquainted, didn't I? Oh my, my, where is my head? I'm the duchess of Thornwood." She broke off the conversation, looking up past Lillian as Lord Steelings approached.

Lillian couldn't breathe. She had inadvertently sought out and conversed with the insufferable duke's mother. His mother and her mother had been friends! She had agreed to take tea at his home! Oh dear. Her mind flooded with images of his home and what she had allowed to happen there. She tried to block out the memories of their night together, and yet that seemed to be the only place her mind wished to travel at the moment.

How could she have tea with his mother under the same roof where she had behaved so abominably? Could she keep up appearances and browse His Grace's collections as if she had never heard of them before? Everywhere she went in this city, she seemed to step a little deeper in the mire. She dragged her mind forcibly back to the conversation.

The duchess stated, "Lord Steelings, do not act as if you do not see me sitting here simply because I am with these two eye-catching young ladies. You are not too old for me to take in hand, you know."

"Your Grace," Lord Steelings offered with an elegant bow. "I would not dream of cutting you in such a manner. I was only temporarily distracted by your company this evening. I do hope my knuckles will stay intact."

"As long as you stay out of my tea biscuits, your knuckles are safe."

"Ladies, the Duchess of Thornwood is known for rapping knuckles if you put one toe out of line. Do beware, especially if you think to sneak and eat her sweets." Steelings laughed. "Or is the rapping of knuckles reserved only for mischievous boys of ten years of age?"

"Dear boy, I have not seen you nearly often enough in recent years," she admonished. "You must come around for a visit now that I am in town. Have you seen my son this evening? He claimed to be attending, which I found most interesting."

"I have not. I haven't seen Thornwood in a few days. He said he would attend this evening? That is curious."

"Indeed." The duchess glanced meaningfully at Lillian. "Dear, you are looking a bit pink. You're not overheated in this warm room, are you?"

"No, Your Grace. I am quite all right. Although perhaps some air would do me good. If you will excuse me." Lillian stood to leave. "Sue, I'm going to the terrace. Would you like to come with me?" She needed time to breathe, time to think.

"I was coming to collect Miss Green for our dance," Steelings stated.

"Go ahead, Lillian. I'll catch up with you later."

"Do not forget you agreed to join me for tea, dear," she heard called from over her shoulder.

Lillian turned and smiled. "How could I forget?" she said quite truthfully before walking quickly away. How indeed? She skirted the ballroom, dipping between groups of chatting ladies and gatherings of men deep in discussion. Finally, she was within sight of the terrace doors when a hand caught her elbow. She turned, expecting to see the duke, who seemed to be everywhere she went, and came face to face with Solomon. This night was going downhill at a speedy rate.

"Lillian, I've been looking for you. I thought we agreed you would make yourself available at the balls you attend."

"Good evening, Solomon. I am ever so disappointed that we are only now seeing one another this evening. When I arrived I said, 'Where is Solomon? Of everyone here, he is truly the one with whom I would like to visit.'"

"There is no need for your sharp replies, Lillian. I have a few people I wish for you to meet. I would wager that your dance card will see a name or two on its lines this evening." He pulled her back toward the entrance to the ballroom and shoved her toward a gangly gentleman with flaming red hair who was busy hovering over three petite young ladies and clearly trying to get a view down their necklines. She tugged her own gown higher and ensured that her fichu was in place before he could turn to look at her.

"Mr. Phillips, it's good to see you this evening. I was telling these lovely young ladies how fascinating the gallery at the Geddings' home is." He turned back toward them. "See if you can slip away after the final waltz, and I will give all three of you a tour of the gallery you won't soon forget."

The ladies tittered at his attention and shot Lillian

reproachful looks as he turned to face her. She felt instantly dirty under his intense gaze. He pulled his gaze from her lace-covered bosom to say, "You must be Miss Phillips. It's certainly a pleasure. I am Lord Hingsworth." His attention shifted to Solomon as he added, "Your sister is quite charming. You didn't exaggerate." His thin face turned back to Lillian, his brown eyes drinking in her form within the yellow gown.

Solomon smiled a thin smile of triumph. "Why don't you dance with Lord Hingsworth, Lillian?"

"Yes, excellent idea! May I have the honor of this dance, Miss Phillips?"

Would she kill her brother? Most certainly, and soon! She would rather be slapped in the face with a fish than to allow that man's hands near her body. Yet Solomon was glaring at her and she did not wish to cause a scene in the Geddings' ballroom. It was only one dance. Surely she would survive in the same manner many other ladies survived dances they did not wish to dance.

"Yes, Lord Hingsworth, a dance would be nice." She almost choked on the last word but managed a serene smile in his direction. As he led her to the floor to join the country dance that had already begun, her fingers itched to be away from his sleeve, her lips tightening into a stern, peevish look sure to turn any man away.

"Your brother has told me about your situation."

"I'm afraid you have me at a disadvantage, then, for I was not aware I had a situation," Lillian replied.

"You are in need of a husband, are you not?"

"I don't know that I would phrase it in such terms."

"Miss Phillips, from the moment I laid eyes on you, a vision in gold, I knew that we must be together. I know this is a bit forward of me and yet I cannot help what my lips must express to you."

"Do you mean you would abandon those three young misses in the gallery for me? Your flattery astounds me."

"It would be my pleasure. Why not begin our future together now? My hands will guide you just as they do now."

Lillian almost stumbled. "I don't believe that will be possible, Lord Hingsworth. You see, I am spoken for during all my remaining dances this evening. I have become popular quite rapidly. It has been very unexpected."

"That is odd. Your brother led me to believe that I could enjoy this entire evening with you if I so chose. I was not aware of any competition for your affection."

"He was mistaken," Lillian chirped.

"I see. I also see that you fit perfectly in my arms. Have you noticed it, too? It's magical, isn't it? I'm amazed by what I feel for you after such a short time, Miss Phillips."

"Lust?"

"Ha, you jest. Quick with the tongue. Your brother warned me of that. Come with me to the gardens tonight. It will be only us together in the moonlight, alone."

"I'm sorry but I really am quite busy." The music ended and she'd never heard such a glorious sound as the final note. Finally. "It is a shame that our dance has ended now. I really must be off."

He grasped her wrist as she turned to leave and placed her hand on his arm. His hand lingered a bit too long over hers. She risked being ill right here on the dance floor if he touched her once more. She allowed him to lead her back to Solomon.

"Solomon, she is quite a gem. Too bad all of her other dances are promised. I would like to…further our acquaintance."

"Her dances are promised, are they? Why don't you join her for the supper hour? She was going to dine with me, but I will gladly relinquish my position so that you might spend more time together."

Lillian's mind raced to find some logical reason why she could not dine with this horrible man. She looked at Solomon with the sinking feeling that she would not get out of this situation. Just then, another gentleman arrived, sidling up to Solomon. Had her brother contacted every degenerate male within the *ton* in an effort to be rid of her? The dark-haired man appeared to already be foxed as he listed to the side with one step. For goodness' sake!

Was she to keep such company for the remainder of the evening? She pushed away the thought that she could very well be forced to keep such company for the remainder of her life. There must be a way out of this muddle. She only needed one good excuse, yet none came to her.

"Have I missed my opportunity with your sister, Mr. Phillips? I was afraid of that. That's what comes of arriving late to a ball." His eyes swept over her with casual dismissal before returning to Solomon.

"Ah, Lord Harrow. Perhaps we could all enjoy the

refreshments together. There is enough of my charming sister to go around."

"Solomon!" Lillian hissed in reprimand at being made to sound like a common strumpet. Her spine straightened a fraction as she touched the pearls at her throat for added strength. She was going to need all of the strength she could muster if she was to survive the coming hour.

Lord Hingsworth offered an arm she did not wish to take as he said, "I'm pleased I get to spend more time with you, even if I do have to share you with the likes of Harrow. Do not fear. I will protect you from his unwanted advances."

"Truly that will not be necessary," Lillian stated just as she became aware of another gentleman approaching at her back. She was beginning to feel like a bone in a dogfight. If this was another of Solomon's friends come to leer at her, he could go well away and rot. She had enough to deal with at the moment.

"Ah, but she promised to dine with me when we spoke not a quarter hour ago."

Lillian spun on her heel and gazed up into Thornwood's face. For once she was glad to see him. "Yes, I did, Your Grace. I'm glad you remembered."

"Shall we?" he asked, though his gaze was narrowed on Lord Harrow at her back.

"Just a moment, Thornwood. I need to have a word with my sister first," Solomon said, tugging her elbow to move away from the other men.

"Solomon, I don't know what you are attempting to achieve by involving me in the gambling books and selecting despicable men for me to entertain, but I will not cooperate!"

"Lillian, we have discussed this and it has been concluded. You have not yet reached your majority and will do what is required as your duty to this family. I am attempting to find you a husband, an effort for which you should be thankful. I don't care what imaginary men you will be dancing with this evening, but you will be saving the last waltz for Lord Hingsworth. I will hear no other talk on this."

"Imaginary? Where do you think the Duke of Thornwood came from? Is he an apparition?"

"He is mad! Not to mention a confirmed bachelor." Solomon stepped closer and lowered his voice. "Lillian, you know nothing of the plans I am arranging for the benefit of our family. Sometimes sacrifices must be made for business to prosper. It is your duty to serve this family in a beneficial marriage. If you are not waiting to dance with Hingsworth when the last waltz begins, I will no longer allow you such liberties as choosing where you reside or wearing those flashy clothes Nathaniel purchased for you."

"One day you will regret your treatment of me, Solomon."

"That seems extremely unlikely."

She turned and walked back to the duke. She took his arm and practically dragged him the first few steps away before he caught up to her. "Hingsworth and Harrow? They don't seem your type, Lily."

"Just because you saved me from having to dine with those poor excuses for gentlemen does not mean you're allowed to torment me for the next hour.

Actually, I was planning on getting some air." She stopped, turning to look at him. "So, I will just leave you here if you don't mind. Thank you."

"Fresh air does sound nice. I believe I'll join you." He replaced her hand on his arm and continued toward the doors just ahead. "The terrace should be clearing off now, with the promise of roast beef in the next room."

"I would prefer to be alone." She stepped through the doors that had been thrown open to the stone terrace at the rear of the ballroom and promptly dropped his arm.

A full moon illuminated the trees that lined the garden, casting long shadows across the lawn. A quiet peace lingered here in the glistening light, one that did not exist inside the overheated ballroom. She took a breath, trying to steady her nerves from the unwanted dance and subsequent argument with her brother. Had anyone heard that quarrel? Her anger had gotten the better of her.

She could not allow Solomon to upset her so. It would do the family name no good for them to be seen having an altercation in front of the entire *ton*. She must be more conscious of her actions. She would adhere to only the most proper behavior from here forward.

"I'm sure my company is preferable to Lord Hingsworth drooling on you for the next hour while Lord Harrow plies you with drink. However, if you don't see fit to thank me, I can go and get them." He made to turn and leave.

"No! Very well, thank you." She glared at him

as he settled back into a relaxed pose, leaning on the terrace wall with a grin.

"You are most welcome, m'lady."

"Why do all men presume to know what is best for me?" She began to pace, her hands balled into fists at her side. "Has it ever occurred to any of you that I may not want to do your bidding?" She paused to turn and level a glare at him. "That I may have my own ideas about my life?"

"You *agreed* to do my bidding, if you recall."

"Of course I recall!" She continued her pacing.

"You do have my sympathies for having the less desirable half of the *ton* gambling over your attentions."

"I don't want your sympathies. I want a fast horse and a place to run."

"Running away from your problems now, are you? You know that will never work."

She turned and walked back toward the insufferable man, pausing before him. "Spoken like a duke who has no problems and nothing to run from."

"Yes, Lily. My life is sheer perfection. I do so enjoy being trapped in the city where I'm of no use to anyone, the sights never change, and my madness is the topic of conversation everywhere I go." He quirked a brow at her.

"How dreadful that must be for you. How ever do you survive day-to-day life under such torturous conditions as surviving a bit of talk? At least you are in a position to choose your own destiny." She walked to the wall he leaned against, looking down at her hands where they lay on its rough surface. "It seems I will not even be allowed to choose my own husband."

"Many ladies are not allowed that liberty, you know. And a husband is what you claim you came to town to find, or is that another of your lies?"

Lillian stared off into the moonlit garden without answering, watching the candles lining the garden path as they flickered in the breeze. His question was too difficult to answer. Yes, that was the reason she was in town, yet no, she did not desire a husband. He wouldn't understand. She was expected to marry, and apparently that was what she would be doing, even if it was against her wishes.

Finally, she turned back to him. "The purpose of my trip to London is to find a suitable husband. Unfortunately, my brother Solomon has despicable taste in whom I should marry—which is fitting, as his taste for everything else in life involves an insatiable taste for money. Vile man that he is." She paused to take a breath, attempting to cool her thoughts. "Of all the gentlemen in London, I would not consider Lord Hingsworth a suitable husband, nor Lord Harrow."

"Lord Hingsworth is well known by every barmaid and courtesan within the country, so I can see your misgivings on the subject. And Harrow is no better. That particular gentleman has plagued me in business for many years and is always willing to sink to a new depth to close a deal."

"How so?"

"We are both heavily invested in shipping. We have stakes in competing businesses. I won't bore you with the details beyond that." His mouth twisted into a grim smile. "Neither man is ideal. I will agree with you on that score."

"And yet it seems I must share a waltz with Hingsworth this evening."

"As potential husbands, at least both gentlemen in question would be away often."

"Is that the life I have to look forward to? Happiness when my husband is not present? A fast horse is beginning to look more appealing."

"It will allow more time for your clandestine activities, such as stealing from dukes, so there is some benefit to that option."

"I do not participate in clandestine activities!"

"Am I the only lucky one who has experienced your skills, then? I'm fortunate indeed."

"Of course you're the only man I ever..." Her voice trailed away with the heat of the blush rising on her cheeks. She turned away from him so he would not see. He was the only man with whom she had ever done anything at all—share a drink, kiss, become intimate. And yes, she'd stolen from him, which he would clearly never let her forget.

"Why are you tormenting me with an event that happened so long ago? Can you not forget it as I have?"

"You have quite the memory to forget that evening entirely," he returned tightly.

"I would like to forget it forever. I wish I had never..."

"Gotten me intoxicated, seduced me, and then emptied my pockets? I can see how that would be a regrettable circumstance for you."

"It was only a watch. You bought it on Bond Street that very afternoon. Buy another!"

"I did, thank you. But that's not the issue. Although

it is nice to hear you admit to following me like a common pickpocket."

"I truly wish you would tell me what the issue is, then."

His eyes were shuttered, revealing nothing. He pulled a parcel from his pocket, unwrapping it as he said, "When you dance the next waltz with Hingsworth, you will place this in his pocket without his notice." He pulled a handkerchief free, holding it between his fingers in front of her.

"I do not wish to be near that man, much less have my fingers in his pockets."

"As much as it warms my heart to know that you only enjoy delving into *my* pockets, this is what you must do to keep my silence. It's for your own reputation, Lily. I can just as easily tell the world what happened between us."

"What is the significance of this handkerchief?"

"It is the metaphorical handkerchief waved at the beginning of a great race. Its whiteness is a symbol of your unblemished past and purity. It's a square of linen, which represents the paths of our lives woven together in this moment." A smile broke across his face.

"You know that's not what I meant. What will this do? What will happen? Does this handkerchief belong to Hingsworth?"

"No, as it happens, it is an old one of mine. But that's of no consequence. Do as I say and all will go to plan."

"What plan?"

"You will see." He grinned. "Supper is ending. We should get back to the ball now."

"Your Grace, you are truly going to force me to do this, aren't you?"

"It's for your own good. And it's Devon, as I believe I've mentioned before."

He left her standing there holding the handkerchief on the darkened terrace. What was his plan? None of this made any sense. Why did he care so much about the loss of that blasted watch? So much that he would go to these lengths to punish her for stealing it? If he thought he could torture her into returning it, he was mistaken. She would never let that piece go, especially not after she had gone to such extremes to acquire it.

Looking down at the square of linen in her hand, she shrugged. What did this handkerchief have to do with anything?

She shook her head, looking up to stare after him as he disappeared into the crowd. He was the most infuriating man she had ever met. She curled the handkerchief into the palm of her hand and entered the ballroom just as the orchestra struck up its music once more.

Lord Hingsworth approached, holding out his arm for her. "Finally I have you alone again, Miss Phillips. The supper hour was dull indeed without your radiance at my table."

"I do apologize. I promised the Duke of Thornwood I would join him, and I am true to my word." She laid her hand on his arm and feigned a slight smile.

"Lovely and noble. I look forward to seeing more of your…" He paused to rake his eyes down her body. "Assets. Perhaps I could call on you tomorrow. We could go somewhere more private to get to know one another."

"I'm busy tomorrow. I'm quite busy every day, you know. I'm not one to be idle." She stared ahead, not wanting to even look at the man much less dance with him.

"I also enjoy occupying my time in the mornings. We have that in common." He led her to the floor and placed his hand indecently low on her back as they began to waltz.

A sick feeling coiled low in her stomach at his touch but she ignored it, gazing over his shoulder at the other couples circling the floor. "Oh? How do you usually spend your mornings?"

"In bed." Her focus snapped back to his face at his statement. His eyes devoured her in a way that caused her skin to crawl in protest.

"Please, do not look at me in such a way."

"If your brother accepts my suit, soon I will look upon you every day—at meals, in your idle hours, at night when I have you in my bed…" he replied with a crooked-toothed grin.

"If it would not draw the attention of everyone in this ballroom, I would slap you for saying such things to me." She glanced at the handkerchief still clasped in the hand that rested on his shoulder. Whatever the reason for planting the cloth in his pocket, she wanted it over with. Not Solomon nor any duke would force her to dance with such a vile excuse for a gentleman again.

"Yes. Such fire. Our marriage bed will be exciting."

"I have not agreed to any marriage arrangements."

"Solomon is handling the arrangements. Don't fret your pretty little head over it. I have not yet won your hand, but I will. You will see."

At the sound of the final chords of the waltz being played, she breathed a sigh of relief. It was now or never. She pulled away from him and feigned a stumble on the hem of her gown. When Lord Hingsworth reached out, all too ready to steady her, she slipped the handkerchief into his jacket pocket. "Oh my. Thank you, Lord Hingsworth."

"I will return you to your brother. I would not want you to have to spend any more time than required with someone like the Mad Duke, after all. Best to keep close to family at events such as these. Ah, look. Your brother appears to be in discussion with Lord Harrow again. Fret not. I will not allow him to make arrangements for you where I am not involved."

"My brother has been busy. I am always surprised to learn how many arrangements he has made on my behalf."

"Yes, you are very fortunate to have a brother like Mr. Phillips."

"I think that same thought so often that I can't recall the last time I thought it."

He looked confused by her response for a moment before replying, "Don't think too many thoughts. It could wrinkle your brow. It wouldn't do to mar your looks with such activity."

"Quite." She dropped her hand from his arm as soon as possible and took a step away from him. "Thank you for the waltz." She gave a quick curtsy and turned to Solomon. "I must return to my friend. I fear that I have abandoned her completely. Solomon, we will talk soon." She shot him a stern look of business before leaving in search of Sue.

Lillian swept the ballroom but did not dare to stay a moment longer or she would be forced to dance with another lecherous gentleman. She turned into the side parlor where she had hidden before and walked straight into a gentleman's broad chest. She felt his hands close around her upper arms as she looked up into the duke's face.

His eyes held concern within their stormy depths as he asked, "Are you well? You look a bit ashen."

"I am perfectly well, thank you. I have completed my task and danced with Hingsworth. I believe I will need a glass of something stronger than lemonade to recover, as well as hundreds of baths to wash his gaze from my person, but it is done."

"The vision of you taking hundreds of baths will give me sweet dreams tonight. Therefore, he has my thanks."

"Pleased to accommodate, Your Grace. It seems I am to be the object of several unsavory dreams tonight. Now if you will excuse me, I am going to find a place to sit and wait for this dreadful evening to end."

"Did you do as I asked?"

"Yes. I told you so. There is no need for you to torment me any further this night." She moved to slip past him, but he caught her elbow to halt her progress.

"You cannot disappear now. This will be the best entertainment of the night. Come with me." The grin spreading on his face held her fascinated for a moment. It transformed him.

She allowed him to escort her out the door. Glancing back over her shoulder, she witnessed the widened eyes of a few of the matrons in the room. Clearly they never saw that boyish grin on the duke's face, either. The duchess caught Lillian's eye for a split second, and she saw the glimmer of hope and encouragement in his mother's eyes.

Was it so rare that he smiled? Or was she the source of their amazement? She would have to ponder that further when she was alone, but now she needed to have her wits about her. Her experience with this gentleman's company proved that she never knew what he might do next.

He was leading her back toward the terrace doors. "Give me your gloves," he said softly.

"My gloves, why?" she asked glancing at her hands.

"Trust me. Just give me your gloves."

"What if someone notices I'm not wearing any gloves?" She wasn't even going to mention to him that the gloves were new. She frowned and began to tug on the white tips of her fingers.

"No one will notice a thing in a moment." He held out his hand and waited for her to strip her gloves from her hands.

She handed him her gloves with a "Humph." Not understanding any of his actions this evening was beyond frustrating.

He leaned in to instruct her, "Wait here. You will have the best view of the spectacle from this location." When she turned to ask what spectacle he was referring to, he was gone.

Eight

Devon left Lily standing by the terrace doors and casually walked toward the garden stairs. Once darkness cloaked his movements, he increased his pace, anticipation driving him to hurry down the garden path. The task ahead of him was really quite simple. He chuckled to himself as he approached Lord Geddings' dog kennel in the rear of the garden. The howling of the dogs pierced the night.

He crouched low and held out a hand through the fencing. "Shhh. I'm not going to hurt you. Who wants to have some fun?" He felt a few licks against his fingers and a nudge of agreement against the side of his hand. "You want to hunt? Who wants the fox?"

The hounds began to dance in the moonlight, their excitement building as they pushed at the gate of their kennel. He waved Lily's gloves before their noses, listening to them sniff. "Are you ready?"

He flung open the gate and watched as five dogs barreled forward. "Get the fox! Go find him!" he called after them as he hurried back up the path to the terrace. He balled up Lily's gloves and tossed them into a bush as he passed. He would have to buy her another pair. He topped the stairs just after the dogs and rounded the corner at a casual pace into the ballroom.

Shouts of surprise and tittering laughter filled the ballroom as the hounds darted around the dance floor. Slipping into the crowd of onlookers, he found Lily and saw she bore a look of wide-eyed amazement. She gazed back at him with accusation in her eyes but said nothing.

"Wait, here comes the finale. You have to watch."

"The finale?" she was in the process of asking when her question was answered.

Three of the dogs closed in on Hingsworth where he stood on the dance floor. The hounds circled and took turns sniffing him and barking. The man twisted and turned, attempting to shield himself while the circle of empty dance floor widened around him. His pale face had grown red. Whether this was the result of anger or embarrassment wasn't clear.

The dogs growled for a heartbeat before one leaped forward, pouncing on Hingsworth's chest like a hungry jungle cat. The orchestra stopped playing, and the musicians were all hanging over the balcony for a better look.

Hingsworth let out a high-pitched squeal as he attempted to push the dog away. The dog, however, was trained not to lose sight of his prize until his master arrived. Another dog dove at the man while the rest of the pack barked and circled him.

"Get this mutt off me!" Hingsworth screamed as one of the animals attached itself to his coattails and began tugging him to the ground.

Devon looked around to see the reaction from the crowd. There was a range of winces to open laughter. Giggles could be heard all through the crowd, along with inarticulate cries involving mutts and some quite colorful language from the man on the floor of the ballroom.

Most ladies hid their smiles behind open fans, as Hingsworth had warmed the beds of more than half of them in the room at some point and then fled when things got complicated. The edges of the ballroom became steadily more crowded as people flowed out of card rooms and parlors to see what the fuss was about.

"Oh my!"

"Is that Lord Hingsworth?"

And one comment that "The punishment seems rather apt, dog that he is" could be heard around the room.

Devon looked at Lily, an amused smile still on his face. This entire ruse had been worth it, if only to see the look of disbelief on Lily's face. Her lips formed a perfect circle and her eyes were bright with amazement above pink cheeks that were twitching in an effort not to smile.

"You did this," she mouthed as she hit his arm with the back of her bare hand in reprimand.

He grinned. "Not without your assistance."

Lily leaned closer to whisper, "He could be seriously injured."

"Would you shed tears over the loss?"

She blinked in surprise at his comment. "No, but he could be hurt for life."

"He'll be fine." Devon began to chuckle, unable to stop himself.

"You're laughing! It's not amusing."

"It's a little amusing."

"It is not." She glanced back to where the man who had fawned over her less than an hour ago lay on the floor weeping as a blustery old man tried to pry the prancing dogs from him. She tried to contain a chuckle and had to bite her lip to do so. "All right, it's a little amusing."

He looked down into her lovely face and laughed aloud. The sound of his laughter seemed to loosen her rein on her amusement, for she began to chuckle with him. There was now such an uproar in the ballroom with giggles, barking dogs, Hingsworth's cries, and the wails of Lady Geddings at the ruin of her ball that no one noticed the two of them slip from the room onto the terrace and collapse in shared laughter.

A few minutes later, Devon was leaning against the terrace wall listening to the continued mayhem inside with a feeling of pride. It was a rare day when society got what it deserved. Those same people hadn't had any issue with ripping his life to shreds, so why shouldn't he return the favor on occasion? And it had all gone to plan.

Lily had played her part to perfection. A small pang of guilt over forcing her to be near Hingsworth in order to make the plot take shape bit at him, but he brushed it away. Glancing over at Lily, he watched as she tried in vain to pull herself together, still fighting bursts of giggles. It was a lovely sound, light and airy like a bird's song in the morning.

"Did you see his face when he couldn't get that dog away?" Lily asked, wiping tears from her eyes.

"Did you hear him scream like a little girl?" Devon returned with a single bark-like chuckle.

Lily turned toward him and tilted her head to the side in thought. "Why did the dogs single him out? Was something on that handkerchief?"

"The dogs have been trained to follow the scent of a fox. In this case, they were under the impression that the fox resided in Hingsworth's coat."

He reached out and ran the back of a finger down the side of her cheek, freezing her movements. "Thanks to your assistance."

The noise of the ball disappeared. There was only the two of them.

Her breasts rose and fell with her quick breaths under the thin lace of her fichu. He wanted to rip the damned thing from her neck to reveal the real Lily under this prim exterior. Was he falling into the same trap again a year later? He needed to get away from her. He needed time to collect his thoughts. He needed to stop touching her.

His rebellious fingers did not listen but tucked a fallen strand of golden hair behind her ear. Finally, managing to rein himself in, he let his hand fall to his side, gripping the wall to keep from reaching out to her again. A minute ticked by in silence as he ripped his gaze from hers and stared unseeing into the ball-room windows.

Lily cleared her throat before saying, "I can't believe we did that."

Devon had to jar his brain into functioning,

realizing she was speaking of the chaos in the ball-room, not anything that existed between the two of them. She had called it nothing today after all. His jaw clenched. "I can. Now, I must leave. Until next time, Lily." He lifted her hand, placed a kiss on her bare knuckles, and left her standing on the terrace watching him disappear into the crowded ballroom.

❧

"Lillian!"

Lillian laid aside her book on aquatic discoveries of the southern Atlantic and looked up at the sound of Nathaniel's excited voice echoing up the stairs outside the drawing room. Just then, the door swung open and he bounded into the room.

"Lillian, you must come downstairs at once!"

"Is something wrong?"

"No, something is marvelous! You received a bouquet of flowers the likes of which I have never seen. You made quite the impression on someone last evening." He pulled her to her feet and began dragging her from the room. "Who is he? There was no signature on the note. You must tell me all, but first let us go bask in the beauty and fragrance of your gift."

"Flowers? Oh, dear. I only danced with Lord Hingsworth last night. You don't think he sent them, do you?"

"No, darling." He paused at the top of the stairs to look at her as if she were losing her mind. He patted her hand and gave her a sympathetic smile. "I don't believe sending flowers is at the top of his list today since he's currently at the center of the most delicious on-dit this town has had in years."

She followed him down the stairs, still thinking of poor Hingsworth.

"Fret not, darling. Most of my acquaintances are in agreement that justice was served last night."

"Nathaniel," she reprimanded. "He is horrible, but we should not speak ill of him when he's in such a condition."

"That's the dead we are not to speak ill of, darling. And I believe he is very much alive, although I'm sure he wishes otherwise at the moment."

Lillian chuckled at the memory of his girlish screams and flailing about. It was true. He most likely wished to be dead this morning from the embarrassment of it all. London would not soon forget that scene. Lady Geddings was the real victim in all of this. Her lovely annual ball would never be the same after last night.

When they reached the bottom of the stairs, Lillian no longer wondered who the flowers were from. "Lilies," she muttered to herself. The flowers were bound together in a large vase with their white heads leaning in every direction. There had to be around fifty flowers, all blooming in perfect snowy white unison. The foyer was already thick with the smell of the blossoms.

Should she send them back to him? That would let him know in no uncertain terms that she wanted nothing to do with his antics in the future. He had forced her to delve into a gentleman's pockets last night. And now that gentleman was the subject of the *ton*'s ridicule. Perhaps Hingsworth did deserve it, but that was not the point of the matter. What would the duke have her do next? She was afraid to think about it. Yet the lilies were lovely…and hers. No one had ever sent her flowers before. She felt a smile tug at the corners of her mouth and quickly controlled the impulse to be pleased.

"I should return them."

"They were left at the door. There was only this note." He handed her a small card. "There's no way to know where to return them, and why would you want to? Enjoy this, Lillian. It's your come-out season. Flowers and callers are a good thing."

She looked down at the card only bearing the words "For Lily" in scrawled writing. She flipped it over, but the back was blank. How was she to explain this to Nathaniel? "I know who sent them and I do not wish him to think I condone his behavior, even if I was amused at the time. It was wrong."

"Oh, now you must tell me all!" He pulled her into a side parlor made for receiving guests and shut the door behind them. "Who is he?"

Lillian sank onto a settee. "You needn't get that look of glee on your face. He's a pest, an arrogant, manipulative, vile, and horrible creature. I don't know why he is involving himself with me," she lied.

"Did you dance together? I only saw you dance with Hingsworth."

"No, but poor Hingsworth. Things for him will never be quite the same, will they? And he only danced with me, nothing more. It is not as if his crime justified that punishment. He is mad!"

"Who is mad? You have me a bit lost, darling."

"The Duke of Thornwood, of course!"

"Yes, they do say so, yet I've never agreed. What does he have to do with Hingsworth? Or the flowers?"

"The duke sent the flowers."

"Why would you think that? There was only that card."

Her fingers traced the lines of ink on the card. He had terrible penmanship. She would add that to his list of unfortunate qualities. "I think that because it's the truth. They have to be from him because…well, because they're lilies." Lilies for Lily was a clever thought. Although she would never tell him so.

"Ah, I see. Actually I don't, but that is neither here nor there. When did you meet Thornwood?"

Lillian colored at the thought of how they met a year ago before saying, "We danced at the Dillsworth ball."

"He danced with you? Why didn't you say so?"

"I don't know. I didn't want to think about it, I suppose." Her fingers kept sliding over the writing on the card.

"I didn't see you dance with him last evening," Nathaniel mused.

"No, we spent the supper hour together."

"I never saw either of you during the supper hour. Lillian! You didn't!"

"What?" Her eyes snapped up to meet his gaze. "No! I didn't do anything with the duke other than chat on the terrace."

"Oh, I am so relieved I won't have to duel with him over your virtue. But you were alone with him? Someone could've seen you. This could have been the latest on-dit. Lillian, you must be careful in London.

It is not like Whitby, where you manage the lands and have not a care for your image. Here, image is everything. Do be careful to act the lady."

"Am I not refined enough?" She straightened her spine at the accusation.

"Certainly, darling. I simply don't wish any harm to befall you. And London ballrooms are vicious places. Now you must tell me of Thornwood. Is he to be a suitor?"

"I can't imagine so. The flowers were only sent as a thank-you for some silliness I assisted him with. It was nothing, really."

"You are a terrible liar, Lillian. Fear not. I won't pry into your personal affairs. Whatever is between you and Thornwood is none of my concern."

"Truly, there is nothing between Thornwood and me. He is mad. He follows me everywhere I go and enjoys tormenting me. It is quite miserable, actually. He owes me those flowers for what he put me through with Hingsworth last night."

"What he put you through? Solomon was the one who required you to dance with him. You don't mean that you and Thornwood had something to do with... Oh, but this is rich!"

"I don't know what you're speaking of," she returned, raising her chin.

"Indeed, darling sister. Indeed. Well, I must go out to take care of some business now. I'll leave you to your thoughts and your flowers. Perhaps when I return, you will be in the mood to regale me with the tale of last evening's events. I do miss so much by milling about the card room."

"We shall see. I may be too weary and in need of a nap when you return for our chat."

"Very well. Keep your juicy secrets. I may never forgive you, but that will be on your shoulders." With a warm smile and a tug of her fingers in farewell he left the room.

The scent of lilies swirled through the open door to fill the empty space her brother had left. She closed her eyes for just a moment and allowed the joy of receiving flowers from a handsome duke to surround her. He might be mad—and maddening, come to think of it—but there were some small benefits to knowing him. He had rid her of Hingsworth. It was done in a most barbaric fashion, but the sentiment remained good. What would he make her do next? She feared it and yet, on some bizarre level, she felt a small degree of anticipation.

❧

A shopping excursion filled the following afternoon. Lillian flicked the end of the ribbon back and forth between her fingers, entranced by the thread of silver catching the afternoon light from the shop window. She'd agreed to come with Nathaniel, who insisted he could find a masculine lace with which to trim his shirt cuffs. At times he truly did fuss over his appearance more than any lady of her acquaintance.

After browsing through the shop twice, Lillian grew bored. Twenty minutes after that, all of the baskets of ribbon on the table before her were sorted by color and the fashion plates on the chair at her side were sorted by date. She was ready to leave. Sinking steadily deeper into this state of dull expiration by the second, Lillian heard the door open and a familiar voice at her back. Turning, she saw the duchess of Thornwood sweeping into the small shop with a girl a few years younger than Lillian trailing in her wake.

"Miss Phillips, imagine seeing you here!" The older woman enclosed Lillian's fingers within her own in greeting and did not let go.

"Your Grace," Lillian said with a smile as she glanced around to see if an introduction for her brother was necessary. But Nathaniel was so consumed with comparing two types of white lace with the shopkeeper that he didn't notice Lillian's new company. She twitched her fingers, but the duchess did not seem to want her to flee, since she didn't release her grip.

"Lillian, this is my daughter, Miss Grey. She will be making the rounds in all the ballrooms and parlors next season. Won't you, dear? Roselyn, this is Miss Phillips."

The young, dark-haired beauty dipped into a shallow curtsy.

"It's lovely to make your acquaintance. Please call me Lillian."

"I look forward to seeing you next year when I'm allowed out of our home," Roselyn stated.

"I look forward to that as well," Lillian returned with a grin over the young girl's saucy response. She had the same gray-blue eyes the duke possessed. On her they looked mischievous, while on His Grace they appeared more all-seeing and intrusive. He had a sister. He'd never mentioned her before. What else was he hiding?

"Patience, dear, patience," Her Grace admonished. "You act as if I have you chained in a dungeon! Your come-out is only a year away. And you're allowed more liberties than I was at your age."

"I should hope so. When you were my age, ladies still wove fabric for tunics while minstrels sang," Roselyn retorted with a grin.

"You should watch yourself or I'll turn my joisting stick on you." The duchess laughed, releasing Lillian's hand to poke her finger into her daughter's side.

"Yes, Mama." Roselyn smiled at her mother. "I'm going to look around."

There was clearly a playful, loving atmosphere in their family. Lillian couldn't help comparing that love to what she had in her own family. Aside from Nathaniel, there was no comparison. How did the duke's arrogant and annoying nature fit into this family? Perhaps he was above their jovial ways since he held the family title. Of course, the Devon Gray she met a year ago had been a laughing, teasing man. And for a brief moment at the Geddings' ball she saw that man again on the terrace. Then, he closed himself off once more and left her there alone.

What had happened to him in the past year to change his nature? Or had that afternoon in the tavern all been a lie? That was when she realized his mother was still speaking to her.

"Are you purchasing a few new things to go to the Amberstall house party? You are going, aren't you? It's always such a delightful event, and Amber Hollow is a fine estate."

Lillian cleared her throat and forced her mind back

to the conversation at hand. "I received an invitation but had not yet decided."

"Oh, you must go. Edwina, Lady Amberstall, is my dear friend. She would certainly want you in attendance. As do I. Her son will be going on about his prize horses, but if one overlooks his constant chatter, it's quite lovely. Edwina's cook makes the best cucumber sandwiches. You must attend if only for the sandwiches."

"I don't usually travel in the name of sandwiches, Your Grace."

"Oh, but you should. They really are worth it. I remember when your mother and I went to this dreadful luncheon at the Earl of Henwick's home. We were starved by the end of the afternoon, the sandwiches completely inedible, you know, and then dessert was brought out. We devoured those lemon cakes in a most unladylike fashion." She began to laugh, her gray eyes bright as she told the story. "I will always remember her that way, with her cheeks filled with lemon custard, trying to carry on a polite conversation with Lady Simperton, of all people. It was quite a sight."

"Yes, Mama always did enjoy sweets." A warm feeling washed over Lillian as she remembered the cakes she had shared with her mother as a child at teatime.

"But fret not. You won't have to resort to such measures at the Amberstall event. Excellent fare. I'll let Edwina know this afternoon that you will be attending. She will be delighted to meet you. She was a friend of your mother's as well. And I'll ensure she puts out plenty of cucumber sandwiches."

"Very well, then. I shall attend. All on the recommendation of a tea sandwich." Lillian laughed.

"That is splendid news! I will leave you to your shopping, then." She gave Lillian's hand one last squeeze as her smile turned sly. "And I believe my son may be there as well. This should be such fun!"

Lillian's jaw dropped as she realized she'd been outmaneuvered. How had she fallen into such an obvious trap?

Her Grace was already halfway out the door, as if she knew Lillian would eventually find her tongue and protest. "Come along, Roselyn. No reason to tarry, dear. I must get to the milliner's to discuss my hat order," she called over her shoulder and left the little shop.

Nathaniel sauntered up to Lillian's side as the door closed behind Roselyn. "Do you prefer this white lace or this one with the hint of candlelight?"

Still fuming over being handled and potentially match-made with her nemesis, Lillian hardly looked at the lace in her brother's hand. "They look the same to me, Nathaniel. And I can't think about lace at a time like this."

"They are two completely different shades of white. How could you possibly think them the same? Wait, what do you mean a time like this? We are having a lovely shopping day together."

"I mean with the Amberstall house party just around the corner and being forced to attend by..." She paused at his confounded look. "Did you hear none of that conversation?"

"What conversation?"

"I have been persuaded into attending the Amberstall house party by the duchess of Thornwood."

"Thornwood? How odd that we were just speaking of her son yesterday morning. Will he be attending?"

"Yes. And now so must I!"

"We'll have to get a maid to travel with you, for I'll be in the country for the next week on a little holiday."

"Where are you going? You could force me to go with you!"

"Oh, no. I will be at a hunting lodge with a friend."

"You don't hunt."

"I know," he said with a wistful sigh. "You can't come with me, darling. Not this time."

Lillian's shoulders sank a fraction as she stared into her bleak future. "I suppose there is no escape from this, is there?"

"No, darling, not if you promised Her Grace you would be there. I suspect that Solomon would have insisted you attend anyway once he heard of it. He's calling later this afternoon to discuss his blasted list and how I need to keep you in line." He rolled his eyes heavenward.

"Oh no! Don't tell me! Amberstall was on the list of approved suitors, wasn't he?"

"Fine. I won't tell you, but he was."

"This little trip is sounding more dreadful by the second. And I will be forced to hide my sorrows in cucumber sandwiches."

"Cucumber sandwiches? I think I would choose to hide my sorrows in a box of chocolates or perhaps a decanter of brandy. But I suppose if tea sandwiches get you through the day, so be it."

"I don't even like…it was something that…oh, never mind!"

"You don't have to get in a huff."

"I am not in a huff or anything else of the sort."

"Is this because your duke will be there?"

"He is not *my* duke!"

"We shall see."

"We shall not see a thing! He is not!"

"Yes, I believe you. Really, I do," he replied with a grin. "Let me pay for this, and we'll go get ices."

"That sounds lovely." As he walked away, Lillian gazed out the window, watching people walk by with parcels in their arms. They were all going someplace happy, Lillian was sure. She was certainly the only one being sold off to the highest bidder by her brother while being blackmailed by a duke. And no amount of ices or dratted cucumber sandwiches would change those facts.

Nine

"Ah, Mother, I didn't realize you were in here. I was on my way to go...so I will just..." Devon's words died as he stared down at his formidable mother in the parlor. There was a gleam in her eye that announced she was plotting some scheme. What was it this time? She had already rid his house of a cook, a rug he was rather fond of in the drawing room, and all sense of order. His eyes narrowed on her as he wavered in the doorway, half wanting to escape, half wondering what havoc she was wreaking now.

"Devon, dear, you have arrived at the perfect time." Her eyes were bright as she clasped her hands together and glanced across the room toward the fireplace.

"The perfect time for what?"

"I need that chair moved a bit to the left. It is in entirely the wrong location in this room. How have you managed without my assistance around your home?" She pointed to a small armchair he'd never given much attention. Come to think of it, had he ever sat in that chair? Perhaps once, although he could not remember the occasion. Its location did not offend him in any way. He shrugged.

"Oh, I get by. Is there not a footman around that can rearrange all of the furniture in *my* parlor to your liking?"

"They're all busy. You will do."

"What are all of the footmen busy doing?" He was almost afraid to ask.

"They are preparing for a few guests to arrive for tea, of course."

"Of course they are." A tea. Wasn't that marvelous? He would have to endure his mother's friends in his home for the afternoon. As long as he didn't have to attend, he might survive the ordeal. He lifted the chair and moved it to where his mother had indicated.

"No, no, no. Move the chair back to the right a bit."

"Is that to your liking?" he asked as he set the chair inches from where it had been before.

"That's not quite right, either. Try it over in that corner." She pointed to the far corner where two windows flooded the room with warm sunlight.

"Mother, how long are you planning on staying here?" He hefted the chair up in his arms and carried it across the room.

"As long as I'm needed, dear. I don't like that chair there, either. Would you place it back over here?"

"Very well." Would she not make up her mind? He had obligations other than to move already adequately arranged furniture around the parlor all day. "How is this?"

"A bit to the left and you'll have it just right."

"A bit to the left and it will be in the exact location as when we began." The indentions in the rug were still evident as he replaced the blasted chair in its original spot before the fireplace.

"Yes, that's nice, dear. Oh look, here are our guests."

"Our guests?"

"Yes, I told you of the tea. And since you are here, you can stay to chat."

"I am *not* staying to chat!"

"Oh, it's only a little tea with your feeble old mother. Surely you wouldn't abandon me in my time of need?"

"Mother, you wouldn't by chance have had me rearrange furniture to trap me into an afternoon tea, would you?" Devon grimaced at the idea of being managed by his mother.

"I would never stoop to such deception, dear." She gave his arm a pat, then left him standing by the chair to greet the arrivals to the room.

It really was too bad there was no alternate door to this room. He would have to add one—soon.

His mother gushed across the room, "Lady Grangish! It's a pleasure to have you here. And this must be Lord Wellsly. So nice to make your acquaintance."

"Your Grace," Wellsly offered with an overly elaborate bow. As usual, the gentleman wore a coat the color of a scarlet macaw's wings. Devon almost expected him to squawk and begin preening his feathers. An afternoon with Wellsly? If this was the best of the company they were expecting for tea, it was to be a long tea indeed.

The older woman with Wellsly was a stylish woman for her age. Too bad her son had taken his tastes for fashion to the degree of being quite a dandy. She nodded her head in greeting to his mother with a smile. "What a lovely home you have, Your Grace."

"Thank you. Have you met my son, Thornwood?" She motioned to Devon.

"Yes, we're acquainted, Mother." Devon leaned against the mantel with one arm and gave a nod to the small bird-like man. "Wellsly." Apparently, one word was all the man needed to engage Devon in conversation. Devon sighed. He would have to remember to keep his mouth shut in the future.

"Thornwood, it's been some time since we've spoken. It's good to see you."

"Yes, I could hardly miss seeing you," Devon offered truthfully, as he eyed the man's coat.

"It's good to be seen," Wellsly returned with a smile, clearly not understanding the jab at his clothing.

"Really? I side more with the chameleon on the subject."

"The what? Is that a foreign title?"

"Yes, it is. The chameleon is above a baron in rank within Sweden. Quite a high title." This was going to be the longest tea in the history of civilization. Why must he stay to endure this torture?

"Ah, yes, I believe I have heard of the position."

Devon looked around for any escape, yet saw none. Ten minutes later, he had plotted his dear mother's demise for the third time in his head, as Wellsly rambled on about the importance of the aristocracy, but then he noticed more guests arriving.

He finally found an excuse to escape Wellsly when he heard his mother say, "Oh, look. Lord Fensworth has arrived with the Misses Yurdlock. This is delightful! Do come in."

As introductions were made and tea was served, Devon quietly endured the standard teatime banter. It had been at least fifteen minutes since he last sneaked a glance at the clock on the mantel. Yet when he looked again, only two minutes had passed. He settled into the chair he had recently moved about the room. It wasn't a bad chair.

He stretched and ran his hands over the arms, testing their strength before bouncing on the seat once with a satisfied frown. Why had he never sat in it before? He needed another chair in the library near the map table. He should move this one there. He nodded.

How long did teas usually last? He felt out of practice since he usually ate at his desk while poring over journals and ledgers. At the first opportunity, he would find an excuse and leave. He had work to do, and tea with mindless members of society did not fit into his carefully planned schedule.

He then noticed his mother looking his way for some reason as she said, "Yes, the Amberstall event always proves interesting."

"Do you know who will be attending this year?" one of the ladies asked.

"Oh, all of the usual people, I'm sure, with the addition of a few new faces to town," the younger lady replied. What had been her name?

"Lord Dashby's girls will be in attendance, I'm sure, with their cousins. They are making such a splash this year." His mother shot an innocent smile in his direction.

Her smile was a bit too innocent. What was she up to?

"I spoke with Miss Phillips only yesterday, and she said she will be attending as well. Such a lovely girl." And then all was revealed. His mother must have seen him with Lily and now thought she would make a good match. He had been spending time with Lily lately, but not for the reasons his mother assumed.

He almost growled at the idea of attending the Amberstall house party. Yet he would not want Lily to have too much fun in his absence. She could meet someone there, become betrothed, get married, and be out of his reach of torment forever. That wouldn't do.

"I will be there as well," he interjected into the conversation.

His mother beamed. "Oh, that is wonderful news! I look forward to your company on the journey out of the city."

She had no clue what chaos she'd just invited to Amber Hollow, but she would find out soon enough. He grinned. A plot was already unfolding in his mind.

"I believe I'll ride there, Mother. Poseidon will need to be exercised. Unlike Amberstall's animals, he enjoys a nice journey."

"Your Grace, I have to disagree. Amberstall is known for his stables of fine horseflesh," Fensworth argued.

"Yes, Thornwood. I'm sure Amberstall's horses would be adequate for a journey as well," Wellsly added.

"Oh, I'm sure his horses would survive a ride or

two down a slow country lane. I am simply stating that Poseidon is an animal trained to the highest standards and, as such, will enjoy the trip." Devon took a sip of tea and waited for the men to accept the bait he dangled so deliciously before their noses.

"Amberstall will want to prove the worth of his mounts to you, Thornwood. Of that I have no doubt. It has clearly been many years since you've visited his stables. You'll be quite impressed," Fensworth stated with his thin nose held high in the air.

"Fensworth, I'm counting on it." Devon took another sip of tea, catching his mother's eye over the rim of the cup. Her eyes were narrowed with suspicion, yet she said nothing.

He picked up a cake from the service on the table before them, holding it in the air as he asked, "Is anyone going to take this last cake? No?" He took a large bite. His cheeks were full of strawberry-glazed cake as he spoke, "Delicious! I'm looking forward to this little journey to the country already."

The ladies exchanged offended glances in response to his poor manners, while the gentlemen smirked in disgust.

"Well, I must be off. Enjoy the rest of your tea. I found it a bit tepid but I'm sure you'll survive." Devon rose and bowed in farewell. The looks on the faces of their guests for tea ranged from shock to wide-eyed dismay. His mission complete, he picked up his chair, hefted it onto one shoulder, and left the room. His mother wanted him to spend more time with society and Lily, did she? He laughed as he strode down the hallway. One must be careful what one wished for.

He had a new chair for his library and some planning to do.

~∞~

Lillian scooped up the poorly folded dress and shook the wrinkles free from the skirt. Nathaniel's home might be well kept, but his maids clearly had no experience in dealing with a lady's clothing. It was true she was being forced to attend the Amberstall house party, but she did not have to arrive looking like she rolled there while wearing all of her clothing. How she wished she could stay in town and read books instead of attending this dratted event!

"This is all your fault, I'll have you know."

Nathaniel turned on the chair at her dressing table to gaze at her. "My fault? How is it my fault?"

Lillian laid the freshly folded muslin in the trunk at her feet. "If you were not leaving town to go on a secret journey to a hunting lodge tomorrow, then you could make some excuse for me to stay in town and I wouldn't have to attend the Amberstall party."

He rose and went to the full-length mirror in the corner of the room, shrugging his coat into place and dusting nonexistent lint from his arm. "Sorry, darling. This has been planned for months. I've spent weeks putting my wardrobe together and making preparations for what we will do while away."

"I know," Lillian replied in a deflated tone. She looked up, watching her brother preen in the mirror for a moment before asking, "So, what will *we* do while away?"

"*We* will enjoy all the freedoms a remote hunting lodge has to offer."

"Which have nothing to do with hunting, I assume, since I have not seen you polishing any guns or sharpening any blades."

He smiled into the mirror. "No. I admit I am a terrible shot and have no patience for chasing small woodland creatures about the countryside."

"Who will you be *not hunting* with at this hunting lodge?"

Nathaniel turned and gave her a sly look of warning. "A friend."

"Does your friend have a name?"

"Yes, but I vowed to never say it."

"I won't tell anyone!"

"I know. Yet I gave my word that I would never reveal his identity, and if I told you, I would know I had betrayed his trust. I could never live with myself."

"I understand. Will I ever meet him?" she asked, picking up a pair of slippers from the bed and placing them in the trunk.

"Perhaps one day."

"That would be lovely."

"Yes, it would. Well, now you have me all maudlin over leaving you, thank you very much," Nathaniel said with a huff of exasperation.

"I want you to have an enjoyable trip, really I do. I only wish I didn't have to be somewhere so miserable while you are somewhere so nice. But I am happy for you. Truly I am."

"Darling, if I could change any of this for you, I would."

Lillian nodded, looking back down at the chemise she had crushed in her hands instead of folding. There was nothing that could be said or done to change her circumstances. She decided to change the subject to a somewhat cheerier topic, the maid Nathaniel had instructed to accompany her to the party. "Thank you for allowing me to borrow Mary for my journey."

"She'll enjoy the trip—change of scenery, fresh air, and all that." He took a step closer, lowering his voice before he continued, "Just don't let her arrange your hair. I saw what she did to one of the downstairs maids once. It was frightening."

"Thank you for the warning. I would hate to frighten the other guests at the party."

"That you would. I'm sure she can button and lace whatever you ladies button and lace, though." Nathaniel paused to examine his cuff before adding, "And she drinks heavily, so I'm sure she will be willing to procure you a few nightcaps to ease the pain of your journey."

"Then she will be a fine maid for this trip, indeed." Lillian laughed.

"I must go now and pack the last of my wardrobe. Have a nice trip, darling."

"Yes, you too," she called out as Nathaniel disappeared down the hallway. She did wonder about the identity of his mysterious friend. Was he involved with some powerful lord? Or was he about to leave the city with some criminal who must remain hidden from the authorities? Perhaps he was a spy? Lillian shrugged. Nathaniel could take care of himself. And she had plenty to be concerned with at the moment.

She crossed the room to her dressing table to retrieve some spare pins for her hair. Pulling open the top drawer, she found the container of pins hiding in the shadows in the back beside the pocket watch. Picking the watch up, she felt the cold gold in her hand. She opened the lid. It must have been some time since she had wound it, for it was frozen at six and a quarter hours.

Possessing the trinket had seemed so important a year ago, having just lost her father. Now she knew better. It had only brought heartache into her life. In an effort to remind herself of the love that she knew had once existed between her and her father, she'd opened the door to a disastrous future. She closed the small lid with a click and returned the watch to the drawer, taking the spare pins back to her trunk.

With introductions to more suitors and torture at the hands of the Mad Duke ahead of her, she now understood one thing quite clearly: Nothing could change her situation now, least of all a watch.

⟡

"If I hear one more word about manes and tails, I'm going to expire of boredom." Sue rested her hands on the stone wall that ran the length of the terrace at Amber Hollow, gazing out over green lawns that cascaded into a grove of trees in the distance.

Lillian shot a sidelong look from the corner of her eye at her friend as she took another sip of tepid lemonade. "Sue, you only arrived an hour ago. You have to last another two days until we can return to the city." Although Lillian agreed about the excessive degree of horse talk among the crowd milling about the terrace that afternoon, complaining about it would do no good.

"Don't remind me. Mama tells me every day I should be pleased to still be invited to events such as this after my woefully disappointing seasons, although we both know my invitation was an afterthought. It is Evangeline they truly wanted to invite. I am the side dish next to her roast. No one orders simple greens. But if I am forced to attend country parties so Evangeline might attend, they could at least keep the conversation interesting. Who cares the distance a horse can race unless there are highwaymen at your back? Honestly."

"Well, I'm happy you came." Lillian gave Sue a smile and a friendly bump on the arm with her elbow. "Horse discussions aside, I find it refreshing to be back in the country for a few days. If you ignore the company we're forced to keep, it's quite lovely here. Did you see the rose garden when you arrived?"

"No, Mama insisted we go straight inside so Evangeline might wash the dust from her face and repair her hair from the journey. Apparently dust and disheveled hair only improve my looks, as Mother and Evangeline are still in the room with the maid."

Lillian laughed. "Oh my. I don't believe I would enjoy being Evangeline. So much of life spent before a mirror seeking perfection instead of outside enjoying life. We are the lucky ones, Sue."

"I agree, but don't tell my mother I said so. She would think it shameful to desire sunshine on one's cheeks over powder on one's nose. Isn't there a nature walk here? We could escape this horse party for a few minutes, if you wish. I would like to try and find the hidden lake I heard was here."

A deep voice rumbled from behind them. "I shall take you to see it, then."

Lillian jumped at the new voice. Turning, she saw Lord Steelings with his eyes set on Sue, who stood there blinking in surprise and unable to answer.

Lillian cleared her throat. "That is very kind, Lord Steelings. However, we were about to partake of some of those lovely sandwiches over on the buffet. I've heard wonderful things about the cucumber sandwiches. Have you tried them?"

"Yes. Dreadfully dry. But I wouldn't want to stand in your way if you wish to try one. Come along, my lady. I'll show you that hidden lake you wished to see. I've been there many times."

"I shouldn't go just now," Sue rushed to say. "I was only thinking…"

"Tomorrow all of our moments will be planned for us as the party begins in earnest. It's not far." He extended his arm to Sue.

"Yes, all right. Lillian, I'll return shortly."

Lillian gave her a shocked nod. It wasn't like Sue to wander away with a gentleman. Lillian had a strange feeling there was more to that encounter than met the eye. She was watching their retreating silhouettes round the corner of the house out of view, feeling rather awkward and alone, when someone joined her at the stone wall.

"Lily, imagine seeing you here." His Grace leaned one hip against the wall in his normal nonchalant stance.

Lillian looked his way long enough to take in his dark windswept hair and tanned skin before returning her gaze to the green lawn before her. He looked as if he had spent all day in the sun. It was a roughened, entirely male look that made her knees turn weak. She stiffened her spine against the impulse to find such a bothersome man attractive.

"Should I feign surprise at seeing you at an event I was forced to attend?"

"Not on my account. But are you implying that I'm following you?" Was there a smile in his voice? She turned toward him to confirm the suspicion. White teeth gleamed against tan skin, matched only by the starkness of his messily tied cravat.

Not for the first time, she asked why her tormentor had to be so handsome. It really was unfair, as it put her at a disadvantage at times such as this. "Yes, of course you are. And it's quite annoying, so you may leave now."

"And end this lovely conversation of ours? Never."

"I was afraid you might feel that way. I was terribly busy enjoying the landscape before you arrived, so if you don't mind, I will continue to do so in silence." She stared off at the horizon, ignoring the man at her side.

"You know you tilt your chin to the right when you're angry?"

"Shhhh. We are enjoying the view in silence," she replied.

"Right."

A moment passed and all the while she could feel his gaze on her.

"The Himalayan goral gets a similar peevish look when you near its young."

Lillian turned back toward him in a huff. He needed to leave soon or she was going to lose what little patience she had left and hit him. "You should go and have a cucumber sandwich. I hear they're delicious."

"Yes, that look right there. Very goral. I knew I'd seen it before. And I've never been partial to cucumber myself, so I think I'll stay here."

"Humph, I am suddenly famished. Until later, Your Grace." She stormed across the terrace toward the table laden with tea sandwiches and fruit. A goral? Wasn't that a breed of goat? She had seen a few goats over her lifetime, and she was quite certain she looked nothing like one. He was determined to torment her at every turn. A goral, indeed!

She placed one strawberry along with a prawn salad sandwich on her plate and turned to walk to the far end of the terrace when she was stopped by the dratted duke in her path. "You didn't get a cucumber sandwich."

She raised her chin in challenge. "I don't care for them either, if you must know. Your mother recommended it, so I assumed you would like to try one—on the far side of the terrace—and leave me be."

"Ah, my mother. She trapped you into this excursion as well, then, didn't she?"

"How did you know?"

"Let's call it a lucky guess. She believes there is…" He paused to motion between the two of them with his hand. "Some sentiment between the two of us."

"How odd. I *am* feeling a few choice sentiments for you at the moment. Would you like to hear them?"

"I fear my pride would not recover from such a blow. Perhaps later."

"Why would your mother think there is anything between us?"

She watched as his jaw tightened, the muscles working in his neck. "I haven't the faintest idea," he returned, looking across the lawn as he answered.

"Oh, I wish I could tell her in extremely clear terms that this is nothing more than a disgusting business arrangement," she hissed as she shifted the plate in her hand.

"Yes, a business arrangement. On that score..." He dug a small parcel out of his pocket and placed it on her plate, beside the prawn salad sandwich. "You need to feed this to Amberstall's prize racehorse tomorrow at precisely one o'clock in the afternoon."

Her jaw dropped for a second before she spoke. "I don't know what your plan might be this time, but I will not poison a horse for you."

"Calm down. It isn't poison. It's oats and herbs." He shook his head in clear offense. "It won't hurt the animal."

She looked at him suspiciously. "What will it do?"

"Ah, that you will have to wait to see."

"And if I fail to feed this to Amberstall's horse tomorrow?"

"Come now, Lily. It's no great task I ask."

"Very well." She slipped the parcel into her pocket. Why did he not answer her question? In the past he had been only too happy to dispense with threats of what he would do to her if she didn't comply with his wishes. Why not now? Her gaze narrowed on him, yet his eyes revealed nothing.

"Good. I will see you at dinner." He nodded and left her standing on the terrace, staring after him. This was becoming a tradition of sorts. He forced her to comply with his mad plots, confused her, and then left her standing alone again. She set aside her uneaten plate of food, vowing the Mad Duke would not abandon her on a terrace again. Next time she was going to do the leaving.

⤬

Lillian arrived early to dinner, seeing no need to sit about her room once she was dressed for the evening. She smoothed the skirts of her peach-colored gown and patted a hand across the back of her head to ensure the knot of her hair was still intact. The parlor where they were to have pre-dinner drinks was empty.

It was a large room for a simple parlor with so little seating, but then the entire home was that way, rather excessive in size yet lacking in ornamentation. She was inspecting one of the two paintings in the room, that of a young blond boy on a horse, when she heard people coming down the hallway toward the parlor.

"That is precisely what I told him, but do you think Thornwood listens to me? Oh no." The duchess paused in her conversation with two other ladies when she spied Lillian across the room. "Miss Phillips! I've been looking forward to seeing you again." She crossed the room with the other ladies in tow. "Doesn't she look the very image of Honoria?"

"Oh yes, I noticed the resemblance the instant we met this afternoon," the hostess of the party returned with an assessing look.

Lillian felt slightly awkward being studied for likeness to her deceased mother. How should she hold her mouth? Should she smile or would that kill the effect? She settled on a bland, inoffensive smile while her toe tapped a violent rhythm under the hem of her dress.

The duchess sighed loudly enough to gain everyone's attention. "Yes, I am sorry I missed the gathering on the terrace this afternoon. I was running a bit behind upon leaving, only to find all of His Grace's belongings sitting in the foyer when I arrived downstairs. Can you believe he departed on horseback, leaving his trunk for me to find room for in my carriage?" She laughed as she added in a quiet tone, "He's fortunate I didn't leave his clothing behind in London and allow him to find his own means of dressing while here."

That explained his sun-tanned features this afternoon when he arrived. He had ridden here. She forced the image of him from her mind, focusing on the conversation.

"The gentlemen in our lives would forget their noses if we were not always there to reattach them." The ladies tittered. Lillian glanced at the door. Where was Sue? At times like these, she could feel her inexperience in society shining through her polished exterior.

"Good evening, Mother." A tall, blond-haired gentleman entered the room with a smile in their direction. "Your Grace, Lady Snellsgrove, it's lovely to see you at our party again this year." He bowed toward the other ladies before turning toward Lillian.

"Amberstall, this is Miss Phillips. I believe you know her family already," his mother supplied.

"Miss Phillips, it's a pleasure to make your acquaintance," he offered in greeting as he joined the conversation.

"Likewise, Lord Amberstall," she returned.

The hostess of the event smiled at the two of them. "Your Grace, Lady Snellsgrove, I simply must show you the new vase I purchased for the foyer. Come along." She looked back at her son before adding, "I don't think we're needed here at the moment."

Amberstall shot a rather dark look at the door as his mother left. Turning back to Lillian on a sigh, he opened his mouth to speak but then closed it again.

Lillian searched for anything to fill this void of silence between them. "You have a lovely home," she offered. "I'm pleased I received an invitation to a gathering in such a nice setting."

"Ah, thank you. It is an amusing group assembled here this year. I'm happy you are able to be counted in our numbers," he replied with a small nod of his golden head. "I trust your accommodations are in order."

"Oh, yes. Very nice indeed." Lillian twined her fingers together before her. An awkward silence seemed to be hanging in the air above their heads, threatening to descend on them. One second ticked by, then two.

"I've known Solomon for quite a few years, you know. Since school, actually," Amberstall said with a smile. "If I'd known he had such a beautiful sister hidden away in the country, I would have made it a point to visit him more often."

"Yes, Solomon does have his secrets."

"Clearly." His eyes twinkled at her in jest.

Lillian searched her mind for some way to move the conversation away from Solomon. Her eyes landed on the painting on the wall. "Lord Amberstall, is this portrait of you?"

"Yes, it is. That was my first horse, Piper. She was of marvelous stock. I trained her myself."

"Really? But you look so young in this portrait."

"I was seven years there. Piper was two. I first sat a horse at three."

"Three?"

"Yes, I began building the stables here at ten." There was obvious pride in his voice but also an edge of something deeper, darker.

"Such a young age."

"Indeed." His jaw tightened around the single word for a moment before his expression cleared and he smiled. "This is now the grandest equine facility in all of England."

Lillian could see her opportunity looming ahead in the conversation to feed Thornwood's oats and herbs to Amberstall's horse. As much as she did not care to tour a stable, she gritted her teeth in the semblance of a smile as she surged forward into the discussion. "That is fascinating, Lord Amberstall. I would like to see the stables."

His golden brown eyes lit with excitement. "Would you care for a tour, tomorrow perhaps? I would like to further our acquaintance while showing you my prize horses."

"I would be honored. One o'clock?"

"I will see you then. Now if you will excuse me, Miss Phillips. I see a few new guests I need to greet."

"Of course," she replied. He nodded in farewell and moved to the far side of the room where a few people were drifting in the door. She watched him go. Amberstall was not so horrible a man. As of yet, he was the most tolerable gentleman on Solomon's list of suitors. His blond hair glistened in the light from the setting sun outside the window. He wasn't altogether unattractive, either. Perhaps her tour of the stables wouldn't be so bad after all.

A movement in the doorway caught her eye and she watched the duke enter. Amberstall's handsome image faded in comparison to the intense look of His Grace. There was something untamed in the way he carried himself. She cleared her throat and blinked away the thoughts as he appeared to be prowling in her direction.

"Good evening."

"Your Grace." His mother's words about his bags being left behind settled back around her, making her smirk. "I'm glad to see you're wearing clothing this evening." The words were out of her mouth before she could think better of them. She had not just referenced the duke's potential nakedness in public—and yet she had. She could feel the heat rising in her cheeks. *Think of something else, anything else.*

"Do I not normally?" His mouth quirked up in a grin.

"Normally?" She had lost the thread of the conversation completely in her need to stop thinking of the muscles hiding under his evening clothes.

"Wear clothes. I can only think of one occasion

when I did not…wear clothes. If I'm not mistaken, you were there as well." He was grinning fully now, the corners of his eyes creasing as the smile stretched across his face.

"It's just something your mother said. I shouldn't have mentioned…"

"Would you prefer it if I didn't…wear clothing? Because I can easily remedy the situation."

"No!" she exclaimed a little louder than she had intended and then smiled at a lady who turned to look at her.

"Apologies. I only asked if she thought your gown was too garish. But I think she approves," she heard His Grace utter from her side.

Turning back to the duke, her smile turned into a grimace as he laughed. Infuriating man! Near the doorway a bell sounded, indicating it was time to move to the dining room. She gave His Grace one last narrow-eyed glare before he turned and walked toward the door, leaving her alone and irritated yet again.

As dinner began, Lillian took a sip of wine to strengthen her frayed nerves. Across the table, Miss Yurdlock was telling everyone who would listen about her journey out of London and the innkeeper they encountered when they stopped off on their way. Lillian stopped listening when she discovered the high point of the story was the innkeeper's poorly tied cravat.

She stole a glance down the table at the duke. It was odd how she could find him infuriating and devastatingly handsome simultaneously. He was busy conversing with Lord Steelings, but he looked up as if he could feel her eyes on him. His mouth tilted up in the hint of a smile before he turned his attention back to Steelings. He seemed pleased, too pleased, anxious even. Whatever he had planned for tonight, she was grateful she had no role to play in it. Feeding snacks to a horse, she could manage. However, causing a scene during a dinner was another matter altogether.

Sue nudged her with an elbow. Private discussions were impossible at such events, but she could read the look of annoyance written across her friend's face. Miss Yurdlock flashed a toothy grin around the table as she said, "I've never been so relieved to get back into a carriage." One gentleman laughed at her tale as everyone else buried their boredom in the smoked fish on their plates.

"Thornwood, I heard you rode here on your gray," Amberstall said from the head of the table.

"Yes, it was a nice day for a ride and Poseidon wanted to stretch his legs a bit."

"I trust he was settled into my stables to your satisfaction when you arrived."

"Yes, his accommodations will certainly do…for such a short visit anyway." The duke took a bite of fish, appearing unaware of any offense he caused with his comment.

The sound of a fork scraping across china silenced the table. "Did you have the opportunity to visit the stables today?" Amberstall narrowed his eyes on the duke. "Fensworth mentioned to me that you might be in need of a tour."

"Oh, I saw all I need to see today. Horseflesh speaks for itself." His Grace stuffed a large bite of potato into his mouth as he nodded in greeting toward another gentleman farther down the table.

"Yes, I was discussing that same topic with Wellsly earlier," Amberstall grated. "Sadly, most cannot discern the difference between quality…and woefully average when it comes to the intricacies of equine breeds." He paused, allowing his words to swirl about the table with an answering series of uncomfortable shifts in chairs and intakes of breath. "It seems a shame not to show off the *premium* horseflesh I have here on the estate."

"Perhaps we could have an exhibition," the man she thought was named Wellsly supplied with a narrow-eyed smile.

"Yes, that sounds perfect." Amberstall sat back in his chair, staring at the duke. "Perhaps then Thornwood's opinion of our stables will improve."

"Doubtful." She heard the word rumble down the table, hidden within a cough as the duke took a drink of wine.

There was a smirk clinging to the corner of his mouth and Lillian's eyes narrowed on him. This was part of his plan. What was he doing? She sat forward to watch.

"Once you see my horses' performance, especially that of Shadow's Light, you won't be able to deny the true talent bred at Amber Hollow. Not like your mount." He waved a hand down the table. "Even Steelings is set to purchase a horse from me."

"I was in the market," Steelings added, shooting a concerned look toward Thornwood.

"Steelings is easily wooed by embossed leather and the handsome color of a mane."

"Who can blame me for the appreciation of beauty wherever it can be found in this world?" His eyes darted to Sue in a quick motion that Lillian didn't presume anyone noticed, yet Sue turned a brilliant shade of pink.

Amberstall was still raging at the end of the table. "Steelings is leaving here with the third generation of the legacy that was…"

"The third generation of some other horse," Thornwood cut in. "Include jumps in the exhibition. Difficult jumps. Watching horses simply prancing about proves nothing. If your horses are able to do more than appear shiny, that is."

"You believe my stables are filled with good looks alone?" Amberstall almost yelled.

"You said it." Thornwood raised a brow in challenge.

Fensworth leaned over the table to say in a loud whisper, "Calm yourself, Amberstall. He is mad, you know."

The duke smiled and raised his glass toward Fensworth. "Life requires a touch of madness at times."

"I will have a course assembled in the morning to include no fewer than four jumps. You'll see how the horseflesh here excels in what I consider to be a standard exercise."

"Yes, I shall see. We shall all see." His Grace nodded.

"Tomorrow at four o'clock." Amberstall's fair features had darkened as he scowled at the duke.

"Let's make it three. No sense waiting in anticipation any longer than necessary." His Grace smiled as he stabbed another potato and stuffed it into his mouth.

Ten

LILLIAN OPENED THE HEAVY FRONT DOOR OF THE ESTATE and walked out into the brilliant afternoon. It was one of those rare days in England when the clouds had all been scared away, leaving a bold blue sky in their absence. A breeze pulled at her hat and she put a hand up to steady it before continuing on toward the stables. She'd spent the past ten minutes waiting in the foyer for Lord Amberstall to meet her for their tour, but when she heard the clock in the parlor strike one, she gave up on his escort.

As she neared the stables, she could see Amberstall in the distance overseeing the grooming of a horse in the paddock nearest the house. He wore a dark green coat which contrasted with his blond hair, making him appear golden in the bright sunshine.

She felt a pang of guilt at having a mysterious parcel of herbs in her pocket. He didn't deserve to be the object of the Duke's scheme and neither did his poor horse. Perhaps she wouldn't adhere to His Grace's wishes. Maybe it was time to call his bluff. She smiled as she joined Amberstall outside the main entrance to the stables.

"Ah, Miss Phillips. Is it one o'clock already? I do hope I'm not in danger of missing our engagement today." He bowed over her hand with a charming smile.

"I would never allow it. I've been looking forward to this little tour."

"Very good." Amberstall smiled as he slid open the large door to the stable. "Down this way is the area where most of my horses are housed."

They walked into a central hall with a cobblestone floor under a vaulted ceiling. Several chandeliers hung from heavy beams to light the area. Ahead was a row of parked carriages, all black and gleaming in the light cast from the open stable doors. They turned down the left wing of the structure, walking past candle-filled sconces bracketed into the brick walls across from an endless string of stalls. Lillian paused when she saw a newborn horse munching on hay in a stall corner.

"Oh my, what grand surroundings for such a sweet little horse," she commented, walking over to the foal and watching it wobble on newfound legs.

Amberstall joined her at the stall door. "His name is Silent Thunder. He was born only a few days ago."

"Silent Thunder," she repeated with a smile, glancing at the man at her side.

"You have a lovely smile—nice straight teeth," he mused.

"Oh, thank you, my lord," she stammered. What an odd compliment to give someone.

He pushed off the stall door and continued down the hall. "If you will follow me this way, you will see we have a well-supplied tack room."

Lillian followed him down the long line of stalls

and turned into the tack room, which looked more like a tack warehouse. Rigging, stirrups, and saddles were hung on giant racks in aisles filling the room. "Goodness, how many saddles do you have?"

"Over a hundred. They have different purposes. Some are for racing, others for jumping." He pointed to the far corner. "Those in that section over there are all suited for ladies." His eyes drifted over her body as he continued, "You would need a smaller saddle since your hips aren't very wide."

"Oh." She could feel heat rushing to her face at his comment.

"It isn't so bad. I once had a filly I thought would never be able to give birth because her haunches sat so close together, yet she produced a prize-winning colt. Of course, she died during the birth." He looked her over again and gave a quick nod of his head. "However, I'm sure you'll be able to bear children just fine—even with those hips."

"Thank you for your professional opinion on the matter, Lord Amberstall." Her teeth were gritted into a smile. Perhaps he was not the shining star of Solomon's list after all. Had he just compared her hips to those of a horse? Her hand patted the hard parcel in her pocket.

"Certainly." He turned and led her through another door to an outdoor paddock. "That is Shadow's Light. Isn't he magnificent?" There in the dusty ring, his prize horse pranced in a circle.

"Yes, quite nice," she offered.

"I've bred him back generations. He's the future of my stables. You see the gleam of his mane in the sun?

That shows his good health." Amberstall beamed with pride.

She watched the chestnut-colored horse toss his head as he was being led closer by a stable hand. Insulting as the man was, she had to admit his horse was beautiful. "His coat does shine in the sun. That shows a horse's health?"

"It does. I see that your hair shines rather nicely in the sun as well, Miss Phillips. That speaks well for you, as does your lineage." He tapped his hand on the top rail of the fence as he considered her with narrowed eyes. "Coming from the Bixley line…one has to consider breeding ability…your family name is old…" he mused aloud to himself.

"Breeding ability?" She must have misheard him. No gentleman spoke of bearing children in those terms. It was indecent.

"Well, certainly. When your brother contacted me and mentioned your desire for a husband, I was concerned about your late age, but I can see you still have a few years ahead of you."

"I do like to think so, m'lord." She was having trouble hiding the grimace from her face. *A few years ahead of you* echoed in her mind as her fingers itched to shove the herbs into his mouth.

Amberstall glanced away for a moment. "Will you excuse me? I see one of my grooms leading the wrong horse out to exercise. I'll return in a minute."

"Of course." She strained to offer him a sweet smile before turning, the look sliding off her face. She stepped up to the fence, gripping the rail until her knuckles were white.

The man leading Shadow's Light around the paddock brought the horse over to where she stood. "Would you like to pet him, m'lady?"

"Yes, I believe I would." Her hand slipped into the pocket of her pelisse, feeling the weight of the parcel there. Palming the snack, she pulled it from her pocket while hiding it in the folds of her dress. She ran a hand down the horse's nose, watching him shift to smell her. All she had to do was get this groom to walk away for a minute. She smiled as an idea occurred to her.

Patting the horse's cheek, she allowed her voice to be honeyed as she said, "You're a good boy, aren't you? Yes you are. Yes you are." She caught sight of the man on the other side of the fence rolling his eyes. It would only take a bit more annoyance and he would leave. "Is it a rough life being a horse? Yes it is. Yes it is." The man tending the horse wandered away, as she had planned. After all, who would want to listen to her babble to a horse?

She opened the package and lifted it in her open palm, sniffing it. It smelled like chamomile tea. Why would the duke want Amberstall's horse to eat tea leaves? She shrugged and allowed Shadow's Light to eat the oats and herbs from her hand. "That's a boy." She brushed her hands off and stepped away from the fence with a grin. Glancing around, she saw Amberstall leading a horse out of the stables.

He looked her way, his features tilting into an apologetic smile. "Miss Phillips, I'm afraid I must end our tour. My work here never ceases. And with the exhibition this afternoon…"

"I understand. You have a lovely facility here." She gestured to her surroundings.

"Thank you. I look forward to seeing you at the demonstration this afternoon. Perhaps we will see one another again this evening?"

"Yes, I can see that you're busy. I'll see you this evening. Thank you for the tour."

"Until this evening." He bowed over her hand before turning to continue on his path with the horse.

"Good luck this afternoon," she called out after him with a smile. She had a feeling he would need all the luck he could acquire.

⌘

Devon leaned against a fence post bordering the field where five of Amberstall's horses were gathered. He watched as Amberstall milled about adjusting stirrups and checking hooves while five of his grooms reviewed the course set up before them. The exhibition would begin any minute now. He grinned and rapped his fingertips on the top rail of the fence in anticipation.

The partygoers were gathered beneath the shade of a tent as they sat sipping lemonade and chatting. He stood some twenty paces away to escape the murmurs containing his name. Where was Lily?

He glanced back toward the house in search of her, only to see her friend Miss Green disappear into the shrubbery beside the path. Were they together? But the question was answered in the next second when Lily stepped outside, making her way toward the exhibition grounds. The corners of his mouth twitched as he watched her move down the path with prim steps and a straight spine as if she'd never committed a crime in her life.

Turning back to the horses, he watched the movements of the animals. Had Lily been successful in her quest, Amberstall's precious Shadow's Light would be feeling the effects of the herbs about now. The horses were being lined up to begin their show. Hooves pawed the ground and heads tossed as they waited for the signal to begin.

They were well-trained, Devon would give them that. He suppressed the current twinge of guilt nagging at him with the fact that Amberstall was an arse who believed himself to be above most of the *ton*. The man's father had thought much the same. He'd led the charge in proclaiming the loss of Devon's father's mind, driving him to prove society wrong and making him leave. His father had left on a mission to find his blasted lost civilization and hadn't returned—not alive, at any rate. But Devon wouldn't run from society's taunts as his father had. He would meet them on the field of battle, as it were. He looked out across the field with a grim smile.

His mother had tried to mend the rift between the families by befriending Amberstall's mother after the old earl's death. Even now, they sat together waiting for the events to begin. She might be able to forgive society for what they'd done to his family, but he couldn't. He shook himself from the harsh thoughts. Today wasn't about any of that. This was about Lily. He wouldn't simply look on as she linked herself to such an arrogant gentleman as Amberstall for the remainder of her life. She deserved better…and he deserved worse.

A shot was fired into the air and the horses were off. They took off across the field with Shadow's Light in the lead. The wind whipped at his dark brown mane as the groom on his back leaned down, urging him forward. The hedgerow they were to jump loomed ahead.

The horses took the jump, soaring into the air. They hit the ground one by one in a thunder of hooves and a cloud of dust. Rounding a bend in the course, the riders guided the animals toward a section of fencing. One by one the horses sailed with precision over the obstacle.

Devon frowned as his hand balled into a fist on the fence post. He glanced across the field to Amberstall, who was already being congratulated by a few gathered lords. His eyes, however, never left his horses, watching them with single-minded focus.

Devon returned his attention to the show just as Shadow's Light landed on the far side of a ditch that had been dug that morning and filled with water. His stride was perfect, too perfect.

It wasn't working. His eyes narrowed on the row of advancing horses, willing his plan to come together.

There was only the one straightaway where the crowd was gathered and the final jump just before them. Shadow's Light showed no signs of slowing. Why wasn't the damiana he'd been given working?

Hadn't Lily given the herb to the horse at one this afternoon? He was sure he'd seen her return from the stables at a quarter past one. The animal should be slowing, and yet the herb seemed to have no effect on the beast.

Perhaps she hadn't fed it to him. Or she could have

given it to a horse other than Shadow's Light by mistake. This would be a rather predictable horse exhibition without the benefit of science on his side—and he would be left eating a great deal of crow. His brow furrowed as he watched, willing the horse to react.

Shadow's Light was stretching forward, edging farther into the lead as he flew down the straightaway. Then, just before the final jump, he slowed with a toss of his head. Pulling back from the lead, he nudged into the gray mare at his side. The gray slowed, turning toward him to stop in the middle of the final run.

"Ah, young love," Devon murmured as he worked to keep the grin from his face. Finally!

Soon three of the five horses were milling about in a fit of stomping hooves and playful nips. Devon chuckled. Now this event was going according to plan. One groom reined his horse in prior to the final jump to assist with the chaos on the track, while the other finished the course before turning back in confusion. None of the riders could control their mounts with Shadow's Light at the center of the scene.

The tent filled with the partygoers began to buzz with chatter as Shadow's Light pranced around the two mares on the track. Damiana—he grinned. He'd discovered the herb on his travels through the Caribbean. The natives there claimed it would entice reluctant ladies to find love. He'd never tried it for those purposes, but clearly it worked on horses. He shook his head. The animals in the exhibition were certainly showing themselves, yet not in the manner Amberstall had envisioned, he was quite certain.

Amberstall had now stormed out onto the course,

bellowing commands. Stable hands were running from the far edges of the crowd to assist their master. And the noise from the crowd was growing.

"What is wrong with the mounts you idiots provided me?" Amberstall's voice rose over the den of tittering coming from the tent.

"What have you done to my Shadow's Light? What's happened?" As he watched in clear horror, he cried out, "My prize racehorse!"

One of the stable hands reached out to steady the animal long enough for his rider to jump to the ground. "He appears to be in an amorous mood, m'lord."

"Amorous? We're in the middle of an exhibition!" Amberstall yelled as he pushed the groom to the side to get a closer look at the beast.

The stable hands were working to separate the animals who seemed intent on flirtation. Shadow's Light finally shoved away from Amberstall to chase after the gray mare, the two disappearing beyond the corner of the stables. Men chased after them as Amberstall kicked at the ground with his boot, churning up a cloud of dust in his anger. Looking back at the crowd, he tried to grin, clearly aware of the audience witnessing the entire scene.

A silence fell over the group, with only a few giggles punctuating the awkward moment. The gentlemen who had been all too willing to hang on to Amberstall's every word only a few minutes ago had disappeared, mixing back into society as if they'd never befriended the man. With a shake of his head and a wry grin, Amberstall turned and left the field.

"Society is fickle, isn't it?" Devon breathed. "Who's mad now?"

He raked the crowd with his eyes. Where was Lily?

He received one clap on the back and he smiled in return. Yet the one person he wanted to see was nowhere to be seen.

He turned and watched as Amberstall vanished into the stables where more yells could be heard echoing off the brick walls.

"What was that herb?" Lily whispered without moving her mouth.

Turning, he saw Lily had slipped from the crowd to join him at the fence. "Shadow's Light is only feeling a bit romantic this afternoon. He'll be back to normal in an hour or two. No worries."

"I can see that, Your Grace. But how?"

"It's an herb I came across a few years ago. Based on the standard rate of digestion for the average horse, I knew it would work within two hours." He chuckled, rubbing a hand across his chin in thought. "Of course, I was beginning to wonder if it would take effect in time."

"How do you know the rate of digestion of the average horse?"

"Doesn't everyone?" he asked with a smile aimed at Lily. She looked lovely today with escaping strands of her blond hair blowing in the breeze. "And it was all due to your assistance." He grazed his hand past hers on the fence rail between them.

"I hardly did anything." Her cheeks were pink. Was it the touch of his hand or the sunshine causing it? "And I almost didn't follow through with it, but then he compared me to livestock on my tour of his stables."

"Compared you to livestock? Well, you are a troublesome filly." He winked at her.

Before their conversation could continue, Lord Wellsly joined them at the fence. "Too bad Amberstall's horse fell ill today or perhaps we could have had a proper showing of good horseflesh."

"Ill? They looked rather *lively* to me. Perhaps a bit too much so." Devon smiled at Lily, amusement flooding him as he watched her struggle to hide her laughter. This afternoon had gone better than he'd expected. With Lily at his side, he couldn't keep the grin from his face. Better than expected indeed.

Lillian excused herself from the conversation with Sue, Evangeline, and their cousins, with complaints of a headache. Truthfully, she only wanted a minute to tick past when the embarrassing showing of Lord Amberstall's horses was not mentioned. The evening had been filled with ridiculous speculations. From the glare of sunlight to untimely spider bites that crazed the animals, the possibilities had all been discussed at length.

She longed to scream, "I did it!" It was torturous to know she had aided in the pompous man's comeuppance but could not gloat over the victory. At least the duke was able to smile at the results of the day. She, on the other hand, had to listen to everyone's silly thoughts on the subject, yet say nothing. She had survived the talk at dinner, but the evening was dragging on a bit now.

She made her way across the crowded parlor, past the card table, and around the group of ladies consoling

Amberstall's mother. Rumor had it, he had been so furious at the outcome of the exhibition that he had fled the house, abandoning his guests. No one knew where he'd gone. Hopefully it was somewhere with no women he could insult with his horsey comparisons.

She offered the ladies a bland smile and headed for the door. Slipping into the relative darkness of the hallway, she stopped just beyond the triangle of bright light from the open parlor door to allow her eyes to adjust. Candles in wall sconces lit the hallway in small semicircles down the long pathway to her room. She blinked again and took a step.

"Lily." The sound brushed past her right ear, causing her to turn with a jerk.

"Your Grace." She put a hand to her heart in an attempt to steady it.

"Lily, when will you say my name once more?"

"You frightened me! What are you doing lurking in dimly lit halls?"

He took a step closer. She could see the hint of a smile playing about his lips. "I'm returning from the stables. I wanted to check on Poseidon. After today's events, I wanted to ensure he wasn't unfairly treated by association with me."

"Yes, today was certainly interesting." She bent her head and bit her lip to fight the laughter that was bubbling up in her throat. But when she heard the deep male chuckle in front of her, she looked up and lost her inner battle instantly. It felt marvelous to release the laughter she had kept hidden all evening.

"You played your part beautifully," he said after a moment of shared humor. Reaching up, he brushed a fallen strand of her hair from her face, his gaze becoming more thoughtful. "Of course, you play every part beautifully."

His fingers skimmed the rim of her ear as he tucked her hair there. Their eyes locked in the darkness.

Lillian didn't know what to say or do. He was paying her compliments in shadowed corridors now? For a moment, it was a year ago and they were simply alone together. Her breaths grew shallow under his gaze. She stood frozen as his hand slipped over her shoulder.

Was he going to kiss her? It had been so long since those lips were on hers. Would they feel the same now? Would he taste the same today as he had last year? Would he make her feel as she did before?

His hand slowly drifted down her arm, his warm grasp lingering on her wrist before falling away.

Perhaps she'd misread the past few minutes entirely. He must not want to kiss her now as he had then. Yet he didn't move away once the contact was broken with her.

She blinked and cleared her throat, forcing her mind to work so he would not guess at her thoughts. "Um, thank you," was all she could think of at the moment, but he didn't seem to be listening anyway.

His eyes were dark as he moved closer to her, gazing down into her face. "Do you know the part I would like to see you play most?"

"What is that?" she asked on a breathless whisper.

"This." His lips descended on hers in a kiss built on anger and forged in tenderness. Her eyes fluttered shut as she melted into him, into the moment. The warm, spicy taste of him on her lips was not enough. She wanted more. She slipped her tongue past his teeth, as she recalled him doing to her a year ago, tangling her tongue with his. One of his hands slid into her hair, while the other circled her waist, pulling her closer. She slipped her hands under his coat, clinging to his hips to hold herself steady. His fingers tightened across her back in response.

He took a step forward, then another, backing her into a darkened alcove off the main hall. They were by no means in a private location, but now they could not be spotted if someone decided to leave the parlor. She could feel his heartbeat through his chest where it was pressed against her. She rose to her toes and leaned farther into him, needing the connection, needing more of him. He all but growled as he broke their kiss to trail his lips down her neck to the line where her pearl necklace lay across her throat.

Her head fell back and her lips made one word, the only word in the entire world, for there was only him. "Devon."

She could feel him smile against her skin at the sound of his name as his mouth came back to hers. His kiss seared her with the heat of the moment and had her winding her arms farther around his back, grabbing at the thick muscles under her hands.

Devon's hand slid down the back of her neck and moved over her shoulder, making her shiver in his embrace. He palmed her breast and she made a small whimper caught by his mouth. She leaned into his touch, into his kiss, wanting all he would give her.

Suddenly, he broke their kiss. A sense of loss

washed over her. He stepped forward, pressing her against the wall of the alcove.

"Shhh," he murmured, his lips close to hers.

Her brows drew together with confusion over what he was doing, and then she heard the voices. She stilled, listening as two ladies made their way down the hallway. She recognized them as part of the group that had been consoling their hostess in the parlor. She sucked in a breath as they passed by. Devon's hand tightened on her shoulder.

"Clearly the horse had some ailment. They should have rescheduled the exhibition."

"Oh, I quite agree. It was all the doing of the Mad Duke. Taunting poor Amberstall over dinner last night."

"And now Amberstall has vanished."

"Truth be told, it's his mother's fault for inviting that duke."

"Yes, all because she is on friendly terms with the duchess of Thornwood now. He would never attend my events. Did you see the gleam in his eye at dinner tonight? I see why he is called the Mad Duke." The ladies disappeared around a corner, their voices trailing into the distance.

Lillian slipped her hand from Devon's back, raised it, and caught the side of his face in her soft grasp. The slight scratch of his beard stubble tickled her hand. She had lived with insults and degrading talk about herself for years and felt a pang of sympathy for Devon at the ladies' callous words.

He turned into her hand for a moment, pressing his cheek into her palm, before leaning back into her and capturing her mouth in a tender kiss. It was quite possibly the sweetest moment of her life. Her heart was breaking for the man before her. Kissing him back with her entire body, she vowed to remember this moment for the remainder of her life.

"I don't think you're mad," she murmured against his lips a minute later.

He pulled back, looking into her eyes, to whisper, "Lily, don't let their words bother you. I've lived surrounded by such talk for years."

"That doesn't mean it doesn't hurt."

"Their comments don't bother me. Not anymore. I've earned the reputation I now have." The bitterness in his tone negated his words of strength.

She shook her head. "Earned or not, how can comments like that not bother you?"

"Because they are society. That is what they do. It's the *ton*'s self-appointed job to degrade and cast out those who step out of line. Apparently, I've spent a great deal of time stepping out of line." He traced the line of her jaw with one finger. "And I have the winnings of a nice little bet placed on the outcome of the exhibition to assuage my anger." He chuckled.

She pulled away from him a fraction. "You gambled on today's events?" Her voice raised an octave.

"Of course I did. I knew what the result would be today, thanks to your help." He grinned.

Her hands fell to her sides. "I should have known you were underhanded, just like my brothers. Gambling everything away without a care for those you hurt in the process. I suppose you don't have an issue with wagering on ladies either...or forcing them into marriages for your financial gain! I can't believe for a moment I thought...but you're the same. All men are the same. And I assisted you in your winnings!" She shrugged free of his embrace.

"I'll give you half, if that's the problem."

"No, that's not the problem!"

"Lily, I'm sorry if I offended you. That wasn't my intention. The bet was just a bit of fun with some of the gentlemen here."

"I can't believe you involved me in a scheme that would make you a profit! You're no better than Solomon and his despicable wager over who will marry me. I thought you were different." She took a step away from him and was running before she knew it.

"Lily, wait! Lily!" She heard Devon's calls but ignored him.

Betrayal. The word rolled around in her gut, twisting her insides and making her eyes sting. How could he do such a thing? She reached her room and disappeared inside. The door closed with a thud at her back as she slid down its surface, collapsing in a heap of skirts on the floor. Her perfect tender moment with Devon—destroyed.

❧

"I don't understand them, Steelings," Devon said as he stared down the dusty road leading back to the city.

"Who?" He shot Devon a confused look while adjusting his seat on his horse. Steelings had offered to ride with the duke on the return journey to London. If he were to be honest, Devon was glad of the company on the ride home, especially after last night's argument with Lily.

"Ladies," Devon grated.

"Ha! And you think I do?"

Devon shrugged as he glanced sideways at his friend riding at his side. "No, I suppose not. After all, you never even found your Suzanna."

"Suzanna was an illusion, it seems," Steelings replied with a smile.

Why was he so pleased? With Steelings, one could never tell. Devon shook his head, problems weighing heavily on his mind. Why had he participated in that damn bet? Lily had been in his arms last night, but now she wouldn't speak to him. She avoided him all through breakfast this morning and then left abruptly to return to town.

"I saw you speaking with Miss Phillips yesterday after the exhibition," Steelings led in, jarring Devon from his thoughts.

"Yes, Lily and I were discussing…"

"Ah, so it's Lily now, is it? How very interesting." Steelings chuckled, clearly enjoying Devon's difficulties.

"It's not so amusing at the moment, if you must know, since she's angry with me."

"It's difficult to keep them happy, isn't it?" Steelings smirked.

"Who?" Devon glanced at his friend, so wrapped up in his thoughts of Lily that he struggled to keep the conversation going.

"Ladies," Steelings supplied.

"Yes, quite." Devon fell into silence as they passed into a wooded area, the sunshine hitting them in patches through the trees.

How could he get back into Lily's good graces after

the gambling incident? Flowers? A gift of some sort? He did owe her a pair of gloves. But that didn't seem appropriate for their tangled relationship. He could cease in blackmailing her. Yes, that would make her smile. At this point, her debt was paid anyway. He couldn't take advantage of her anymore. He smiled as he increased Poseidon's pace. Surely, this would make her let go of her anger. Then, perhaps, she would again say his name.

Eleven

Lillian swallowed her misgivings about accepting the duchess's invitation to tea as she knocked on the door. Being forced to speak with Devon after their argument had her wringing her hands all morning, yet the invitation could not be ignored.

Her only hope was that Devon would not be at home this afternoon. She twisted her pearls around one finger. What would she say if she did see him? Her disappointment in him had not lessened since she'd seen him two days before. Gambling was such a vile activity. And yet he had some indescribable hold on her that had nothing to do with blackmail or plots against gentlemen in society. She pushed Devon from her mind, focusing on the large oak door before her and what stood behind it. She needed to keep her wits about her if she was to chat with the dowager duchess all afternoon.

A moment later, an austere butler appeared at the door...the same austere butler she remembered from a year ago. "Good afternoon, m'lady."

She froze, unable to speak. My, this day was

certainly spiraling toward disastrous at a rapid rate. Blast it all! Why had this possibility not occurred to her? She had been so focused on Devon that she had not thought of his servants! Of course the butler that witnessed her fleeing the house would still work here. Perhaps he wouldn't remember her. Perhaps all would be fine. Perhaps…She blinked, resolving herself to the task at hand.

Pulling herself up to her full height, she lifted her chin in an expression of superiority.

The butler's eyes narrowed on Lillian's face for a moment as he swung the door wide, then stepped back to allow her entrance. "Welcome back to the Thornwood residence."

Oh blast, blast, blast! She stumbled into the foyer, attempting to think of a retort. "Welcome back? I don't know what you mean." Lillian's heart raced and she could feel the heat rising in her cheeks. "I'm Miss Phillips. I'm here for tea with the duchess."

"Certainly. I must have confused you with someone else." The knowing look in the butler's eyes did not match his words.

"Yes, you must have. This is my first time here. Yes, the first time…ever." Lillian forced her mouth to close, as she was looking guiltier by the second.

"My apologies, Miss Phillips. I won't say another word on the subject as I am clearly mistaken. Right this way."

"Thank you," Lillian returned with a thin smile.

He nodded, leading her to a parlor just inside the door. "Her Grace will be with you in a moment."

Lillian was overcome with appreciation for his

silence and his retreat as he bowed and left the room. She sank into a chair and ran a shaking hand over the knot of hair at the back of her neck, forcing her lungs to work. Accepting this invitation had been a terrible idea. The butler knew her secrets. Devon could walk into the room at any moment. She clasped her shaking hands together as she stared out the window across the room.

"Lillian!" the duchess exclaimed as she glided into the parlor in a swirl of lavender skirts. "I'm so pleased you could join me for tea today."

Lillian got to her feet, trying to hold her crumbling thoughts together. "Your Grace, thank you for having me." She curtsied.

"I thought we would take our tea in the gallery today so that you might see some of the treasures this home holds."

"That sounds delightful, Your Grace." Although Lillian did not think it was advisable to be inside this particular home, she was excited to finally see the gallery and all the foreign artifacts it held.

"Excellent. It's right this way, dear." She led the way out the parlor door and up the stairs.

Lillian's hand tightened on the handrail. She could feel the ghosts of memories slip around her as she ascended the stairs.

It was here that Devon had held her against the wall. She forced her eyes forward. It was here that Devon had ripped her corset from her body. She kept moving.

Her heart was pounding in her ears. She must divert her mind or she would never survive this tea. *Say something, Lillian. Anything!* "Your home is lovely," Lillian blurted out in a breathless squeak.

"Thank you, dear. It's my son's home now, you know. I do enjoy visiting, though." As they reached the top of the stairs, Her Grace turned to look back at Lillian, alarm creasing her brow.

"Visiting family can be quite nice." Lillian tried to smile.

"Dear, you are as white as the first snow of winter." She guided Lillian by the elbow to the railing at the top of the stairs. "You need to sit. And of course the settee that has been in that alcove as long as I can remember has been removed."

"Removed?" Lillian's eyes fell on the empty patch of floor where the settee once sat. She blinked away the memories that took place there, focusing on the duchess's voice to keep steady.

"It was a lovely piece, too. I shouldn't say so, but it was one of Thornwood's wild hairs, I'm afraid. A maid told me he had it hacked to bits in the garden and used it as firewood. It was a pleasant settee. I don't know why he disliked it so. And now, when we are in need of it, we must press on to the gallery where we may sit."

"Yes, that is unfortunate," Lillian murmured as she moved down the hall. It had been there on her last visit—that much she knew. It had been there that she'd allowed him to... She blinked away the memory. Was Devon so angry that he didn't want a single reminder of her in his home? Obviously he was. She shook her head, looking back over her shoulder at the empty alcove once more.

Double doors stood open, allowing the light from

the gallery to warm the hallway. Stepping inside, Lillian did not know which direction to look first. The large room was filled with displays of exotic plants, ancient pottery, and maps. Exotic fabrics were draped over tables, and native garments hung on dressmaker's forms. Every corner seemed to be filled with pieces of Devon's travels. "It's amazing," she said with a smile.

"I thought you would appreciate it, dear. And your color seems to have returned a bit. Would you care to look around or take tea first?" The duchess moved to the center of the room where she walked in a slow circle, looking at everything at once.

"I do feel a bit more myself, thank you. If you don't mind, I would like to look at everything now." Lillian walked to a window on the far wall, bending down over a small purple flower with spoon-like petals. "His African daisy!" Lillian beamed as she ran a finger across the soft petals.

"Yes, it is… Has His Grace mentioned it to you before?"

"What? Oh, yes, he spoke of it once," Lillian replied, absorbed in all the sights the room had to offer.

"I see."

Lillian moved to investigate a bookshelf in the corner filled with travel journals and articles. She clasped her hands behind her back as she read the spines of a few books. Turning, she asked, "Do you have the journal article His Grace wrote about his Himalayan expedition?"

"Yes, I believe it's on the second shelf, just there." She pointed to a stack of journals by Lillian's right shoulder. "I had no idea you knew so much about his travels already," Her Grace replied in a pleased voice.

Lillian frowned in thought. "I find it fascinating— exotic lands, foreign cultures, new sights..." She sighed as she thumbed through articles in search of the one Devon wrote.

"You have a great deal in common with my son, Lillian."

"Yes, I suppose I do." She laid down one journal to pick up another. "Although Devon has gone so many places and I have only read of them."

"Devon? I can see you are on better terms than I realized."

Lillian snapped to attention, her head whipping around to look the duchess in the eye. "Oh, I mean His Grace. My apologies. I don't know where my head was."

"I do." She smiled, her gray eyes creasing at the corners. "Come and sit, dear. Our tea will be here in a moment."

"Yes, Your Grace." Lillian crossed the room and joined the duchess in the seating area set up near the fireplace. She sat opposite the other woman, arranging her skirts around her in the chair. How could she have been so thoughtless? Devon? *You can't call him that, you ninny!*

"This is one of my son's favorite places in the house. When he's not working in the library, I can usually find him here. This room represents his life's work."

"And extraordinary work it certainly is," Lillian added in agreement.

"I want you to know, Lillian, no matter what his

reputation in society, this…" She waved the back of her hand toward the artifacts in the room. "This is the true Thornwood. Do you know he achieved all of this while searching for his father? Most people are unaware. They think him mad for boarding a ship bound for some distant land just as his father did. But they don't know the truth. He did it for his family. For me."

Lillian was unsure how to reply. The duchess clearly loved her son. But why was she telling Lillian of Devon's true nature?

Just then a maid arrived carrying a silver tray laden with cakes as another brought in the tea service. Her Grace poured the tea and handed a cup to Lillian. Once they were alone again, Lillian took a fortifying sip of tea. She looked the woman in the eye and asked the one question that had been burning in her mind for the past two days. "Does His Grace often gamble?"

His mother was clearly thrown by the question. Her cup clattered against the saucer in her hand as she began to laugh. "Heavens no," she managed to say between bursts of laughter. "What would make you ask such a thing?"

"I meant no offense. It's only that he gambled at the Amberstall party."

"Did he? Well, that is unlike him. He only uses the funds in his pocket to play on a hand of cards. His father, God rest his soul, taught him that. Although Thornwood hasn't been himself lately."

"Truly?" Lillian leaned forward in her chair, anxious to hear of Devon's flaws.

"Yes, he's spent the past year locked away in his library poring over his work."

"Oh." That wasn't quite the fault Lillian was hoping to discover. Working in one's library was rather…honorable. Perhaps the wager had only been an individual occurrence and not an ongoing proclivity for gambling. Lillian pulled her attention back to the teatime conversation.

"He's had a fit of the doldrums for quite some time now. Always focused on his boats and the profits of shipping here, there, and everywhere… until this season, that is. Now he attends balls. He even danced—once." She smiled at Lillian over the rim of her teacup. "Do you understand what I'm saying, Lillian?"

Did his mother believe Lillian's relationship with Devon made the difference of happiness in his life? Surely not. "He danced with me, but that was only because…" Lillian broke off, taking a sip of her tea to stop the words from leaving her mouth.

"Lillian, I don't need to know the whys of it all. It isn't my place to pry. I would never involve myself in such a meddlesome fashion with the lives of those around me. No, no, no, dear. I am only here to enjoy a spot of tea with the lovely daughter of an old friend."

Somehow Lillian doubted the duchess's lack of involvement in the lives of those around her. She took a cake from the platter between them and enjoyed a bite.

"I see you have a sweet tooth, just as your mother did."

"It seems to have diminished slightly within the

span of a generation, but I do enjoy sweets." Lillian chuckled, feeling more at ease already.

"I remember once when Thornwood was a boy he swiped some candies from the kitchen when Cook wasn't looking. I would never have found out if he had not felt inclined to share them with his sister. I found her a sticky mess in the corner of the nursery." She laughed in wild contagious bursts.

After a moment, she wiped her eyes as she picked up a cake. "He has always shared all he has with those around him. I look forward to the day when he has a duchess to share all of this with." She gestured around her to the exotic plants and maps of foreign lands.

For a moment, Lillian pictured sailing off to distant places with Devon at her side. Then she set aside her teacup with a wistful smile. No matter what the duchess believed, that future was simply not to be.

❨✿❩

"It's none of your concern, Nathaniel," Solomon's quiet yet sharp voice sounded from Nathaniel's library.

"Lillian *is* my concern!" Nathaniel snapped back in response.

Their voices echoed through the house. Lillian took another careful step down the staircase, peering around the corner where her brothers were arguing. Wasn't this a lovely way to begin the day? She took another step, listening to get a grasp on the "discussion" before entering the chaos.

"You cannot believe you have a say in these matters when you were tossed from the family years ago."

Solomon picked up one of Nathaniel's porcelain trinkets from a table, weighing it in his hand.

"Someone needs to speak on Lillian's behalf. You certainly don't have her best interests at heart." Nathaniel paused, sneering at their brother.

Left alone, they would kill one another, and then she would have even more problems on her hands. Lillian sighed and descended the last three steps, entering the library. Nathaniel was poised at his desk, leaning down on clenched fists as if he were about to vault over its shiny wooden surface.

Solomon turned, regarding her with little interest. "Lillian, I'm pleased you have decided to join us."

"I was unaware we had a meeting this morning," she stated, raising her chin in defiance.

"I decided I needed to visit when I heard the unfortunate news yesterday of Lord Amberstall's situation." Solomon's dark eyes narrowed on her. "I heard he left immediately in search of solitude. No one can find him."

Lillian chuckled in spite of her better judgment. "Yes, I suppose when one's horse gets romantic notions in the middle of a show of its skill this is what can happen."

"You find Lord Amberstall's fate amusing, do you?" Solomon laid Nathaniel's breakable on the table at his side as he took a step toward Lillian.

"Lord Amberstall brought his situation upon himself. And I'm not sure why it warrants a family meeting before I have been able to wake properly." Lillian clasped her hands in front of her in a grip that could break bones.

"Tell me, Lillian, did Lord Hingsworth bring his situation upon himself?" Solomon spoke in the same low, deliberate voice that always turned Lillian's stomach on end.

"He was set upon by hunting dogs." Lillian shook her head. "I'm not sure what any of this has to do with me."

"I find it peculiar that the gentlemen on the list I gave you of approved suitors seem to be fleeing town as soon as they near you." He took another step toward her with a menacing prowl. "Do you find that peculiar, Lillian?"

"Not at all, Solomon," she bluffed, hoping her complexion was not growing pink at the lie.

Nathaniel stepped around his desk, joining the conversation. "Solomon, she had nothing to do with those gentlemen's fates. Why would you think such a thing of Lillian?"

Solomon held up his hand to stay Nathaniel. "This is between Lillian and me, Nathaniel. You have no business here."

"This is my home." Nathaniel gestured to their surroundings. "I have business here whether you approve of it or not."

Solomon ignored Nathaniel, continuing his interrogation. "Lillian, whatever charades you have been carrying out cease now."

"I haven't..." she began, but he cut her off.

"You will be attending Lord Erdway's garden party this afternoon. You will accept any advances he makes toward you and be glad for them."

"I will do no such thing!" she exclaimed.

"You will honor my word on this, Lillian. I have been in correspondence with Josiah, and he is in agreement with me. The family needs one of these alliances."

"Why? Why these men, Solomon?"

Solomon didn't answer.

"What if I refuse?" Her jaw tightened around the words.

"Don't test me, Lillian." Solomon's face grew tight, the only outward sign of his anger. "Where will you go without the assistance of this family? What funds do you have?"

"I will live here with Nathaniel," she stated, looking at Nathaniel for confirmation of that truth. His face contorted with discomfort. He ran a hand through his hair as he considered before answering. The moment drew out in silence as Solomon grinned across the room. Lillian's fingers twisted together tighter. It hurt, but not as much as the betrayal written on Nathaniel's face.

Finally Nathaniel answered, "Darling, I love your company, but…" He looked down at his desk, unable to complete his statement of refusal. Then, turning on Solomon, he stalked across the library to look him in the eye. "I will not stand by while you bully her in this manner, Solomon."

Lillian couldn't believe what was happening. She truly had no options. Not that she blamed Nathaniel for wanting his freedom, but what of her freedom? She listened as the argument swirled around her like thick smoke, cutting off the breathable air in the room.

"I don't *bully* anyone. She has not yet reached her majority. Josiah and I can make her do anything we please. She has a responsibility to this family, after all."

"Yes, but Erdway? He's vile. I saw him kick a dog not a week ago. You can't doom our sister to live with him," Nathaniel said in outrage.

"I'm sure the dog in question had some fault. Erdway is a prominent gentleman in society. Lillian would do well to marry the man." Solomon shook an invisible wrinkle from his sleeve.

"You can see the anger in his eyes. He'll lift a hand to her one day, I have no doubt. Have you never met him?"

Solomon looked past Nathaniel to sear her with his dark eyes, daring her not to obey. "Lillian, my word is final on this subject. You will attend Lord Erdway's garden party and act according to the dictates of this family." Solomon pushed past Nathaniel and left the room.

Lillian turned and left the room after him, not heeding Nathaniel's calls for her to return. This turn of events wasn't new, only surrounded by different circumstances. She left the house in need of air and sank onto a bench in the front garden. Every difficulty in her life always came back to a man. And it all began with Papa.

She blinked away tears as she gazed at the grass at her feet. She gave up everything for him, for the family. If he had been well…if she hadn't had to bear that burden alone…perhaps she would be wed now. Solomon would only be a brother she rarely saw. She pulled a yellow rose from the bush beside her, gently tugging on the petals until her palm was filled with a pile of soft yellow.

Fate, it seemed, had other plans for her. Solomon had other plans for her. She looked down, realizing she'd crushed the rose in her hand, and tossed the crumpled rose petals to the ground. Now she would be forced into yet another situation in the name of family responsibility. She tried to breathe. But the scent of roses surrounded her, making her feel nauseous. She needed to walk. She needed distance from her present situation. She needed...Devon.

Twelve

DEVON GUIDED POSEIDON THROUGH THEIR STANDARD morning ride, dipping between trees and jumping the log that crossed the path into his favorite clearing in Hyde Park. The sun was threatening to reveal itself from behind the bank of altostratus clouds. Reining his horse to a stop, Devon looked up, watching the wind blow the puffs of gray across the sky. He caught a glimpse of the bright sun just before it disappeared again.

"At least it's not raining on us, Poseidon," he said as he slid to the ground, pulling an apple from his satchel. Devon laughed as the horse nipped at it before he could get his hand open. "Always so eager," he mused.

Devon took a few steps away, feeling the desire to walk for a few minutes in the fresh air. The tall grass bent with a gust of wind, brushing the tops of his Hessian boots. Just then, a movement caught his eye in the corner of the clearing. Who had discovered his hidden corner of the park? He had only seen one person here before. Had she come to find him? Squinting, he could now see it was a lady in a green dress.

"Lily?" he muttered, taking a few steps in her direction. It was a little concerning that she was seeking him out here where there were no witnesses. She must be planning to berate him for gambling once more. He had to apologize or she would never move past this. Bracing himself to endure her fit of pique, he sighed.

As soon as she was within earshot, he began, "Lily, I'm sorry I gambled over horses. The gentlemen at the party were all placing bets. I was the last to join in, but there I was with a pocket full of money. So I tossed a bit in. I didn't mean any harm by it."

"None of that matters now," she muttered, staring off at Poseidon where he stood grazing and swishing his long gray tail.

Had he truly just used the "Everyone else was doing it" excuse in reference to the bet? He hadn't said that since he was twelve and caught throwing rocks! What was wrong with him? He cleared his throat and tried again. "Yes, I realize that was a terrible excuse. But believe me when I say it won't happen again—my wagering on anything that remotely involves you."

"I'm glad to hear it. You're forgiven," she replied a little too quickly, bending to snap off a long blade of grass, then tear it in half.

Had he heard her wrong? He shook his head, watching her rip the grass into tiny shards. Speaking in slow, deliberate words, he tried to grasp the purpose of their conversation. "You aren't here to rail at me more for gambling?"

"No, although I should." She shot him a narrow-eyed look, dropping the last of the grass to the ground at her feet.

"Oh. Well then. It is a lovely day for a stroll in the park." He smiled up into the cloudy sky before looking back toward Lily.

"Lovely day indeed!" she grated, crossing her arms and looking across the clearing.

Devon couldn't seem to gain his footing with her this morning. He studied her pensive frown for a moment. "Is something troubling you, Lily?"

"Yes, something is troubling me!" she fairly shouted.

He could hear Poseidon pawing the ground in agitation a few feet away, as her voice carried to the trees on the far side of the field. "I see," he proceeded carefully. "Do you mind telling me what might be the matter?"

She took a ragged breath before meeting his gaze. "My brother Solomon has guessed at my involvement in recent events—Hingsworth, Amberstall…"

"How would anyone possibly know that?"

Her voice was bleak and her eyes vacant of expression. "He called it 'peculiar' since they were associated with me at the time they fell victim to dogs and, I suppose in a way, horses."

He took a step back, running a hand through his hair. How could Solomon know of Lily's participation? He'd been careful. If Solomon had guessed at Lily, would he discover Devon's involvement? He didn't want to think of what could happen with his ships if that occurred.

His family's welfare hinged on the expansion of his fleet, and Solomon held the key to that happening. Devon should have never gotten involved, but it had been because of Lily. He hadn't been expecting to find her, but then he had. He looked back into her eyes. "Surely he has no proof."

"He doesn't need proof!" She spat the words, her face twisting in anguish. "I'm a female! He can force his will on me anytime he chooses. Solomon can make me do as he sees fit. He's run our family for his purposes for years now. Do you think I'm here seeking some vile husband because I desire it?"

Her voice rang out, the pain of her situation visible in her eyes. "I'm here because Solomon wants to be rid of me, and as with everything else, he seeks to make a profit from it. I want nothing more than to have him out of my life for good. And yet, here I am…all by the wave of Solomon's hand." She turned, taking a step away from him.

He watched her shoulders rise and fall with labored breaths. What was he to say? He was the Mad Duke, yet even madness couldn't save him today. He couldn't very well go against the man constructing enough ships to almost double his fleet. He'd thrown every shilling in his possession at the endeavor. But then, this was Lily. He opened his mouth to say the right words but no words came out.

Pivoting back toward him, she added, "It has been decreed that I attend Lord Erdway's party this afternoon and accept his suit."

Rage began to boil up under his skin. Devon could feel his face pulling tightly into a scowl. "Erdway? The hell you will! That bastard beats his horse!"

She took a step forward, a look of bewilderment creasing her brow as she twisted her pearl necklace around her finger. "What am I to do, Devon?"

"You certainly are not accepting any suits!" The image of Lily at Erdway's side floated through his mind, causing his stomach to clench. He had to stop this from happening. Yet how was he to do that? The problem was that Solomon held a better hand of cards with the possession of Devon's ships and his money. His jaw tightened over the thought that being the Mad Duke didn't have its advantages at the moment. What good was a blasted title if not for situations such as this?

"Do you have a plan for how I am to avoid that fate?" She was looking to him for answers and he had none.

"No, I don't." He needed time to think, time to plan.

"You don't?" she asked in disbelief. "I'm in this situation because of you!"

"Yes, and I have decided to end the blackmail." He nodded in agreement with his own words. That much he knew. Whatever must be done to save Lily from Erdway's clutches, it would not involve blackmail and preferably it would not involve Lily. "I won't ask you to do any more tasks. Your debt is paid and I can't ask you to take another risk. You have my word that I will never tell anyone of your past."

Her head tilted to the side and her jaw dropped for a moment. "What good does that do me now?"

"It will keep you safe from your brother's ire, for one thing," he stated. He had to get away. He needed time to plot something, anything. He glanced back at Poseidon, still grazing. The horse clearly was in no hurry to leave the park. He turned back to Lily.

A wild look of desperation entered her eyes. "What if I tell all of society about us?"

He froze in his retreat. "What? Why would you do that?" He strode toward her, closing the space between them.

"I would be undesirable to marry if everyone knew of my past. Solomon wouldn't be able to throw me at any gentleman he pleases. I would be free of this situation." Her words rushed out of her mouth as if chasing careening thoughts. "All I would have to sacrifice is my reputation."

He reached out and grasped her arms, holding her still. "I will not allow you to soil your own name, Lily."

"You will not allow? This is entirely your fault!" she exclaimed, turning wounded eyes on him. "I will tell the world of our involvement a year ago. See if I don't!"

He moved his hands in small circles on her shoulders, trying to rub away the pain he had caused her. "Lily, do you really think your actions will stop your brother's pursuits? You will be married off even faster to hide the family shame. And you don't deserve to have your name dragged through the mud."

"Don't I? You've said otherwise."

He pulled her a fraction closer and tilted her chin up with the touch of a finger to look her in the eye as he spoke. "I don't know why you stole from me last spring and I don't want to know. None of it matters now. That's in the past." He had to tell her the truth: his family's low funds, the ships, how he never meant to hurt her, and the bit about destroying her reputation having been a bluff... He sighed. "I shouldn't have blackmailed you. If I hadn't plotted against your suitors..."

"What can I do to get Lord Erdway away from me?"

"Oh no. You are not getting involved in any more schemes, Lily. Too much lies at stake for you." He should never have thought up those ridiculous schemes to begin with, and he'd be damned if he allowed her to become entangled in potential scandal again. Not if he could stop it from happening.

"That is precisely why I must be involved," she implored.

"I told you, your debt is settled. I don't want you wrapped up in this anymore. It's over." His hands slid down her arms to grasp her hands in his.

"Then I will blackmail you." Her voice was thin. She licked her lips and swallowed before continuing. "Help me be rid of Lord Erdway, or I will tell all of London society we were intimate and you, Devon, will be forced to marry me."

"Lily." He couldn't believe what he was hearing. Forced to marry Lily? What of Solomon? He shook his head. "I can't."

"I know you don't wish to marry, so what are we to do? What is our plot?"

"Lily." His grip tightened around her fingers. The world seemed to be closing in on him. His heart was pounding the beat of her name in his ears.

"I don't wish to marry you, either, if you must know. So think of some scheme to get me out of this mess."

He dropped her hands and turned away with a grimace. Of course she didn't want to marry him. And he couldn't marry her, so he should be relieved.

Stalking a few strides away, he took a breath, forcing his mind to function. He turned back to her a moment later. "Very well. We will do this together. Are you attending the charity ball tomorrow night?"

Her lips pursed in thought. "If Erdway is to be there, I'm sure I am. Why?"

"Erdway has several estates. Any one will do. However I'm thinking the one on the Welsh border would work best for our purposes."

"Devon, what are you speaking of?" Lily clasped her hands in front of her, twisting her fingers together.

He turned his attention back to her with a smirk. "This task should be perfect for you, Lily. For, to make this work, we need to steal from Lord Erdway. His seal and stationery from his desk, to be exact."

"How are we to accomplish that?" she asked with wide eyes.

"During this afternoon's garden party, of course," Devon returned.

"Steal from him...at his garden party? And I thought this would be difficult."

❧

"At least his gardens are pleasant," Sue offered, a frown creasing her face.

Lillian didn't care a whit about the pristine condition of Lord Erdway's hedgerows; she would not be marrying him. She looked out across the green lawn where most of London society was gathered this afternoon. A smile tugged at the corners of her mouth as she thought of the plot that would be unfolding for Erdway. "I suppose I shall just live in the gardens if I'm forced to wed him," she teased Sue, knowing if all went to plan, no such thing would happen.

Sue grinned politely, pausing their conversation for a moment while two society matrons passed on their way to watch the croquet match. "Yes, you see? It wouldn't be so horrible. You could make your home over there between the rosebushes and the stone fountain." Sue pointed with her lemonade glass across the garden to a corner holding only a bench.

"I agree. It looks quite the cozy place to live out my days." Lillian twisted her pearl necklace around her finger. This would be the last time she would ever set foot on Erdway's property, yet she couldn't tell that to Sue. She smiled and swept her eyes across the crowd.

Where was Devon? She had already made Lord Erdway's acquaintance this afternoon. He was a middle-aged man of meticulous grooming. In fact, she had never seen hair parted so severely. She had then chatted with Sue for twenty minutes. He should be here by now. What if he didn't come? She would have to go into Erdway's home alone.

Her nerves were causing her toe to tap a rapid rhythm under the hem of her dress. She cast her eyes over to the large brick home at their backs. Did she truly need Devon? She could sneak in and take what she needed to complete their task. And hadn't she spent enough of her life waiting for a man's assistance?

Lillian glanced at Sue with a smile. "Will you excuse me? I need to find the ladies' retiring room."

"Oh, I'll come with you. My nose could use some powder, I'm sure. Mama is always saying my face is too shiny. And yet she tells Evangeline how nicely she glows. What is the difference between a shine and a glow? I've never understood it." She sighed. "But alas, I'm expected to be dull, so dull I shall be." Sue set her lemonade aside on one of the small tables that were scattered across the lawn.

"You aren't the least bit shiny, Sue. You look perfect, in fact. I wouldn't change a thing." Lillian's eyes widened. She couldn't accomplish her task with Sue at her side.

"All right, but I should keep you company. I saw Lord Erdway heading into the house with a footman a moment ago. Someone needs to keep you safe from unwanted advances."

"I'll be fine, Sue. I'm quite tough, you know," Lillian bluffed.

"Quite." Sue eyed her friend's thin frame with a dubious glare.

"Enjoy the party. I'll be back in a moment." Lillian slipped away from Sue's side, weaving her way past a cluster of gentlemen and through a group of giggling younger misses.

Crossing the terrace, she entered the home through a side door hidden in the corner behind a potted palm. She hoped not to encounter anyone, yet as she walked into a drawing room, her eye was drawn to a line of servants marching up and down the hallway outside the door.

The seal and paper she needed were likely in the library. Where was the library? And how was she to get there without being seen?

Perhaps she did require Devon's assistance with

this little endeavor. But it was too late for that. She must press forward now—alone. As she moved with slow steps toward the open door, trying not to catch anyone's attention, she noticed the maids and footmen moved with efficiency and a sense of order she had never witnessed before. She stood watching them for a moment as they walked with military precision. How odd.

Her eyes darted around the room, taking in her surroundings in an attempt to get her bearings. The entire room was the same shade of taupe. It looked as if everything had been painted with porridge. Every lamp, book, and vase sat squarely on its highly polished table. Every pillow in every chair had been placed at the exact center of the back cushion and fluffed to the same degree. And the fringe on the edge of the rug under her feet looked to have been combed into perfect order.

The clatter of metal on marble sounded from the hallway, jolting her attention back to the open door. She scooted to the far corner during the chaos, watching the activity and waiting for her chance to leave the room unseen. "Erdway!" She breathed the name as she saw the man step into her line of sight.

"Watch your step!" Lord Erdway bellowed at a boy no more than ten years of age.

The boy dropped to his hands and knees, attempting to retrieve the food that was now strewn across the hallway. "Sorry, m'lord. It won't happen again, m'lord."

Erdway swelled in his well-tailored coat, his round face growing red. "I know it won't happen again because you no longer work in this home." He waved to a footman a few paces away. "Get him out of my sight!"

The boy looked up at Erdway with large eyes. "M'lord, please. Mama is sick and…"

"That is none of my concern!" Erdway flicked a crumb off his sleeve as if it were a poisonous spider. "You should have thought of your dear mother before you decided to dump tea biscuits on my boots!"

"Please, m'lord," the boy groveled.

"Haul this boy out of my home this instant." Erdway pointed to someone out of Lillian's sight, yelling, "You! Dust the crumbs from my Hessians before my guests notice my absence."

There was a chorus of "Yes, m'lord." She could hear Erdway growling his discontent.

Lillian held her breath, taking a small step to the side—farther from view. Surely there was another way out of this room. If Lord Erdway saw her sneaking about his home while he was in this state of rage, she wasn't sure she could defend herself against him. Nathaniel and Devon had been right; the man was pure evil. That poor boy. She tiptoed to the far side of the fireplace, and there she saw a door. Turning the knob with a silent twist, she opened the door and slipped through.

She took a breath, trying to steady her nerves. The room was dim with the curtains closed, yet she could see walls of bookshelves through the darkness. The library! She smiled her relief and hurried over to one of the windows.

The tall ivory curtain on the window overlooked a

side lawn where only a few guests lingered. Drawing the curtain, she turned back to the library. She needed to complete her task and be gone from here. She shuddered to think what Erdway would do if he found her here or—even worse—if she failed and ended up married to the man. Spying his desk in the center of the room, perfectly centered with a large window on one side and two chairs marching in precision before a fireplace on the other, she moved toward it.

She tugged on the center drawer only to find it locked. Blast! Carefully sliding all the other drawers open, she sorted through neat stacks of ledgers and spare quills. Where was the seal? What of his spare paper?

Flipping open a box sitting on the corner of the desktop, she found only a stack of cheroots within its depths. What she needed must be in the locked drawer. Where would the key be hidden?

Her hands dipped with frantic grasps into the other drawers, feeling for what would be a rather small key. Sliding the drawers closed, she gave the room a quiet huff. Her eyes slid over the polished desk surface topped with a brown leather blotter. Perhaps the key was under the blotter. She picked up a tidy stack of parchments and made to set them aside.

"There you are!" A deep male voice murmured from across the room.

"Ahh!" The breathless noise escaped her throat as sheets of parchment flew into the air. She looked up, dreading the sight of Erdway's angry form filling the doorway.

Her heart skipped a beat as she saw Devon closing

the door at his back and walking toward her. "Devon, what are you doing in here?"

"Helping you." He grinned, his gaze turning to the parchment now covering the floor at her feet.

"I'm getting along just fine, thank you," she stated, bending to pick up the mess around her.

"Yes, I can see that." He chuckled as he stooped to help her pick up the papers littering the floor.

"I had everything well in hand until you scared me out of my wits." She shot him a narrow-eyed glare before quirking the corner of her mouth in a smirk.

Handing her a messy stack of gathered parchment, he mused, "I always thought thieves had nerves of steel and cat-like reflexes. That doesn't appear entirely accurate in your case."

"That is because I'm not a thief," she said. Honestly, how long was he going to believe the worst of her? She jostled the papers in her hands, trying to shift them into some kind of order.

He chuckled as he straightened the papers. "So what do you call what we're doing now? Borrowing?"

"Acquiring the tools necessary to live my life in peace." She lifted her chin and whipped her head around, turning her attention back to the desk before her.

"Procurement of resources, then." He leaned one hip on the side of the desk and crossed his arms, watching her. "That does make theft sound more official, anyway." He looked around the room for a moment before his eyes returned to her. "It's quite clean in here. Have you noticed?"

"Stop talking so loudly. Someone will hear you,"

she hissed. "I'm fairly certain thieves are rather quiet in nature." She tapped the edges of the papers on the desk to realign them into a neat stack. Setting them aside, she lifted the leather blotter, seeing only the highly polished surface of the desk beneath. Frowning, she looked down at the small lock on the drawer.

"You would know better than I, Lily." He leaned farther over the desk to whisper close to her ear, "My little thief."

She paused, her gaze turning to his. Had he said "my"? Perhaps she'd imagined it. This, however, was not the time to muse over such things. "We need to find the key to this locked drawer."

"Ah, that I can assist with." With one quick movement, he reached up and pulled a pearl-tipped pin from her hair.

She felt his hand brush down the top of her spine just before the knot at the back of her neck began to slide steadily down, her hair cascading down her back. How had he found the one crucial pin that held her entire style in place? She huffed, looking at him as he held up the pin between two fingers. "Why did you do that?"

"For the lock," he explained. "It's a skill I acquired over the course of a misspent youth. Although I can't say I've ever enjoyed the side effects so much as this." He stepped toward her to slide one hand through her unbound hair, watching as it fell in ripples over her shoulder.

She could feel heat rising in her cheeks as his fingers drifted through her hair. "Devon," she tried to warn, but even to her ears it sounded more like an invitation.

His eyes held a dark glimmer of desire as he pulled her close, his lips descending on hers with a soft caress. One of his hands twined into her hair while the other slid down her spine. Her body melted into his as he kissed her again.

She heard the tiny ping of her hairpin hitting the floor. They shouldn't be doing this, not here. Yet the excitement of their dangerous location and the risk of being caught in Devon's arms pushed her to slip her arms around his shoulders. Her hands wound around the back of his neck as she deepened their kiss.

Before she knew what was happening, he had lifted her from the ground and deposited her on the desktop. She pulled back from the kiss to read his intentions in his eyes—eyes heavy with wanting. Tugging at the lapels of his coat, she brought his lips down to meet hers once more as he stepped closer into the void between her thighs.

His hand slipped to her hip, holding her to him as he guided her head back to the surface of the desk, leaning over her, devouring her mouth with searing kisses.

She held his shoulders as if he anchored her to a world that had been tipped on its side. Their tongues tangled together in a desperate dance for more. His hips pressed into hers. She arched instinctively into his growing arousal with a whimpering plea.

Cool air met her skin as he pulled her skirts up around her waist, only to be replaced by the warmth of his hand on her knee. She opened to him as his fingers moved steadily up the inside of her thigh, tracing lines of need toward the apex of her legs.

He broke their kiss to trail his lips down her neck, tugging the neckline of her dress down with his teeth. His tongue drew circles around the hardened peak of her breast before catching it between his teeth to tug gently. Her hands tightened on his broad shoulders. Placing a soothing kiss on her breast, he moved to kneel on the floor below her feet. "Are you leaving?" she asked in a raspy whisper, feeling disappointed and alone.

"I'm not going anywhere." He kept one hand on her hip, holding her still with a gentle grasp as the backs of his knuckles grazed the apex of her thighs. Her head fell back to the desk with a thud.

He caressed her damp heat, gently stroking her until she arched her body into his touch. His tongue descended on her. What was he doing to her? She held the edge of the desk to keep from pulling away. Every flick of his tongue was intoxicating yet maddening. He circled and licked until she whimpered "Devon" into the silence.

The tension was building in her and about to drive her over the edge into insanity. He slowly slid one finger into her depths, then added another before finally sucking on the little bud he had been tormenting for the past few minutes. She released the desk to reach down and slide her hands into his dark hair, holding him close. "Don't stop," she breathed.

She felt herself careening out of control as he increased the rhythm of his fingers inside her.

His mouth pulled her, willing her until she flew, shaking, into a million pieces and came to rest in his capable hands.

Lillian released her hold on him to collapse on the desktop and catch her breath. Devon stood from his kneeling position between her legs. He looked at her with heat and awe wrapped in desire visible in his stormy eyes.

She wanted to touch him, to taste him, to pleasure him as he had done her. She sat up, watching Devon as he brushed the tousled hair from her face and slipped his arms around her. She slid off the edge of the desk, holding his waist as she gained her footing for a moment. Then she knelt down on the rug and began to fumble with the buttons of his breeches.

She could hear his surprised intake of breath at the direction she was clearly headed. "Lily, you don't have to do this."

"Yes, I do." As she released the last button, he sprang free of the confining fabric of his breeches. She blinked, having forgotten his size.

With a slight smile, she ran her fingers lightly over the length of hot, smooth skin. She could hear his answering groan as his fingers delved into her hair. Just as she slipped her fingers around him, she heard voices in the hallway outside the door.

Pulling free of her grasp, Devon refastened his pants and dropped to the floor at her side. There was a soft creak as the library door swung open.

Devon pulled her lower to the floor and into his embrace. He held her there, hidden in silence behind the desk, as footsteps moved across the room. Above the sound of Devon's rapid heartbeat, the scrape of something sliding from a bookshelf sounded from nearby before the footsteps retreated.

When she heard the door close, Lillian breathed for the first time in over a minute. She turned her head toward Devon, watching as his gaze dipped to her still exposed breasts. A roguish grin covered his face, creasing the corners of his eyes as his head dipped to place a kiss on the top of each mound before tugging her dress back into place with a defeated sigh.

Picking up her forgotten hairpin from the floor, he held it up as he said, "I suppose we should go ahead and be thieves so we can return to the party before anyone notices we're missing."

"It may be too late for that. I left quite a while ago. I wasn't expecting this *theft* to take so much time." She smiled at him as he pulled her to her feet.

"My apologies," he offered.

"No apology is needed." She blushed and looked down at the floor. "I'm sorry I didn't...that we couldn't."

"Lily." He ran a hand over her shoulder, pulling her into his arms as he continued, "I enjoyed our time together today and I thank you for it. Now, let's pick this lock, take what we need, and be gone from this place."

Lillian nodded against the warm comfort of his shoulder. He released her and set to work on the lock. Only a few moments later, the drawer released and Devon handed her hairpin back to her with an easy smile.

Devon stuffed a sheet of Erdway's vellum into his jacket pocket and picked up the small ring from the drawer. "Got it," he exclaimed.

"Oh, good! Now, let's leave." Lillian refused to celebrate until they were well away from Erdway's library. She straightened the desk back to its meticulous state, repinned her hair, and followed Devon to the door. "How are we to leave without being seen?"

Devon smiled. "Leave that to me."

She watched from a crack in the door as he slipped from the room and crossed the hall, picking up a vase from a table. "Is this French?" The question was directed to a passing maid.

"I'm not sure…" the maid was answering as Devon dropped the vase to the floor with a crash.

Devon shot a quick glance to Lillian as he said, "Oh no. I seem to be all thumbs today."

She slipped from the room, walking straight for the door without a backwards glance and leaving Devon in the middle of a group of clamoring servants. She didn't take a breath until she had accepted a glass of lemonade from a passing footman and mixed back into the crowd on the lawn.

A few minutes later, she saw Devon emerge from the house and stride across the terrace. He gave a nod in her direction and disappeared around the corner toward his carriage. The only thing for her to do now was wait and hope his plot worked. Until tomorrow night's charity ball, their scheme could still go horribly awry.

Thirteen

LADY HEYWARD WAS BUSY GREETING A NEW GUEST TO her charity ball. While her back was turned, Devon slipped the sealed letter from his pocket, stepping closer to the table at the foot of the stairs.

He took a sip of his drink, considering who else might be watching him. With a quick flick of his wrist, he dropped the letter into the glass bowl set out for charitable donations and turned away.

"Thornwood, good to see you again," the Marquess of Elandor offered with a nod of his head.

"Elandor, it's a nice evening to be charitable, isn't it?" Devon asked, wondering how much the man had seen as he walked up beside the table for donations.

"Certainly. Although I must admit I'm here more to see a friend and less to take the orphaned children of London under my wing." He gave what could be considered a chuckle for such a serious gentleman. "Have you given further consideration to joining His Majesty's Treasury?"

"The Treasury? Oh yes, of course. Funding for foreign endeavors."

"Among other things. I truly could use your assistance, Thornwood." He clapped Devon on the back. "Think about it. Now, if you'll excuse me, I see someone I need to speak with."

"Yes, I'll let you know soon." Devon watched Elandor walk to the edge of the dance floor to greet Lily's brother Nathaniel. What business could they have together? The thought slipped away as he watched Lily sweep by as she danced with Erdway.

Devon stepped closer, watching them with narrowed eyes. The dance was ending and Erdway was leading Lily back to Nathaniel's side. Devon heard him say, "If I'm to be honest, dancing with you was the only reason I attended this evening." He smiled as he added, "I see no benefit to charity. The street urchins should be put away somewhere so their presence doesn't interfere with the view out one's carriage window."

"Well, that is an interesting idea, Lord Erdway," Lily responded with a tight smile. "Thank you for the dance."

"Yes, I would like to dance again, perhaps later in the evening."

"Yes, I look forward to later this evening," Lily offered as she stepped away from him.

Erdway bowed and walked away as Devon closed the gap between him and Lily. As he reached her, she smiled. It wasn't the tight-lipped smile she had given Erdway. Instead, it was a special smile and all his. It held untold secrets and was wrapped in excitement.

She wore a pale rose gown. It clung to her tall, willowy frame and dipped low in the front to reveal an expanse of pale skin. Her hair was swept up in the same loose style she had worn the day they met. His throat closed as his eyes slid over her, and a smile crept across his face. "Lily, you look lovely this evening."

"Thank you. You look quite dashing as well." She blushed. "Now tell me, is it done?" she asked in a low voice. "Did you...you know?"

"Fret not. We are waiting for the letter to be delivered. It's out of our hands."

"Fret not? How can I fret not?" She ran a finger over her necklace in a gesture that grew from her nervousness, he had discovered.

He needed to distract her, or she would spend the remainder of the evening standing here looking guilty. "Would you care to dance to pass the time?"

"Oh. Well, certainly."

Devon held his arm out to her, enjoying the feel of her slender fingers wrapped around his forearm. He led her toward the floor. However, before they could move forward to take their places for the quadrille, they heard the dinging sound of a spoon on crystal. He glanced over his shoulder to see Lady Heyward practically bouncing where she stood on the staircase above the ballroom, a large grin covering her face.

"Ah, and now for the show," he whispered to Lily. Devon laid a hand over hers as he guided her back into the gathering crowd at the foot of the stairs.

"What if it doesn't work?" Lily asked through teeth clenched in a smile.

"Shh," he implored, rubbing his thumb over the back of her hand. "All will be fine." He only hoped his words of comfort were true. If his plan didn't work... He couldn't think about that now. It must work. It simply must. For Lily. He squeezed her hand briefly before letting it go.

"Ladies and gentlemen, if I may have your attention for a moment," Lady Heyward chirped from her elevated perch on the stairs. "I have just received word of a most generous donation to our cause. Lord Erdway? Has anyone seen Lord Erdway? Ah, there he is. Would you be so kind as to join me while I make this announcement?" She beckoned and there was a small scuffle as Erdway went to the base of the stairs and took one step up to join Lady Heyward. A baffled look creased his brow into a deep vee.

Ha! The letter had fooled the lady. Thievery, forgery…he was becoming quite the deviant, Devon realized. All for Lily, which was fitting, really. Devon smiled as he waited for the culmination of his work to be made evident to all of London society.

"Lord Erdway has generously bestowed on our charity the use of his home on the River Severn. He wants it to be used as a home for disadvantaged boys and girls. And he will be overseeing renovations to the property at his own expense to make it fit for the new use!"

There was a round of applause that died suddenly at the sound of Erdway's "What?"

"Oh, now, Lord Erdway, there's no need to be modest. We are all so grateful for your donation. Just think of all the beautiful children this will benefit! Join me in congratulating Lord Erdway this evening for, as his letter stated, he will be leaving tomorrow morning to begin his work. So enthusiastic, Lord Erdway! If there are any more donations, please seek me out here

at the donations table over the course of the evening."
She turned with a smile, signaling the orchestra to
begin the music once again.

"You did it! I don't know why I doubted you,"
Lily said at his side. Her hand slipped around his arm,
giving him a tug toward the dance floor. "Your Grace,
I do believe you owe me a dance."

"I wouldn't want to disappoint," he returned,
glancing back over his shoulder to see Erdway push
a footman from his path and storm off down the
hallway uttering a rain of curses. There were shocked
gasps as those in his vicinity moved away from him.
Devon grinned. The man wouldn't be pursuing Lily
anytime soon.

The first few notes of a waltz filled the ballroom
around them as he led Lily to the floor. His hand slid
so naturally around her back to guide her through
the steps. It felt like a dream. It was as if the past year
had never occurred and the Lily he'd met in that
tavern had never fled. His anger with her had disappeared, replaced by some tender feeling he would
rather not define.

Her eyes shone with untold happiness as she gazed
at him. Did she feel the same? He pulled her with him
through the steps of the dance. She laughed as they
rounded the corner of the floor, almost careening into
another couple. His heart clenched at the sight of her
smiling in his arms. He tightened his hold on her. He
never wanted to let her go. *My Lily*.

When the music ended, as all music eventually
does, he released her. They stood there trapped in one
another's gaze for a moment before he shook himself

and led her to the side of the room. "Would you like something to drink, m'lady?"

"Yes, that sounds lovely," she returned, her clear blue eyes shining in the light of the ballroom.

He took only one step away from her before he noticed Lord Harrow scowling at them from across the room. That man had only brought trouble into Devon's life for years, and there was something in the deep set of his eyes this evening that signaled more was to come. Did this have to do with the shipping routes for which they were in constant competition? But as the man's eyes drifted to Lily with a smirk, Devon knew there was more to this than competition on the high seas. Turning back to Lily, he said, "On second thought, why don't you walk with me to the refreshment room?"

Solomon twisted the letter opener in his hand, spinning it on the wooden surface of his desk. Harrow was late. His lip curled in disgust. The very idea of waiting for some undeserving, overfunded lord to sweep into his office and deign to meet with him was revolting. Yet he must wait. For this particular lord held the key to his success. Hingsworth, Amberstall, Erdway...he was glad nothing had come from his proposed alliances there. Harrow's deal put them all to shame.

Solomon's eyes flashed in anticipation as he leaned back in his chair. He was pleased with his own cunning in this situation. He drummed his fingers on the arm of his chair. He truly was a genius in matters of business. And there were those who sought to stop him? Ha!

Now, he was one signature away from attaining his goals. One signature, and riches would be his. One signature, and he would become the primary shipbuilder for the Crown. He grinned. It had a rather nice ring to it.

The door to his small office on the London docks opened and Lord Harrow was escorted inside.

"Mr. Phillips," he nodded in greeting, moving to the chair opposite Solomon's desk.

"Lord Harrow, I'm pleased you could join me this morning." Even if it's almost afternoon now, Solomon finished silently.

"Yes, but was it necessary to meet this early? I had a rather late night of it, you know." Harrow slouched in his chair and crossed his legs, his reddened eyes showing the truth of his statement.

"Ah, and how was the charity ball last night? I regret I couldn't attend. Charity is not my particular interest. Although I heard it was quite interesting."

"It was unusual, to say the least. You've heard the news, then? Erdway donating his estate on the Welsh border?"

"Yes. I wasn't aware of his interest in charitable endeavors." He suspected Lillian was behind Erdway's change of plans, but thanks to this business deal, none of that mattered now.

"Quite. And there was another curiosity at the ball last evening," Harrow offered with a wry smile.

"What would that be?" If Lillian had done anything else of report, he would throttle her!

Harrow leaned forward in his chair. "The Mad Duke of Thornwood spent most of the evening in the company of your sister…again. I told you I noticed them together at the Geddings' event."

"It seems our arrangement is quite timely." It was good he was around to keep her from making foolish decisions.

"Indeed. I'm pleased with the arrangement we've come to," Harrow said, drumming his fingers on the arm of his chair.

The corners of Solomon's mouth turned up in a slight smile. "As am I, Harrow. As am I."

"Very good. Did you have the documents drafted as I requested?" Harrow asked while rubbing his unshaven chin.

"Yes, everything is in order." Solomon slid the parchment across the table toward Harrow. "It is as we discussed."

"Including the bit with Thornwood's ships?" Harrow asked, taking the document.

"Yes, all should be in place." Solomon watched him, not daring to move. It was finally happening!

Harrow's eyes drifted over the document. He lifted the quill from the corner of the desk and signed the bottom. Solomon had done it! Wealth from a prospering business was within his grasp! Now, to send for Josiah. He smiled as he stood to shake Harrow's hand. "I trust I will see you tomorrow evening."

"I wouldn't miss it."

❧

"Good morning, Your Grace," Lillian said while dipping in a curtsy. Her eyes paused on Nathaniel's butler as he turned and left the parlor. Taking a step forward, she dropped her voice to say, "Devon, I wasn't expecting you this morning."

"I know, but I thought perhaps you would like to go for a ride with me in the park."

"It's only nine o'clock in the morning. Isn't the fashionable hour for a ride this afternoon?"

"It is. If you would rather sit in carriage traffic on a dusty path with the rest of society, I can return later."

"When put that way, an afternoon ride does sound appealing, but I think I'll just get my hat and gloves now."

"I was hoping you'd say that."

"I'm going for a ride in the park," she called out to the butler as she picked up her things from the table by the door.

Devon followed her out through the garden. Indeed, it was a perfect summer day. She paused on the path, looking up into the morning sunlight and allowing the warmth to settle on her cheeks. Devon tugged her arm to pull her through the open gate. Laughing, she followed him to a black phaeton harnessed to a matching pair of coal-black horses waiting on the street.

"My lady," he said with outstretched arms ready to offer her up into the conveyance.

As his strong hands slipped around her waist, her heart did an odd sort of flip. His stormy eyes lingered on hers as he lifted her high into his vehicle. She paused before climbing in, allowing the warmth of his hands to sink through her pale-blue day dress. She offered him a smile and slid onto the bench seat high above Nathaniel's garden gate.

"I'm glad you were at home and without plans for the morning," he mused, taking the reins from a young boy in livery and settling on the seat beside her a minute later. Once the boy jumped on the back of the vehicle, Devon set it in motion.

"There was a book I had intended on finishing, but it can wait," she returned as the phaeton rolled down the street. Glancing at Devon's profile as he concentrated on maneuvering through the morning traffic, she wondered why she felt so safe at his side even though they sat so far above the ground. She could feel the solid, muscular brush of his thigh against hers as he rounded a corner. Her heart flipped once more.

"I recently finished a guide to the behaviors of wild game in the Americas. It was fascinating, if you would like to borrow it," he offered as he turned into the park's entrance.

"That does sound interesting. I saw a bit of your book collection while taking tea with your mother on Tuesday." She smiled, thinking of the room filled with his artifacts and belongings.

Devon looked sideways at her before returning his eyes to the path ahead. "Tea with my mother? Don't tell me she has taken to hosting teas in my private library now." He looked truly disgusted by the idea of anyone in his home.

She hadn't meant to offend him. "Oh no, it was only the two of us," she said in a rush of words. "She gave me a tour of your gallery. It was nice to finally see it." She blushed as she spoke, looking away at the buildings they passed so he wouldn't notice.

"I had hoped to show you the collections myself," Devon replied in a grumpy fashion.

Lillian then understood. He wasn't upset she had seen his collection; he was upset by his mother's actions. "She means well, Devon."

He shrugged. "I know. It's only that she tends to turn my life on end when she visits. It's quite annoying to be mothered so completely once one is grown."

"I think she's lovely. But then I've been alone so long, perhaps..." Lillian's voice trailed away as the image of Mama floated through her mind. Turning back to Devon she asked, "Did you know she was friends with my mother?"

"No, she never mentioned it."

"Yes, they were the best of friends in their youth." She smiled wistfully at the tree branches stretching across the path as they drove beneath them.

"Lily, it wasn't my intention to bring up such a painful topic for you." He shifted the reins into one hand and gave her fingers a squeeze with the other. Their fingers tangled together, neither wanting to let go.

"Mama's been gone from my life for a very long time. It's easier to speak of her now, although I don't believe I will ever cease missing her." She looked down at their entwined hands lying on her knee. "I've begun to feel that there is some happiness to be found in the future. I've spent so much of life in mourning..." Yes, perhaps there was happiness to be found here with him.

"I'm glad to hear it. I don't like to think of you wrapped in sadness forever over the loss of your parents." He shook his head and chuckled, his eyes glittering as he looked over at her. "How do we always circle back to these serious subjects?"

"I'm not sure," she said on a giggle. She was at ease with him. Happy. Was that what she felt for Devon—happiness? Or was it something more? Did she love this man? She was studying his face for clues to her feelings and wondering about his feelings when she saw his eyes narrow.

"Elandor," Devon grated all of a sudden.

"What was that?" she asked, not following the path of his thoughts.

"The man riding this way on horseback," he murmured in a low voice only she could hear. "He is the Marquess of Elandor. Do you mind if we leave the path for a few minutes? I don't wish to speak to him just now. We can walk down to the bank of the Serpentine just there." He nodded with his head toward a grassy slope leading toward the water.

"Certainly," she returned as he pulled the phaeton onto the grass and stopped beneath a large oak. "May I ask why you are avoiding this Marquess of Elandor?"

"It's nothing." He motioned for the boy riding on the back of the phaeton to take the reins as he leaped down. Circling the rig, he came around to her, lifting her to the ground. "He wishes for my participation with some group in the House of Lords," he continued as he led her away from the vehicle.

"And you are against this?"

"Parliament is but a room filled with old men all in disagreement. No benefit seems to come of it." He led her down the grassy slope toward the banks of the Serpentine. "And I have the shipping business to contend with. In my free time I want to discover unknown plants, map untraveled lands, and better the world in some way, not sit and chat with a room full of men." He gestured to the city surrounding them. "There's no place for me here."

"I see." Her brows were drawn together in thought. He wanted to run from his responsibilities as a duke and representative of his country? But he had so much to offer. He was a brilliant man. He couldn't allow his frustration to drive him away. "And you don't believe the House of Lords could benefit from your experience with other cultures?"

He grumbled in response, looking away.

"Devon, from what I have seen of the gentlemen of the *ton*, the House of Lords could use your mind if our country is to survive the day, let alone the week."

He chuckled. "That may well be true, Lily."

"Just as I have decided to stop living surrounded by grief, perhaps it is time you start living surrounded by society. Show them you're brilliant instead of perpetuating this silliness about being mad." She paused to smile at him. "Distasteful though it may be."

"Perhaps," he conceded with a wry grin. "Although I believe I would rather spend this morning with you than in discussions over whether or not the Royal Navy should be allowed new cannons."

"Indeed. You have many days after this one to be the Duke of Thornwood this country requires of you. Today I require you to escort me over there to see those swans."

"With pleasure." He pointed toward the water. "Look at those two swans near the bank."

"Yes, they're beautiful creatures, aren't they?" She watched as one swan preened its white feathers before straightening and nudging the swan at its side.

"That they are," he replied, although she could feel his hot gaze on her instead of on the swans in the lake.

She tried to focus on the nature around them to keep from blushing at his attention. "I think those two swans are friends. They look as if they're having a lovely conversation. It's about the chill in the water today, I'm sure." She laughed, turning to look at Devon.

"Those swans have likely been swimming together in chilly waters for some time," Devon mused.

"You think so?"

"Of course. Swans mate for life. Each cob— the swan gentleman—finds some enchanting, similar feathered pen, and together they spend the remainder of their days swimming about chatting over the weather." His eyes danced as he added to her tale of conversing birds.

"That's rather romantic." *As is this moment*, she finished in silence as she allowed her hand to slip farther around his arm.

"Yes." He leaned in to murmur close to her ear, causing her skin to prickle with awareness. "And occasionally, I've heard tell, one of the females plucks a few feathers from the male, causing him to follow her all over the lake until he finally falls into her trap and they live together happily ever after." He straightened with a mischievous grin covering his face. "All due to her theft of a few feathers."

"Ah, and does this *gentleman swan* blackmail this *lady swan* along the way around the lake?" She held her breath. What was he saying? Happily ever after had the general meaning of forever. Or had it simply been talk of swans?

"I believe he might. Swans are prone to blackmail, you know."

That response, unfortunately, didn't answer any of her questions. Her heart pounded in her ears. "Devon, where is this leading?"

"I was hoping to that grove of trees over there where I might kiss you without being seen," he offered, pointing to a nearby grouping of trees.

"No, I mean this…whatever this is between us."

"I'm not sure, if I'm to be honest." He ran his thumb over the back of her hand where it rested on his arm. "Does this mean I cannot interest you in the grove of trees?"

"Do you desire to…um…live like the swans?" she asked, not sure how to say the words that were currently shredding her nerves.

"What I desire…there are certain caveats between me and what I desire. It's rather an involved story and I'm presently unsure of the ending," he replied, his eyes dimming from their jovial state a moment ago.

"Where does that leave us?" Her voice came out as a scratchy whisper because of her fear of hearing the answer to her question.

"I don't know, Lily." He turned, dropping her hold on his arm as he faced her. "All I know is that I want nothing more on this day than to be here with you, or rather in the previously mentioned grove of trees," he teased.

Why wouldn't he take this conversation seriously?

If he desired only her lips, her body, then that's what she would give him. She glanced around and saw no one in their area of the park at this time of day. Rising to her toes, she kissed him. It was a brief kiss—all she dared in the public park—yet when their lips met, delicious warmth filled her.

She had meant to prove a point with the kiss. She had planned to then tell him to continue their discussion without the mention of kisses within groves of trees. Yet, now with the taste of him on her lips, all she could think of was kissing him again.

He slid his hands to her waist, pulling her closer. "Lily, I'm as confused by this as you are. I was angry with you for so long, and now…" He shook his head. "Can we not enjoy one another's company today and decide what it means later? I need time to sort out some things."

She nodded in agreement, still wanting more answers but knowing he didn't have them, either. What did he need to sort out? His life could need sorting but so could his feelings for her. What did he think of her now in the absence of anger? Fondness, perhaps friendship? For her part, her feelings were a bit stronger. She loved him.

Oh dear, she loved him!

She wasn't sure when it had happened but she knew it was true. But what did he feel for her? She was sure she would discover the answer to that question soon enough. For now, she was curious what he would do once in the shelter of that grove of trees.

Fourteen

Lillian entered the house, humming an indistinct tune. Her heart was filled with sunshine, swan's songs, and Devon. Pulling off her hat and gloves and tossing them on a table, she grinned at her reflection in the small mirror. "Nathaniel, are you at home? I've had the most marvelous morning!" She took a few steps toward the rear of the house, continuing, "I must tell you of it." The words died on her lips as she rounded the corner into the library.

Solomon stood by the window facing the front garden. His dark hair was slicked back and seemed to melt into the dark collar of his coat, making him look like a tall shadow clinging to the draperies. Nathaniel rose from his seat at the desk when he saw her enter. He looked pale. What had happened?

"Lillian, do come in," Nathaniel offered in a tight voice, gesturing to a seat opposite his desk.

She entered the room, walking with slow steps to the chair he indicated. Her smile had seemed fixed on her face only moments ago, but now it fell as concern took its place. "Nathaniel, is something wrong?"

When he was silent, she turned her attention to her other brother. "Solomon, has something happened?"

She waited in silence as Solomon turned and went to the table filled with decanters in the corner, pouring a glass of dark liquor. When he was done, he replaced the crystal stopper and swirled the liquid in his glass before the light from the window. Turning, he said, "Lillian, I have reason for celebration today."

"Celebration of what, exactly?" She couldn't breathe. Her palms began to sweat as she sat looking at Solomon. He was pleased about something, too pleased.

"You have cause to celebrate as well, dear sister. But as it's unacceptable for ladies to drink liquor, I will toast for you." He lifted his glass and took a swallow.

"Why?" she asked, dreading his answer.

"Today is a joyous occasion, Lillian. For today we celebrate your betrothal."

"My what?" *Nooooo*, her heart screamed, yet she didn't twitch a muscle.

"Your betrothal," Solomon repeated. "Really, Lillian. It's the only reason you're here in London this season. You would think this would not come as such a surprise."

"And who does this betrothal arrangement involve?" Her throat was tightening as she spoke. They had gotten rid of Erdway. Who could it be?

"Lord Harrow, of course." He took a drink from the glass in his hand. "He's been admiring you from afar all season, you know."

"No, I didn't know." Lillian blinked in surprise over the information.

"Well, he has. We have discussed matters and

entered into an agreement only this morning." Solomon's dark eyes glimmered with excitement. "I've sent word for Josiah to come to town immediately. I'm sure Harrow will not want to wait long after announcements are made."

"How can this be?" she muttered. "Lord Harrow doesn't even know me."

"I don't see how that affects things." Solomon shrugged one shoulder and took a sip of his drink. "You look pleasant enough."

"If he's to be my husband, I would like to think our marriage is based on more than pleasant looks," she grated. Her husband. This Harrow was to be her husband? Her mind flew to Devon. She didn't want this. She wanted a life with Devon. How could this be happening?

"There are no *ifs*, Lillian. He will be your husband. I have a signed contract."

"This isn't a business deal, Solomon. This is my life!" she pleaded, knowing all the while it would do no good.

"Marriage agreements are serious business, Lillian. Your interference forced me to push this issue. And now all is settled."

"Solomon, I can't marry Lord Harrow. We won't suit."

"He is a titled gentleman of relative means. What's not to suit?"

"There are more important things in life than money!"

"Were you hoping for a love match, dear sister?" Solomon asked, laughing.

"Solomon!" Nathaniel warned from his seat behind the desk.

"No, I only thought…" Lillian's eyes burned with unshed tears. She would not fall apart here. Not in front of him.

"You were!" He chuckled again, walking closer to her. "You were hoping for a love match. Did you truly think the Mad Duke was going to swoop in to save you?"

"How do you know about…" she began, but Solomon cut her off with his cool tones as he leaned over her chair.

"You don't know about him either, Lillian. Did he tell you he's been involved in business with me for a year now?"

What? Devon in business with Solomon? "No, he didn't."

"Yes, I've built quite the fleet for his shipping business. He's terribly indebted to me at the moment. You didn't know? He won't save you from this, Lillian. Not at the risk of his family's welfare. He may be a duke, but he has no funds, no influence. Not like Lord Harrow."

The world seemed to be crashing around her feet. "He never mentioned…"

"We've met on numerous occasions to plan the growth of his shipping venture. He's mentioned expeditions in his future…" He leaned closer to her to whisper, "A duchess has never entered the conversation."

"That's enough, Solomon," Nathaniel cut in, rising from his seat.

Solomon smiled as he continued, his soft words

hanging in the air mere inches from Lillian's ears. "The Mad Duke of Thornwood is but a man entertaining himself in London until his ship leaves the harbor. Did you think you were more important than that? Foolish girl." Solomon straightened and turned away from her. "Nathaniel, have her at Bixley House tomorrow night for her betrothal ball." He set his empty glass on a table and moved toward the door. "Good day, Lillian," he offered over his shoulder as he left the room.

❧

"Thornwood, is there a reason you look so pleased this evening even though you've lost at every hand of cards?" Steelings asked, leaning close so all of the Angry Rabbit Pub wouldn't hear their discussion.

"Life is good this day, Steelings. Let us leave it at that," Devon stated as he stared at his cards, not truly seeing any of their markings. He couldn't pull his mind from the morning he had spent with Lily in the park. Nor could he wipe the grin from his face. *Lily.* The name repeated in his mind like a sweet melody. He had walked around town in a daze all afternoon before winding up at the card table with his friend.

"Very well. We could go up front to have a drink if you feel I've taken enough of your money already," Steelings teased.

"Perhaps that would be wise." Devon laid his cards on the table and looked over at Steelings with a mock grimace. "My losing streak does seem to be stretching out a bit."

"After you, then," Steelings said, offering the table of gentlemen around them a nod of farewell.

Devon went to the only open table, which was regrettably near the busy bar area, and sat down, signaling for a drink. Steelings had just joined him when a group of already foxed gentlemen staggered in the front door.

"It's a bit early to be in their condition, isn't it?" Steelings remarked in an undertone as they accepted glasses of scotch.

The men swarmed the bar area at Devon's back like a hive of angry bees. "Only a few drinks here, then we'll go visit Madame Amelia and her girls," a gentleman instructed to an answering round of cheers.

"Gin all around! Oh, take your time with the pouring, why don't you?" a voice called out from somewhere in the pack at the bar.

"I say, would you like to come home with me for the night?" one gentleman asked.

"Let 'er pour the drinks first, Harrow," someone called out. There was a round of laughter.

Harrow. Devon should have known that particular gentleman would be involved with this group. He shot a look of annoyance at Steelings. At least the group of idiots wouldn't be here long. If Devon had ever been so obnoxious when foxed, he couldn't remember it. He smiled at the irony of that thought.

"Harrow can do as he chooses this night. Once the leg shackle goes on, he'll be chained to his home," someone called out.

"Chained to my bed, you mean," Harrow returned, to the sound of more laughter.

Good God! Some poor lady had agreed to marry Harrow? She had his sympathies. Devon shook his head, trying to shut out their conversation in order to talk to his friend. However, Steelings seemed to be distracted by the scene as much as he.

"And you'll win the bet over her as well. Most of the *ton* has a stake in that wager! Think of the winnings, Harrow!"

"There's more to be won here than a little bet, although I do enjoy winning," Harrow replied, chuckling.

Devon's fingers gripped the glass in his hand until it threatened to shatter. How many ladies had wagers placed on the books over their betrothal status this season? Surely more than one. There had to be more than one. He turned, looking up at the crowd leaning on the bar.

"How'd you do it, Harrow? Miss Phillips is quite the ice queen!"

Devon's vision blurred. How could this be? How had this happened?

"She may be an ice queen now, but I'll have her melting as soon as the banns are posted." Their cheers and laughter filled Devon's ears. "I entered into an agreement with her brother this morning. The prim Miss Phillips will be mine in a matter of weeks."

Devon couldn't hear beyond the blood coursing through his ears. He couldn't see beyond the bastard currently leaning against the bar discussing his Lily. He couldn't feel anything beyond the desire to rip Harrow apart as a lion would on the African plains.

His chair slid back with a screech across the wooden

floor. He rose and took two steps toward Harrow in an instant, curling his fingers into the frilly cravat at the man's neck. Devon pulled him closer with his left arm while his right fist met Harrow's eye with a sickening thud.

Devon reared back and pounded him again. Harrow crumbled to the floor, yet Devon lifted him up again to slam him into the bar. There were yells as hands grasped at his shoulders, but he shoved them away.

He leaned close to the half-unconscious man, watching blood trickle from his nose as he grated, "You need to watch your mouth when speaking of a lady." His elbow shot out to collide with the shoulder of one of Harrow's friends who was trying to intervene.

Harrow tried to smile around his swollen lip. "She will soon be *my* lady. I can say whatever I please."

"Never," Devon murmured as his fist collided with Harrow's jaw once more. The man's head hit the bar with a loud crack.

Harrow fell to the floor as Devon released his hold on the man's cravat. Harrow rolled to his side, a moan escaping his lips. Devon stepped over his limp form, stalking toward the door. He needed air.

"Thornwood!" Harrow called out, causing Devon to pause. "You should know, I won't be bested. Not at sea and certainly not here in London."

Devon's fists clenched. He turned, prepared to pummel the man again, just as Steelings reached him.

"Thornwood, it will do no good. Let's leave," Steelings murmured as he shoved Devon toward the door.

With one final glare at Harrow's form on the floor, Devon swung open the door and stepped out onto the street. How could he stop Harrow? He couldn't allow this to happen to Lily. And it was entirely his fault. His dealings with Harrow went back years. He swore under his breath. This was no coincidence. Steelings matched his pace. They walked in silence until they reached the corner.

"He deserved that. It was a nice hit, the one that bloodied his lip. Nasty cut," Steelings mused. "But what are we to do now?"

They turned the corner and continued down the street. Steelings kept shooting glances in his direction, but Devon said nothing.

"Thornwood? Can you at least tell me where we're going?"

"To track down Lord Bixley and see what can be done to stop this," Devon stated, stepping out to cross the street.

"Would you like company?" Steelings called out after him, still standing on the walk.

"Not tonight, Steelings. Not tonight," Devon returned as he stalked off into the growing darkness, his heavy footfalls echoing off the stone walls of the buildings as he passed.

Harrow's declaration of not being bested had hit a nerve. They'd been in competition at sea for years with Harrow always finding some way to win—usually by rather dishonorable means. Devon was always left picking up the pieces and trying to mend them back into a profitable business to provide for his family. He shook his head free of the thought as he turned onto the street where the Bixley residence sat among a row of stately homes.

He wished now he'd never attended the events this season. If he'd never danced with Lily, spent time with her where they could be seen, none of this would have happened. Of course, he couldn't stay away from her. That much he knew.

Lily… How was he to save her this time? He ran a hand through his hair in frustration. There was only one course of action he could see. When had his life become so complicated? He raised a hand and knocked on the door to the Bixley home, wincing at the sting of his knuckles as he did so.

Fifteen

DEVON WAS SHOWN INTO THE HOME BY AN UNHAPPY-looking butler. As they rounded a corner into the library, he saw a plump man puffing on a cheroot and holding a drink in his other hand. The only family resemblance he bore to Lily was perhaps his nose, but, as he had his feet propped by the fire inside the Bixley library, he must be Lord Bixley. The man rose from his armchair in greeting as Devon entered. "Your Grace, I don't believe we've met before."

"No, we haven't. Call me Thornwood," Devon offered as he neared.

"Likewise, I'm Bixley. Take a seat." A confounded look covered his face as he sat back in his chair to eye Devon. "May I ask the reason for your visit so late in the evening?"

Devon sat opposite him as far as possible from the oppressive heat of the fireplace. "I have come to discuss the betrothal agreement involving your sister."

"Ah, that is the very reason I just arrived in town." Bixley smiled as he tapped the ash from his cheroot into a potted plant on the table at his side.

"And I am happy you have come. I have only tonight heard of this arrangement." Devon paused, stretching his sore fingers. What was the best way to discuss this? His brows were drawn together in concern as he continued, "And I would like you to reconsider."

"Reconsider? Why would I do that?" Bixley leaned back in his chair, drawing smoke into his mouth as he did so. His next words were thick around the chimney of smoke pouring from between his teeth. "My brother has finally arranged a marriage. Everything is set. We're hosting a betrothal ball under this very roof tomorrow night."

Devon watched him, knowing the next words he must say. "I would like you to reconsider because…I want to marry your sister."

"What?" Bixley's head tilted to study Devon in more detail. "My brother hasn't mentioned you in any of his letters to me."

"My interest in your sister has been beneath Mr. Phillips's notice. Yet I would like to offer for her." Devon leaned forward, his eyes never swerving from Bixley's questioning gaze. "She would be happy with me, I believe."

"Thornwood, this is all well and good, but my brother has already gone into negotiations with Harrow." Bixley waved a hand in the air. "There is a contract of some sort."

"Tear it up. I'm sure we can come to some understanding." Devon was a fine line away from begging the man for Lily's hand in marriage. He took a steadying breath.

"Thornwood, you're a man who knows business, are you not?"

"I am."

"Yes, of course you are. My brother builds ships for you." He paused to take a sip of his drink. "To put this into terms of business, it wouldn't be profitable for the family to allow a match with you."

."Not profitable," Devon repeated.

"Not with what Harrow is offering in the bargain."

"I have a dukedom. Surely that is of some value to you." Devon ran a hand through his hair in agitation. There was some detail in this he was missing.

"Unfortunately for both of us, titles don't pay the servants' wages and provide the life to which we are accustomed."

"What did Harrow offer?"

"You would need to discuss that with my brother. I'm not at liberty to say."

Devon stood, unable to contain his agitation any longer. This was Lily's life they were talking about. "You must! For your sister's future."

"I'm sorry, but my hands are tied," Bixley returned with a shake of his head.

"I see." Devon paused, trying to think of some other argument to sway Bixley, yet there was none. He blinked. "I'll show myself to the door then," he stated, shock settling into his limbs as he made his way out.

"Thornwood, I do regret this."

Devon nodded in reply and left the house. He wasn't aware of the route he was taking through the city. He never saw the homes he passed. His booted feet fell to the ground with wooden movements. He could only think that with every step, he was moving farther from Lily. Their morning together in the park seemed to have happened in a different lifetime. Today, in this reality, he was going to lose her all over again.

He didn't realize he had walked all the way home until his hand wrapped around the familiar doorknob. Pulling the key from his pocket, he unlocked the door and entered his dimly lit house.

Stomping up the stairs, he gazed at the spot on the wall where he had held her in his arms last year. He never seemed to be able to traverse these stairs without thinking of Lily. After this evening's disappointment, he would have to rip the damned stairs from the house.

He reached the top, pausing to look at the empty alcove where the settee once sat. His grip tightened on the banister. Why had he thought destroying that piece of furniture would erase her memory? Lily's hold on him was too tight. It always had been. And now she was beyond his reach.

A growl of anger wrenched from his throat. He reached out and wrapped his fingers around a vase on a side table. Hurling it through the air, he watched it smash against the alcove wall, shattering into tiny pieces on the floor and scattering flowers everywhere. However, it didn't ease his pain.

Scowling at the roses now strewn across the hall, he took a breath. He would be forced to live with the results of today's news for the remainder of his life. He felt the flowers squish under his boots as he headed for his bedchamber. Walking into the empty room, he went immediately for the decanter of brandy on the table by the fireplace. He poured one glass, drained it, and poured another.

"Devon dear, I heard something crash," his mother's voice sounded from the doorway. "Do we have an intruder?"

"No, Mother. Go back to bed." He glanced at her as he took another drink before turning back to face the fire.

"Dear, is something wrong?" she asked, moving into the room.

"I'm fine," he returned, wishing she would leave him be.

"I don't believe you," she replied. He heard a soft squeak as she sat on the edge of his bed. "A mother knows these things, dear. There's no need to pretend otherwise."

Devon shook his head and walked to the window, looking down on the garden below in the light of the moon. "I've lost her," he muttered. He didn't think his mother heard him, but it didn't really matter anyway. What could she say or do to make this problem go away? Nothing mattered anymore.

"Dear, come away from that window. It's quite drafty in here." She rose from the bed, walking to the window closest to the door. "Oh my! It's a wonder you don't catch your death in here, Devon."

"It feels fine to me, Mother." All he wanted was to drink himself into oblivion, collapse on his bed, and end this horrible evening.

"Celia, Mary!" his mother called out into the hallway. Turning back to Devon she explained, "We must bring some more blankets in here until these windows can be repaired properly."

"My windows are in fine repair." He turned,

leveling a glare at her that was meant to force her to flee.

One of the maids arrived in the doorway, catching his mother's attention. "Oh, Mary, there you are. Will you get someone to stoke this fire and bring some extra blankets?"

"I don't need extra blankets," he grated.

"Dear, there's a chill in here." She held her hand out as if to touch the nonexistent chill. "Can't you feel that?"

"No, I can't. I'm fine, Mother."

"But you look pale. Perhaps you need something to eat. Yes." She turned once again, calling for more maids. "Celia? Celia! Could you bring up a tray with some sandwiches for His Grace?"

"Mother, I'm not hungry."

"Go sit in the chair by the fire and warm up until your blankets arrive."

"Mother!" he bellowed.

"Yes, dear?" she answered with an innocent smile as she shoved him into the chair by the fireplace.

"I'm fine. I just want to be left alone," he pleaded.

"Sitting around this drafty house alone is what got you into this mess."

"My home is not drafty!" He watched her as she sank into the other chair by the fireplace, her froth of ruffled lavender nightclothes held in place by a dark purple robe cinched around her waist. She didn't appear to be leaving anytime soon. He sighed.

"That is not what I meant. If you had courted Miss Phillips in the proper fashion from the beginning, you would not be encountering such difficulties with her today. Ladies like to be called on with flowers and such, you know. Why is she upset with you this time? I set her straight on your gambling. Really, Devon. Betting on horses?" She clucked her tongue in disapproval.

"My difficulties are not with her." He shifted in his chair and ran his hand through his hair. "The trouble is her brothers."

"Oh? Perhaps I can assist in some way."

"I don't see how that will help, Mother." He drained the last of the brandy in his glass and stared into its empty depths. "Lily has been promised to Lord Harrow."

"Harrow? Well, that is dreadful news. The poor dear."

"Yes." He set the glass on the table at his side, watching the flames in the fire lap at the coals, consuming them.

"And what are you going to do to stop this travesty from happening?" his mother asked after a moment of silence.

His gaze snapped up to meet hers. "What can I do? She is going to marry another. And not just any other—Harrow. He's keeping her as some sort of prize. It's the trade routes to Asia all over again, only this time…" He shook his head. This time he would lose Lily.

"Devon dear, do you wish to marry her?"

"I told Lord Bixley as much tonight," Devon replied with a shrug of his shoulders. "Yet his hands are tied in the matter."

"I see. But you want Miss Phillips as your duchess?"

He was surprised at the ease of his answer. "Unfortunately for me, I do."

"I've never known you not to take what you wanted in life," his mother said with a hopeful smile.

"Take her? Is that the wisdom you are suggesting?" he asked with narrowed eyes.

"I'm not suggesting kidnapping, for goodness' sake!" She pursed her lips in exasperation. "I'm merely saying that you need to step up to the challenge you are facing and not back down."

"What if I'm too late?"

"Dear, you are Thornwood. Whenever you decide to arrive, it is always precisely the right time."

⁓

Lillian took another sip of tea to shake off the morning fog that had settled on her mind. Her life had changed yet again within the span of a day. She had spent most of the night tangled in her bedclothes, lost in thoughts of Devon's clandestine dealings with Solomon and a future wed to Harrow. Now, in the light of day, it still didn't make sense.

Had Devon been playing her for a fool all along? How many times had she mentioned her hatred of her brother to him? At least twice, if not more. She rubbed her temple, forcing some explanation for Devon's actions to settle there, but nothing occurred to her. He'd allowed her to ramble on, never mentioning he was in business with Solomon. Why would he keep that knowledge from her? *He's a man entertaining himself in London.* Solomon's voice sounded in her head. Her heart clenched at the obvious conclusion—Devon, like every other man in her life, had used her.

A knock sounded at the door. "Come in," she said, her voice a scratchy monotone.

"Darling, how are you surviving the day?" Nathaniel asked, poking his head inside her room.

"One sip of tea at a time," she replied with a grave smile.

"I suppose I shouldn't mention the dark circles under your eyes?" he asked as he entered.

"They will only enhance my looks for the ball this evening." She glanced in the mirror to see the dark smudges under her eyes looking very pronounced above her pale cheeks. "Perhaps I should fix my hair to match and scare Harrow away with my appearance."

"It's a nice thought, although I don't think it would work at this point." Nathaniel sat on the edge of the bed, wrapping one hand around the poster at the foot.

"I suppose not." She shifted on the chair at her dressing table, staring down into her teacup before she took another sip.

"Lillian, I'm sorry you can't live here with me," Nathaniel blurted out as if the idea had been weighing heavily on his mind. "I feel responsible for this mess you're in."

She twisted to look him in the eye. "Nathaniel, it's not your fault. You have your life to live. You can't have your little sister tagging along after you for the remainder of it."

"Yes, well, it's not just that." He paused, looking down at his hand where it lay on his leg. "You see,

Lillian, this house was a gift, as is everything I have, really. A friend gave it to me. He visits occasionally…"

"Oh?" Lillian paused with her teacup halfway to her lips. "Oh! Your gentleman friend."

"Yes." His gaze returned to hers. "Anyway, I didn't feel right allowing you to live here permanently when I…when he…when he and I…"

"Nathaniel, you need not say another word. I don't blame you for my fate."

He nodded in acceptance. "I do wish I could help you in some way." A thoughtful frown covered his face as he continued, "Perhaps I can help."

"You've done enough, Nathaniel." She continued to speak though her throat seemed to be closing. "There is nothing more to be done. I will attend the ball tonight and accept the future that will be announced there."

"I will still try, if you don't mind," Nathaniel offered, rising from the bed. "I couldn't live with myself if I didn't attempt to stop this."

"Do what you wish." She attempted to smile up at him as he crossed to the door, but she was sure her lips refused to make more than a grimace. "I will be here trying not to think about all of it."

"Very well. There is liquor in the dining room to assist you on that score."

"Thank you. I may have need of it before this is over."

As he left the room she set her tea down on the dressing table. Comfort within this storm did not reside in her teacup or one of Nathaniel's liquor bottles. She slid open the drawer before her, pulling free the pocket watch. She squeezed it tight in her hand, yet no sense of peace could be found there either.

Prying her fingers loose from its surface, she looked down at the small fox and smiled. No matter what had transpired in her life due to the watch, she was happy to have it within her grasp today. Her future may be devoid of love, but this was proof that for one small moment in time she'd had love in her life. Her father had loved her. He'd taught her to tell time on this watch while she sat curled by his side. No matter what happened after that, when he became frail and angry over his ailments, she would always have that day—the day she was loved.

She ran a finger over the small engraving of the fox. Truly she'd had the same with Devon: a small moment in the grandness of life when she'd laughed, when she'd loved.

Of course it had all been a lie on his part. He'd used her for his own entertainment, all the while doing business with Solomon behind her back. The worst part was that she loved him, truly loved him.

She shook her head, refusing to shed tears over someone who had betrayed her so horribly. Perhaps the only love she would receive in this life was represented in the sapphire eyes of the small fox. She slipped the watch into the pocket of her dress.

"On second thought, I believe I could use a drink of something stronger than tea." She gave the empty room a nod of agreement and walked out the door.

Sixteen

SHE HAD BEEN ABOUT TO POUR A DRINK TO STEADY HER nerves when she received word she had a caller. Setting her glass aside, she left the dining room. Who would be visiting her? She hoped it was not Lord Harrow, for she might be sick if that was true.

"Devon." Her weighted steps slowed further as she entered the parlor, pausing just inside the door.

He was here. Had he heard her news? If not, she must tell him. He could keep his secrets from her, but she couldn't do the same. She was weary of hiding, of plots, of all of it. Only, how was she to speak the words aloud when she could not even utter them in her heart?

He stood in the center of the room with his arms folded behind his back. He looked troubled. Good. Perhaps he knew she'd discovered his deceit, in which case he deserved to be troubled. Once he'd heard her news, he would no doubt leave. It would be over.

She stiffened her spine, opened her mouth, and forced her horrid truth to be said. No more secrets. "I'm glad you're here. I need to tell you of some new, um, occurrences in my life."

He said nothing.

She took a few more steps into the room, stopping before him.

"I am to be…" Her throat closed around the next word, not wanting to release it into the world and make it real. She swallowed. "Wed. My brothers have chosen Lord Harrow for me."

"I've heard."

"Oh." Did everyone in town know by now? "It will be announced formally at the ball tonight." She looked down at her fingers as she continued, "I thought I could keep this from happening. I thought I could…" She broke off with a shake of her head. "But I have no choice."

The room fell silent with only the sound of her heartbeat filling her ears. She'd been foolish to think she had a future with him. This was for the best. With her betrothal confirmed, he would leave. She clearly meant nothing to him anyway. A light began to fill his eyes, filling the room with the intensity of a storm on the high seas. "Run away with me."

"What?"

"We can be to Scotland by tomorrow. Married by nightfall." Devon grasped her hands and wrapped them in his as he gazed into her eyes.

"Scotland." Her legs were numb. Married by nightfall… She would have said yes only yesterday, but now? He'd lied to her. Even now, this could be some plot set forth by Solomon to achieve some evil end.

"Yes, Lily. Forget all of this madness here. Forget your family and come with me."

Even after all he'd done, a small part of her still

wanted to say yes. It was the same part that liked seeing flowers about to bloom and reading stories about love, and that believed the best of people, even liars. But he was in league with Solomon. She could never trust him, not now. He was no different from her brothers after all. "Devon, I can't. What kind of future could we possibly have together?"

"I don't know, Lily. I may not have funds the likes of which Harrow has clearly offered, but I can offer a pleasant life."

"A pleasant life," she repeated. "Pleasant for you or pleasant for me? I've spent years doing as my family requires, living their version of pleasant, and this is where it's led me."

"Your family doesn't care for you." He released one hand to tilt her chin up, looking her in the eye as he said, "I do."

"No, you don't." This discussion was getting them nowhere. He didn't care for her; he couldn't. Why had he kept the truth of the ships from her if he cared?

"Of course I do."

"If you ever cared for me, you would have told me you were in league with Solomon. You would have told me about the ships."

"The ships? Is that what this is about?" He looked lost.

"So you do recall having business dealings with my brother." She shook her head. "How could you, Devon? After all he's put me through? Have you been on his side from the beginning? Is that why you never mentioned it?"

"Lily, I didn't mention it because it has nothing

to do with you, not to mention that it's rather shameful."

"That it is!"

His grip tightened on her fingers as he looked into her eyes. "I'm sorry I didn't tell you. I don't make a habit of going about town discussing my failed investments and how Solomon's ships could keep my family from starvation. I need those ships, Lily. Don't let this stop you from leaving with me."

"If I run away with you, you would be further linked to Solomon through marriage. Is that what this is about? Ships? Money?"

"If you run away with me, I'll likely be destroyed financially, but that's a risk I'm willing to take."

She shook her head. Was he using her again? A marriage couldn't be built on so little trust. "How can I believe you?"

He stepped away from her to run a hand through his hair, tousling it in every direction in the wake of his fingers. He turned back to her with the menacing look of a madman. "Is the alternative to believing me so appealing? A life spent at Harrow's side?"

"I know little of Harrow, but at least he's never tried to control me for his own financial gain."

"Neither have I. Think about what you're saying, Lily! You will be forced to lie with that man for the rest of your life."

"I am aware of the implications of marriage and I am prepared to face them…"

"Will you think of me when you're with him? When he falls drunken and lusty on top of you and has his way with your body, will you regret this moment?"

"Stop. Please, stop." She closed her eyes against the image his words brought to mind.

"When you are forced to bear his children, will you think back to this day? I am offering you a better life, Lily! Come with me."

"I can't!" she yelled, her breaths coming out in small bursts of fire. The room fell silent except for the echo of her words off the walls.

He nodded. "If that is your final word…"

"It is," she replied, yet neither of them moved. She looked into his stormy eyes, not wanting to ever look away. If they could but stay here unmoving forever, if time would stand still for them, she might be able to continue breathing. There would be no secrets, no lies, only the present and the two of them.

"I suppose this is good-bye, then."

"Good-bye." She began blinking to force her eyes to clear. There was no other way. She'd rather commit to a marriage that was loveless on both sides than to hopelessly devote her life to someone who could never return the love she was giving. And he'd made it abundantly clear he didn't care for her the same way she did for him.

"If you choose it to be the end." He did not flinch, staring into her eyes and through them into her very soul.

Of course she didn't choose it to be the end, but he had lied to her, used her. How could she trust him now? No. She couldn't. It was over.

"I…" She closed her eyes to hold back the tears that were pooling at her lashes, shaking her head as they slipped down her cheeks in rebellion. "I have something for you." She reached into her pocket and closed her shaking fingers around the cold metal of the pocket watch. Pulling it out, she looked down into the small fox's sapphire eyes once more. The watch felt heavy in her palm. "I should never have taken it."

He shook his head. "I don't want it back."

"No, it's yours. I only took it because...well, it doesn't matter why anymore." The tears were streaming down her face now and she wiped them away with her fingers, sniffling so she could continue. "I see now how silly I was. I've learned I can't hold on to love, not in the palm of my hand. Not like this. So I want you to have it back." She turned his hand over with her own and dropped the watch into his grasp.

"I can't take this."

"It's yours. It was always yours. I'm sorry."

He looked up from the pocket watch in his hand to her face in confusion.

Her chest seemed to be collapsing under a great weight. She licked her lips and breathed in a shaky breath. Her words escaped her mouth on a whisper. "Good-bye, Devon. For my part, anyway, I will always love you." She dropped his hand and turned, running from the room.

৵৹

Devon stared into the palm of his hand for a moment. He didn't want the damned watch! Had she said she loved him? How could she say those words yet still agree to marry another? He dropped the watch into his pocket and began walking at a leaden pace toward the door.

She loved him. His heart pounded with the news.

But she would not go with him. What option did that leave? Was he doomed to see her at Harrow's side for the remainder of his life?

Stepping into the foyer, he paused at the bottom of the stairs, gripping the railing. Lily was somewhere at the top of the stairs. He could go after her. He could make her see reason. He took two steps up toward her. What could he say to change her mind?

"Thornwood."

Devon stopped. Turning, he saw Lily's brother exiting the library. Nathaniel, he believed he was called. "Mr. Phillips."

"Where are you going?"

"I need to speak further with Lily."

"From the sounds of your conversation in the parlor, I believe my sister has said all she intends to say to you."

"Pardon me, but you have no idea what you're talking about."

"Don't I? Why don't you enlighten me then, Thornwood?"

"I don't have time to explain things to you. I need to speak with Lily!" He turned back toward the stairs, bellowing, "Lily!"

"Thornwood! I will not have you cracking the plaster on the walls of my home with your yelling. Now, if you would please come back down *my* staircase, we can discuss this."

Devon turned, sneering at the man. "Yes? And what good will that do? She will still be wed to Harrow as soon as the banns can be posted. All because of those blasted ships!"

He took one step down the stairs, his knuckles turning white where he gripped the railing. "I offer her everything I have and she gives me back the damned pocket watch she stole from me a year ago." He took another step down the stairs. "It's not what I want! It was never about the watch. It was about her. It's always been about her." He ground the words out through his clenched jaw.

"The pocket watch she stole from you a year ago," Nathaniel repeated, his eyes narrowing. "Do you mind if I see it?"

Devon pulled the watch from his pocket, holding it out in the palm of his hand. Nathaniel stepped closer to take a look. "Father's watch," he uttered in a quiet voice. His gaze snapped up to Devon's. "How did this come into your possession a year ago?"

"I bought it from a shop." Devon leveled a glare on the man before him. "Just before your sister stole it from me in the dead of night while I thought she was sleeping."

"You thought she was sleeping." He paused to blink. "Thornwood, what exactly is the nature of your relationship with Lillian?"

"That is far too complicated a question when I need to be speaking with her or someone who can stop this betrothal." He ran a hand through his hair in frustration. He needed to be doing something, not standing around talking to Lily's disinherited brother. "I don't have time for this." He made to push past the man and head for the front door. But a hand caught him on the shoulder, impeding his progress.

"If you've had relations with my sister, you need

to damn well make time for this." Nathaniel straightened, dropping his hold on Devon's shoulder. His lips were pursed in the same manner that Devon had seen Lily's purse when angry.

"Mr. Phillips, my quarrel is not with you. I have asked Lily to elope with me to Scotland and she has said no."

"I see." Nathaniel paused to glance back at the open library door, a look of calculation drawing his brows together. "Thornwood, the disasters that seem to continue to befall every gentleman that nears Lillian this season…they were your doing?"

Devon blinked at the turn of their conversation but didn't offer an answer.

"The men my brother has set forth for her to marry, Hingsworth, Amberstall, Erdway, and Harrow. Do you know what they all have in common, Thornwood?"

"Aside from the fact that they would all make your sister miserable for the remainder of her life?"

"Yes, aside from that."

"Does there need to be more? I can't imagine any gentlemen less suited for marriage to Lily." He paused, rubbing the bridge of his nose in thought.

"I agree with you," Nathaniel finally said. "And yet I, like you, can do nothing to stop it from happening."

There was something he was not saying. "If you know something, I demand to know what it is," Devon said. "If there is some piece to this puzzle I have missed, you must tell me. Your sister's future happiness is at stake!"

"Tell me, Thornwood, do you love her?"

Devon's gaze shifted to the table across the room.

He swallowed, knowing Lily's brother was watching his every move.

The answer to the question caught at the back of his throat. All he could do was nod his head. God, yes, he loved her. He had loved her since the day she wandered into his life in a giant blue dress. He had loved her while he searched the city for her. He had loved her when he saw her again across that ballroom, and he certainly loved her now.

"Then you need to speak with my brother Solomon. In our little family, Josiah may hold the title, but Solomon holds the cards."

Devon looked back at Nathaniel. "We both know he'll only be swayed by money, and that is the one thing I'm low on at the moment."

"You can try."

With one last look at the stairs that led to Lily, Devon nodded. Turning, he was almost to the front door when he caught sight of the Marquess of Elandor standing in the library. Devon wasn't sure what the man was doing eavesdropping at Nathaniel's library door, as he rarely left Parliament, but he did not care. Right now he needed to get to Solomon Phillips.

Seventeen

Devon reined in Poseidon outside a warehouse overlooking the London docks. He paused before dismounting to eye the gray stone building. Solomon had to be here. He was always here. The soot built up on the building's surface from years of sea breeze and chimney smoke gave the structure the look of abandonment, though many workers moved in and out of the large bay doors loading and moving crates. A small sign bearing the name "Phillips Shipbuilders" hung above the door. It swung in the breeze with a gentle *squeak, squawk.*

Devon gave his horse a reassuring pat as he slid to the ground and tethered the reins to a nearby post. What was he to say once inside? He was unsure, but he had to do something. Taking calculated steps, he traversed the plank walkway to the main door of the office.

"Thornwood!" called a familiar voice before he could reach the door.

Devon sighed. So much for making this little visit alone. Turning, he saw Steelings tying up his horse beside Poseidon.

"Thornwood! I've searched the entire city for you." Steelings crossed the distance between them with long strides. "At least I caught you before you did something rash to Mr. Phillips," he added as he slowed beside Devon.

Devon shot him a look of disbelief. "When have you ever been able to stop me from impulsive actions, Steelings?"

"True. But still, we require a plan. We can't simply storm in there and demand that Mr. Phillips allow you to have his sister."

"What do you know of it?"

Steelings shrugged. "Your mother filled in a few of the details I was missing."

"Of course she did."

"Don't be angry. I'm here to assist you with your leg shackle." Steelings grinned.

Devon turned a narrow-eyed glare on his friend. He was in no mood to joke about the matter. Behind this door stood the man responsible for Lily's betrothal to Harrow. What could Devon possibly say to change her brother's stance on the issue? His fingers curled around the doorknob.

"Slow down, Thornwood. Shouldn't we think this through first?"

"No. We shouldn't." Devon swung open the heavy oak door and strode inside, Steelings at his back.

They walked into the dimly lit office, approaching a small, pointy-nosed man where he sat perched behind a desk on the far wall. The man's gaze was on a ledger spread across his desk as he said, "Welcome to Phillips Shipbuilders of London, building quality vessels since aught five." He looked up, his eyes widening. "Oh, Your Grace. My apologies, I wasn't expecting you today." He stood, rounding the corner of his desk. "I suppose you're here about the ships."

Devon grimaced at the question. "Not today."

"Are you certain? The two flagships of the fleet are in the berth just outside the building. You must have walked right past them."

Devon's jaw tightened. He'd heard enough about the damn ships today. If only he didn't need them so badly. "Actually, I am here to see Mr. Phillips."

"Oh." The secretary deflated slightly. "I will see if he's in."

Devon nodded in agreement. Once the man left the room through a door on the far wall, Devon turned to look at Steelings. How he hated to wait at a time like this.

Steelings scratched his head in thought. "Don't the ships you're having built by Miss Phillips' brother muddy the waters a bit in all of this?"

Devon's eyes narrowed on his friend. "You have no idea."

"I can guess."

"You would most likely be correct."

The secretary returned with a rather pinched look about his mouth. "Mr. Phillips is busy and unable to speak with you at the moment."

Devon clenched his fists at his sides. "He's too busy?"

"That is what he says, Your Grace."

Devon was already striding toward the door in the far wall. Before the man realized what was happening, he had been shoved aside as Devon and Steelings entered the back offices. They only needed to open two incorrect doors before they found the door to Solomon's lair.

He sat reclined with his booted feet crossed on the corner of his desk. A glass of dark liquor rested in one hand on his chest while the other thumbed through a document.

Devon stepped inside the opulently appointed room. "I can see how dreadfully busy you are, Phillips."

"Thornwood, who allowed you access to this office?"

"I allowed myself access." He crossed the room to take the seat across the desk from Solomon while Steelings stood sentry at his back.

"You received my note, I assume?" Solomon asked with a gleam in his dark eyes.

"No, I have come to discuss the arrangement you have agreed to with Lord Harrow regarding Miss Phillips." Devon stared down the man in front of him without blinking.

"This is awkward, then."

"You know of my opposition to this match already?"

"I admit I'd suspected as much. However, my decision is made. Harrow is to marry my sister and I'm quite happy about the outcome."

Happy? How could he be happy? Devon's hand clenched into a fist on his thigh. "I'm sorry to hear that, for I am asking you to break your agreement."

"Break my agreement? Why would I want to do that?" Solomon set his drink on the desk.

"I would like to marry your sister." It was amazing how easy those words were to say.

"I'm afraid it's too late for that, Thornwood." Solomon dropped his feet to the floor and sat up from his reclined position in his chair. "Her betrothal will be announced at the ball tonight. As a matter of fact, I need to get changed into appropriate evening attire for the joyous occasion. So if you don't mind…" Solomon broke off with a meaningful glance at the door.

Devon bristled at being asked to leave but did not allow his face to show it. "Actually, I do mind. I would like the chance to discuss this with you."

"Thornwood, there is nothing you can say that will change the outcome of these events. In fact, if you had received my note you would know…"

"You aren't interested in having my title in the family?" Devon could not understand Solomon's stance. Didn't everyone clamor over connections to titles and such?

Solomon steepled his fingers in front of him in a show of power. "No. What Harrow offered serves my purposes perfectly."

Devon leaned forward in his chair. "I can offer your sister a good life."

"That is neither here nor there," Solomon returned with a small shrug.

"Your sister's happiness is not of importance in this decision?"

Solomon sighed. "Thornwood, the betrothal will be announced in a few hours' time. I really must get ready to leave."

"What has Harrow offered you?"

Solomon leveled a glare at him yet said nothing.

"Surely, there is room for some negotiation. I could make some sort of arrangement…"

"No, Thornwood. You can't," Solomon said with a slight shake of his head.

"Is there nothing I can offer to change your mind?" Devon was almost out of his seat in protest.

Solomon's mouth twisted into something resembling a smile. "Gentlemen, I must ask you to leave. We have nothing further to discuss on the subject. My sister will marry Lord Harrow as soon as the banns can be posted." Solomon stood. "My decision is final. She is as good as married. Thornwood, it would be best if you were to go now."

Devon stood to his full height before leaning over the desk to look down on Solomon. He truly was a greedy, heartless bastard. How could anyone throw his own sister to the wolves for financial gain? Yet there was no reasoning with the man. Devon could see the resolve in his eyes. He had lost her.

His fingers gripped the edge of the desk to keep from knocking the superior smirk off Solomon's face. How had he been so unfortunate as to have business dealings with this man? Devon had been blinded by his own desperate need for the ships Solomon offered. But no more. "You will regret this, Phillips."

"Somehow, I doubt that."

Steelings spoke for the first time at his back. "Thornwood, we should go."

"Yes, Steelings. There's something I need to take care of as soon as possible." Devon turned and stalked out of the office.

His stomach twisted over the knowledge that Lily would marry Harrow and he could do nothing to stop it. She should be his. He swung the door open onto the harbor. He had allowed this to happen. He paused outside the office to look out at two of his new ships. The gentle slap, slap, slap of the water against the wooden hull was like a slap to his face.

He had failed. His desire to have a respectable income for his family—and even more than that, his desire to use those ships as an excuse to leave London—had overshadowed all reason. He'd known Solomon wasn't a good sort, but his price had been attainable. Ha! He now saw the price of this endeavor and it was too high. Looking beyond the ships to the harbor, he paused to watch as the sea tossed and carried ships out to the horizon. That wasn't where he belonged. Not anymore.

His place was here, fulfilling his responsibilities as a duke, with Lily at his side. Lily. He closed his eyes. It was too late for that part of his future to come true but it was not too late for everything. He gritted his teeth as anger seeped steadily into his veins. He began walking, his boots landing with loud thuds on the wooden walkway.

"Ah, look, there's a tavern," Devon tossed over his shoulder in a voice that could be considered too calm for the circumstances.

"Yes, perhaps a drink is exactly what you need. We'll go get foxed and not think about life for the remainder of the evening," Steelings returned as they crossed the road.

The Boar's Hoof Inn stood opposite the London

docks. A steady stream of sailors was treading in and out of the establishment in search of either a first drink on land or a last. Smoke seeped from the open door, swirling around Devon's shoulders as he edged his way into the crowded tavern. He and Steelings pushed their way to the bar past a dirty collection of the sea's finest ruffians.

"Two bottles of your finest whiskey," Devon stated, dropping a bag of coins on the wooden bar top.

Steelings stepped up to the bar, nudging his friend in the elbow as the bartender got the bottles from a crate in a back room. "Two bottles? Well, that should do the trick. If it takes more than that to numb us, we have larger problems than I realized.

"We'll need glasses as well," Steelings told the man with the whiskey as he neared.

"That won't be necessary, thank you."

"Thank ye, come back soon." The man pocketed the money and turned his attention back to a group of rowdy men at the end of the bar.

Steelings took one of the bottles and popped the cork out with his teeth. "Drinking from the source, are we? All right, then. On days like this, I suppose it is appropriate."

Devon said nothing. He pulled the cork from the top of the whiskey in his hand and took a long draw on the sweet fire in the bottle. He held up the glass bottle, analyzing the level of liquid left inside before taking one more gulp. Exhaling, he turned to look at Steelings. "Take one more drink."

"All in the name of friendship," Steelings offered before downing a large gulp.

"There. Now, hand me your bottle," Devon said with an outstretched hand.

"You need them both, do you? Well, you have had a rough go of it today." Steelings passed Devon the container, the brown liquid swirling inside.

"Yes, two bottles should do," Devon said as he stepped past Steelings.

With the necks of the two bottles wrapped in the grasp of one hand, he made his way for the door. Pausing to rip a lit candle from its perch on the wall by the door, he stepped out into the setting afternoon sun with Steelings at his back. The dirt on the street crunched under his boots as he walked back toward the shipbuilder's office where Poseidon was still tethered to a post.

"Thornwood, where are you going? You're beginning to worry me a bit," Steelings said beside him, but Devon ignored his friend.

Passing the candle to Steelings, he reached into his pocket and pulled his handkerchief free. Pausing beside his horse, he poured a portion of the whiskey onto the fabric until it dripped with brown liquor. Stuffing the handkerchief into the top of the bottle, he set it at his feet. One down, one to go. He reached into his pocket in search of another piece of fabric and pulled from its depths the silk stocking he'd taken to keeping with him. Lily's stocking. His lips twitched in an attempt at an ironic smile.

He kissed the lace top of the fabric before drenching it with the liquor and stuffing it into the other bottle of whiskey. Picking up the bottle at his feet, he took the candle back from Steelings and began to walk toward the plank path that led to the office.

"Thornwood, what are you doing?" Steelings grabbed his shoulder. "This is madness, Thornwood! You cannot do this!"

Devon threw off Steelings' attempt to hold him back, striding forward down the plank walkway.

"Think about what you're doing, Thornwood!" Steelings yelled from behind him.

Devon lifted the candle flame to the fabric in his hand. He lit the edges of handkerchief and lace that peeked from the tops of the containers in his hand. He watched for a second while the lace that once caressed Lily's thigh singed and burned in his hand.

"Devon, stop!"

"For Lily," he growled as he threw the first bottle onto the deck of the new three-masted frigate floating in the berth beside him.

He took a few steps forward before lobbing the second bottle onto the ship floating at its side. There was a burst of flames as the bottles shattered.

Fire seeped across the wooden planks of the ships. Sparks floated up on the breeze and hit the sails where they hung loose in the sky. The flames crept up the masts, singeing lines while spreading across the decks.

The crackles and pops of the flames were interrupted a moment later by the main mast falling from one of the ships with a crash across the bow of the second ship.

"Good God," Steelings muttered at Devon's side.

Devon watched as his dreams for his future burned in the London harbor and yet he felt nothing. There was no sense of loss. But there was also no sense of righteousness. There was no victory in this moment.

None of it mattered anymore. He had lost Lily because of these damned ships. Now, even with them destroyed, he couldn't get her back. The sun was setting. Soon her betrothal would be announced. All was lost.

Just then the door to the office burst open and Solomon came outside. "What have you done?"

"What I should have done long ago. Our business dealings are over, Phillips," Devon stated as the ships continued to burn. Embers fell around them and smoke filled the air.

"You're burning my ships!"

"They were mine to burn."

"You truly are mad," Solomon said, gazing up at the column of flames from the ships. Solomon turned, bellowing to the group of his employees that had made their way outside to see what was happening. "Seize him!"

Four large men walked Devon's way, grabbing at his coat sleeves. He didn't care anymore. Let them take him. Throw him in prison. Kill him. It would make no difference. Lily was beyond his reach. She was like the smoke that swirled around his body; she surrounded him but he couldn't grasp her in his fingers. He felt callused hands wrap around his wrists only to be replaced by rope. At some point, Steelings stepped in, throwing punches.

"You will not be taking him anywhere!" Steelings cried as he cracked one man's jaw, then caught another across the eye. "Thornwood, you want to assist me a bit?"

Devon didn't answer, only stared at the flames crawling higher and higher into the darkening sky.

When he glanced back, three men had Steelings pinned against the stone wall of the building.

"I'll have you brought up on charges!" Solomon was screaming beside him. "You can't do this and get away with it!"

Devon observed another mast cracking and falling with a crash into the water before them. "I believe I just did."

"But you won't get away with it, Thornwood!" Solomon moved closer to where Devon stood with his hands tied behind his back. Looking into Devon's eyes with a gleam lighting their darkness, Solomon smiled. "Do you think this will change my mind about my sister's betrothal? Because that will never happen!"

"I didn't think it would. I simply didn't want the ships you built," Devon offered with a shrug of his shoulders. He could hear Steelings struggling against the men a few feet away, but he didn't turn to look at his friend.

"You don't even know what you've begun. You see, I sold a fleet of ships to Harrow just yesterday, your ships. These ships," Solomon stated as he rose up on his toes in an attempt to look Devon in the eye. "I sent a note this morning to let you know of the change."

"Harrow's ships?" Devon quirked his lips as the railing of one ship finally gave way to the flames and crumbled into the water.

"He doubled your payment, among other things…"

"Then he's a fool."

Solomon turned at the splash of wood hitting water. When he turned back toward Devon, his face was twisted into an expression of victory. "Say what you will. You'll be in chains within the hour for this, while I celebrate my new alliance with Harrow. I have much more to gain than these two…" He pressed a finger into Devon's chest. "Little ships." "

"And what gain is that, Phillips?" Devon looked down at the man with a sneer.

"He is going to turn my small business into a pinnacle of modern achievement."

"Ha!" Devon let out a bark-like laugh. "How is that?"

"A contract for the Crown." Solomon laced his hands behind his back and rocked up onto his toes.

Devon's eyes narrowed on him. "Building ships for the Royal Navy? That is what you're after?"

"You've attended meetings at the House of Lords. You must have seen this unfolding, Thornwood." Solomon stalked away from Devon. Stopping to turn with a snap, his eyes widened before narrowing to slits. He took several paces back toward Devon to add, "You knew all along, didn't you? Hingsworth, Amberstall, Erdway, Harrow…They all have seats on His Majesty's Treasury. And you thought you could be rid of them, didn't you?" Solomon asked with a snarl. "You thought you could pull off your little schemes without notice. So you could give the contract to some friend of yours, I'm sure! Some peer who thinks he's better than I am. I come from a titled family, too, you know! But none of that matters now, because you didn't succeed."

Devon couldn't believe what he was hearing. A ship-building contract? That was what all of this was about? "I have no interest in your business or that damned contract! All I want is your sister. All I want is Lily."

Solomon clearly hadn't heard him since he was still speaking. "I'm going to hold the contract for all the Navy's vessels and you will be left with nothing."

"You're selling your sister off for rights to a contract? Are you mad?"

"No. I'm the sane one here. I saw a business opportunity and I took it."

"And what of Lily?"

"*Lillian* will marry Harrow, of course. I'm sure she will live out her days at his estate in the country doing whatever ladies do with their time." Solomon waved away the thought with the back of his hand.

"All so you can build more ships? She's your sister!" Devon began to pull at the bonds holding his wrists behind his back.

A man stepped through the swirling smoke, and another voice entered the argument. "He won't be building anything more than a shipping rig if I have any say in the matter." The Marquess of Elandor neared from a carriage parked at the end of the pier. "And I believe I do have a say in the matter."

"Elandor, what are you doing here?" Devon shook his head in wonder at why the man kept appearing wherever he went today.

"I followed you here from a friend's home," he replied to Devon before turning toward Solomon. His stance said he was unaffected by the burning of ships or the argument he had walked into. The air of power about him was truly something to be admired.

"Mr. Phillips, from what I've heard, you have

entered into some agreement with Lord Harrow involving naval ships, offering the winnings of a wager at White's along your sister, Miss Phillips, as some sort of prize. I regret to inform you that this action will not succeed."

Devon's chest contracted at the possibility of the truth in his words. "Elandor, what do you know of this?"

Elandor was calm, his tone unhurried as he spoke. "Thornwood, when I asked you a month ago to join my little group within the House of Lords, I was sincere. As titles are passed from generation to generation, we do not always retain the most devoted gentlemen in power." He shook his head with a look of disappointment clouding his eyes. "I truly could use you to balance the weight of the corruption I have found. I only apologize that your involvement had to come about in such a fashion."

Solomon stepped forward. "While this is a lovely scene of heartfelt love among the peerage, I fail to see what it has to do with the ship-building contract that is now mine. You see, Harrow has already agreed to my terms." Solomon pulled a piece of parchment out of his pocket and waved it in the air.

"Mr. Phillips, what you fail to see is a great deal." Elandor paused to give Solomon a look filled with pity. "As it happens, Lord Harrow has no power or authority to grant such a contract to any company without my approval...as I am head of the Treasury, not he. If I'm correct, he only wanted to possess Miss Phillips as some sort of personal vendetta against Thornwood here. Why else would he offer you twice the worth of the ships due to Thornwood?"

"He can keep his blasted ships," Devon stated over the sound of wood crackling and burning.

"It's true they don't seem quite seaworthy at the moment," Elandor mused.

Solomon's face was turning a deep purple as the knowledge sank into his thick skull. "That cannot be! He signed a document! The contract is mine!"

Elandor stepped forward and pulled the document from Solomon's grasp. "The word of a deceitful man is of little value." He tore the parchment in half, stacked the pieces, and tore them again. "You would do well to remember that," Elandor offered as he moved past a shocked Solomon to where Steelings was trapped under the weight of three dockworkers, with his mouth bound.

"Let him go." Hearing the simply stated words spoken with the marquess's customary tone of authority, the men gave up the fight and stepped away. Steelings shook out his coat and tugged on his cuffs with a menacing glare aimed at the men.

"Are you hurt, Steelings?"

"No, I am fine, thank you," Steelings said, stepping forward to unbind Devon's hands.

"Wait!" Solomon bellowed. "You cannot let them go! They burned the ships I spent the better part of a year building! They can't get away with such action!"

Devon shook the feeling back into his hands. "By rights they were my ships and I can burn them if I damn well want to."

"This isn't over, Thornwood! Harrow will set it right. This is but a small battle, when the announcement of my sister's betrothal will be taking place in only a few minutes' time. Once that is done, she is as good as wed in the eyes of the *ton*—with or without a contract. I will see to it that she is never yours." Solomon shook his coat into place. "If you will excuse me, I have a ball to attend." He turned and walked away, stepping up into Elandor's carriage, and was gone.

Steelings stepped forward with a look of amazement on his face. "Elandor, he just stole your carriage."

"I know. Let him go. We'll make better time on horseback anyway."

"Better time where?" Devon asked.

"To the ball," Elandor returned with a smile.

"But it's too late. You heard Solomon. She's as good as wed."

"Not if we get there first," Steelings cut in.

Devon looked the two men over as if they were the mad ones. "Once we arrive, what are we to do? Push Harrow to the floor while I steal his bride?"

"If a more diplomatic resolution cannot be reached, then yes, that is exactly what we do," Elandor stated.

Devon couldn't believe any of this. "Elandor, why are you doing this? Why do you care?"

The marquess ran a hand across weary eyes before answering. "Because I happen to love the brother of the lady in question. And he is quite upset by all of this."

Suddenly everything fell into place. Elandor's presence at Nathaniel's house. His confirmed bachelor status. His involvement tonight. Devon's eyes widened. "I see." He glanced at Steelings to discern his reaction, only to see a concerned nod of agreement. "Elandor, you have my word, this information remains on the London docks this evening."

"Good. Now, we must hurry."

The three men ran for their horses. Poseidon was pawing at the ground in anticipation when they reached him. Devon unwound the tether and gained his seat on the large gray's back. Looking back toward his ships now lighting the night sky, he took a breath. His dealings with Lily's brother may be over but he had not yet won Lily's hand.

His and Lily's fate was affixed to the hands of the clock that ticked steadily past. It was a fool's errand. He would never make it to the ball in time. And once there, if they tried to interfere, the chances were strong they would be thrown from the ballroom. Would they even be allowed entrance? The ball was at the Bixley residence, after all.

"Elandor, what will you ride?" Devon heard Steelings ask.

"If Mr. Phillips can steal my carriage, I believe I can return the favor without fault." He swung up onto the back of a chestnut mare and turned with a grin.

"Let's go, then." Devon glanced over his shoulder one last time at the crumbling black mass of wood in the harbor. Urging Poseidon into a gallop, he turned up the street toward the Bixley residence. He had burned his old dreams and his future security to ashes tonight; he only hoped it wasn't in vain.

If he arrived too late, he would be forced to watch as Lily held Harrow's arm at events. He would have to endure the knowledge of what would happen in their marriage bed. He would see Lily about town one day large with Harrow's heir.

His speed increased with every passing thought.

Buildings soared by as he raced up the street. He was going to be too late. *Lily, wait for me. Wait for me.* He knew she had no control over any of this, but he sent a silent plea into the cool night air anyway.

"Thornwood, you know, I was thinking…" Steelings shouted, bent over the mane of his horse to gain additional speed as they galloped down the street. "I believe this might be the first time you've raced toward a ball." He laughed as they turned a corner and picked up their pace again. "It seems you've always been going in the reverse direction."

"You'll excuse me if I don't laugh just now," Devon growled as he pulled into the lead of the three once more. The Bixley home was four blocks away. Time was passing. The announcement could have been made already.

Three blocks away. The guests could be toasting the couple's future happiness at this very moment.

Two blocks away. Lily could already be dancing with Harrow by now.

Finally, Devon saw his destination in the distance. Carriages lined the street, indicating a large crowd. It must be due to the resolution of that damned bet on the book at White's. How he hated Solomon for what he was doing to Lily.

Gritting his teeth, he veered through the carriages, startling two horses along the way. Barreling down the sidewalk, he watched as one driver, then two gentlemen dove out of his path. He pulled up on Poseidon's reins, slowing the horse to a stop at the bottom of the steps to a large brick home with candles blazing in every window.

He dismounted and gave his horse a quick pat on the shoulder before bounding up the stairs. A moment later he was inside, and Steelings and Elandor had caught up to him. The sound of music from the orchestra filled the air as he made his way through the foyer.

He forced his way around ladies and past gentlemen. They all seemed to be giving him looks of shock and disdain. Glancing down, he realized he was not wearing evening attire and also was covered in soot. Heston may murder him later, but right now, he didn't care. He had to find Lily. He rounded the corner of the hallway leading to the ballroom and came face to face with Lord Bixley.

Eighteen

A WOMAN TWIRLED PAST AS SHE TURNED THE CORNER of the dance floor, her skirts brushing the edge of Lillian's light green silk gown. She had chosen the color because it was almost the exact color of the painted walls in the ballroom. With any luck she would simply disappear into the wall at her back. Excited smiles were thrown her way by everyone who passed, but so far no one had stopped to chat. Grateful for this small blessing but not sure how long it would last, she took a step backward into the shadow of a large potted palm.

She smoothed her skirts for the third time in five minutes and twined her gloved fingers together in front of her to keep them still. Her entire life came down to this. It was depressing, really, to think that she had lived for the purpose of serving those around her, namely her family, only to end up bargained off and gambled upon. All of London seemed to have come out tonight to witness her shame. As the minutes ticked by, dread filled her, turning her stomach and making her throat clench.

Sue arrived at her side with two glasses of champagne. "I thought you could use this."

"Thank you," Lillian offered with a wooden smile as she turned up the glass, finished it to the last drop, and set the empty glass on a nearby pedestal.

Sue laid her hand on Lillian's arm in reassurance. For once, her friend appeared to be at a loss for words. Across the ballroom, Harrow shook hands with gentlemen and laughed in great guffaws. For some reason, he was sporting two blackened eyes and a broken nose. She was going to be sick. "Sue, what if I run? Where could I go that no one would find me?"

"I have a seldom used wardrobe in my bedchamber," Sue offered.

"I somehow don't think I could live out my days inside your old wardrobe." Lillian stared ahead at the swirl of colors on the ballroom floor.

"Under the servants' stairs, then?" Sue asked with a raised brow.

Lillian pulled her gaze from those dancing. "No, I suppose I must face this fate with dignity, not hide under stairs. How bad could it be, anyway?" she bluffed.

Sue's head tilted to the side with a look of extreme pity. "Oh Lillian," was all she said.

"Let's not speak of it. Let's talk of…" But Lillian's mind was blank. Only the bleak future that was going to be announced soon filled her thoughts.

She should have accepted Devon when he asked for her hand. She should have left with him. This was all because she was upset over some silly boats. In the face of her present circumstances, that mattered less and less by the second. What had she been thinking?

She was glad she had confessed her love to him. At least he knew now how she felt. Even if it was of little consolation to her now.

Would he come tonight? Her eyes searched the crowd before coming to rest on the floor before her toes. He wasn't here. Not that she expected him to be. He had said good-bye. She might never see him again. Her chest tightened. Surely she would see him at some point around town, even if from a great distance. Of course, he would eventually move on. He would dance with other ladies. He would marry another. He would have children.

"The influence of Italian opera on British composers," Sue blurted out, her eyes wide with excitement.

"Pardon me?" Lillian had been woolgathering but the subject did seem to change rather abruptly.

"It's a topic to discuss," Sue pleaded. "I'm sorry, Lillian. I just hate to see you like this."

"I know. But I will survive."

Nathaniel slipped through the crowd to join them in their corner of the ballroom. "Ladies," he offered, coming to Lillian's side. "I thought you could use some company. I spoke with Josiah a bit ago. He's waiting for Solomon to arrive before the announcement is made. Of course, if Solomon takes much longer…" He broke off to glance at his watch. "Josiah will go ahead with things."

Lillian nodded in acceptance. There was a moment when silence fell over them, with Nathaniel and Sue exchanging uncomfortable glances.

Sue's eyes darted around for a moment, clearly in search of a pleasant topic to discuss, before she said,

"Mr. Phillips, I do like your waistcoat this evening. The blue suits you."

Nathaniel looked down at his attire. "Oh, this? I got it ages ago and never wore it."

"Is that a thread of gold woven into the fabric?" Sue asked with a little too much interest for someone who never wore much ornamentation herself.

"Yes, it is." Nathaniel beamed.

"Would you two please stop making conversation to pass this dreadful hour? I would rather wait in silence, if you please. Sorry, I know you mean well, but..." She broke off when the music died and Josiah stepped up onto the platform where the orchestra sat.

Her heart hammered in her chest. This was it. Her life as she knew it was over. Perhaps it was good for it to be over. If she hurried to marry Lord Harrow and could survive her wedding night, then perhaps he would abandon her at some estate in the country and she could live out her days alone.

The image of Devon floated through her thoughts. But she must stop thinking of him. He was out of her life forever. Her fingers tightened where they were laced together.

"Ladies and gentlemen, I want to thank all of you for coming tonight to celebrate this most joyous occasion for our family."

Lillian froze. Nathaniel gripped her elbow to keep her from swaying. Sue shifted uncomfortably at her side.

She glanced once at the door leading to the garden, not six paces away. Turning her focus back to Josiah, she saw Lord Harrow making his way to the front of the room, gentlemen clapping him on the back as he went. Josiah tucked a finger into his collar to loosen it. She swallowed and licked her lips in an effort to paste on a smile. However, her face would not cooperate.

Just then, some sort of altercation occurred near the doorway. Josiah turned with an alarmed look. She rose to her toes to see over the crowd. She could hear a few screams. Then something crashed. What was happening? She looked over at Nathaniel to see a gleam of anticipation in his eyes.

"You will not get away with this!" The cry came from the entrance to the ballroom. There was a thud and another crash. Josiah's eyes widened for a moment. He turned and watched whatever was happening before nodding to someone Lillian could not see. Harrow had stopped at the front of the crowd, his dark hair just visible over the crowd.

Josiah cleared his throat and attempted to speak over the commotion. "Please excuse the interruption." There were a few grunts and a thud from the doorway. Then the room grew silent except for the buzz of whispers across the crowd. "It is my pleasure to announce tonight the betrothal of my sister, Miss Lillian Phillips, to..." He glanced toward the doorway with one of his superior looks of smugness. "The Duke of Thornwood."

Harrow roared in anger.

Polite applause filled Lillian's ears. Had she heard that correctly? Had she imagined his name being said? Devon stepped up onto the platform. How had this happened? Tears stung the backs of her eyes. Devon! How could this be?

"Thank you, Lord Bixley, for bestowing on me

this great honor. I am pleased to soon be part of your family." Devon lifted a glass to more applause and chatter over the news. He smiled to the crowd, his white teeth gleaming in his dark face.

Why did he look so dark? His face was blackened, as were his clothes. And he was still wearing his clothes from this afternoon. Lillian started walking forward. He clearly had not yet seen her, since his gaze roamed the masses packed into the room.

"Excuse me." She moved past groupings of gathered people. "Pardon me." She elbowed her way past others. The crowd seemed unaware they were blocking her way. Then once they noticed her, everyone wanted to offer their congratulations. Devon. She didn't want to stop and chat now, all she wanted was Devon.

When she finally neared the front of the room, the crowd parted and she could see him fully for the first time. He was covered from head to toe with what appeared to be soot. Where had he been these last few hours and how was he here now? Her betrothed? All she could do was stare. He watched her come near, a question lurking somewhere behind his eyes and drawing his brows together.

Devon stepped down from the platform, setting aside his glass of champagne. He walked toward her, closing the gap between them, his storm-cloud eyes never leaving hers. Stopping before her, he grasped her hands in his. Everyone paused their continuous stream of whispers to listen.

He must have noticed their audience for he signaled the orchestra to begin playing again. Turning back to her, he rubbed his thumb across the back of her hand in a caress that left dark smudges on her white glove. He pulled her to the side of the dance floor as a dance began. "Lily, I know we quarreled this afternoon."

"Yes." She could not tear her eyes away from their joined hands. He was here? He was here and they were to be wed?

"When I left here, I thought I might never see you again," he murmured in a deep rumble so only she could hear.

"I know." She looked up, her eyes catching his and refusing to let go.

"But I want to spend my life with you by my side. If you will…"

"How?" How could this be real?

"I suppose through marriage. Living in the same home and all that our nuptials entail." He spoke in a slow, deliberate tone, nodding his head as if explaining life to a child.

"No…" That hadn't been what she meant.

"No?" he asked, his eyes flaring with emotion.

"No…I mean, yes…um…how is this possible?" Confusion washed over her in great waves.

"Circumstances changed in the agreement with Harrow. As soon as Bixley heard the full tale…" Devon glanced toward the doorway.

She shook her head in disbelief. Looking around at Josiah, she watched him walk toward the ballroom entrance. It was then that she saw the aftermath of the argument she could only hear earlier. Was that Solomon lying unconscious on the floor? Her eyes widened. Two men seemed to be guarding his body. When the crowd shifted, she could see they were

Lord Steelings and the Marquess of Elandor. Why were they standing over Solomon? Their faces were blackened just like Devon's.

Broken china littered the floor, and a broken mirror hung on the wall behind them. Oh my. Harrow was there now as well. He appeared to be having words with Josiah as he nudged Solomon's limp form with his toe. Just then Elandor slammed Harrow against the wall with a thud. She looked back to Devon in dismay.

"The new arrangement was not without incident," he said cryptically.

"I can see that." She was not sure what had transpired this afternoon. She only knew she was standing here with her hands wrapped inside Devon's warm grasp.

The soft chords of a waltz began humming around her.

"Why don't we continue this discussion while we dance."

"Yes, that would be lovely." As Devon swept her into a waltz, she could hardly believe she was in his arms again. This afternoon she'd thought she had said good-bye to him forever. Now, here she was dancing with him, her future husband. His face held a look of trepidation as he guided her around the floor.

"I only hope that in time you can forgive me for not telling you of the ships."

"It did hurt to discover their existence from Solomon," she conceded. The muscles in his shoulder tensed under her hand.

"I promise, Lily, it will never happen again." He pulled her closer as they revolved around the floor.

The warmth of his hand on her back seeped into

her bones, relaxing her into his open arms. "Good. But really, I should have guessed as much. You mentioned your shipping investments, and then there are your explorations. I've known that since we first met. Ships *are* usually required to travel to foreign lands. I was simply surprised that my brother was the one keeping you in ships. You could have told me. I would have understood."

"I know that now. If I could go back and change my actions, I would."

"Will it happen again? Can I trust you?"

"Lily, I will never keep things from you again. But also, it will never happen again because I no longer have the ships."

"You sold them?"

"No, I burned them."

"You...burned them." Her eyes raked over his soot-smudged face and the smears of black across his cravat and shirt. "You said you needed them."

"Not as much as I needed to burn them." He grinned down at her.

"You do look a bit like a chimney sweep this evening." She laughed. "You truly burned them...are you mad?"

"Well, they say I am. Perhaps they're right. I know I'm mad for you right now."

"Devon, shhh. Don't say such things in the middle of the ballroom."

"That, Lily, is an easily solvable problem." He shifted their direction in an instant, waltzing through the open door to the garden.

When they were outside the edge of yellow

candlelight coming from the ballroom, he stopped their dance, yet didn't let her go. Their arms tangled together as he dropped their joined hands to his sides. The moon dripped silver streams of light between the tree branches, pooling at their feet.

"Devon, are we really to be wed?"

"Yes, although I believe I have neglected to officially ask you." He cleared his throat. "Lily, marry me."

"That wasn't a question."

"Hmmm, all right…Lily, will you be my wife?"

"That ballroom just there is filled with the finest members of the peerage, who tell me I will in fact be your wife. And yet you still have not asked me."

"You're enjoying this, aren't you?"

"Now that was a question, and yes I am. After all you put me through, I believe I deserve some enjoyment."

"Lily." He said her name with narrowed eyes that contradicted the grin tugging at his mouth. "Would you marry me?" His hand tightened on her waist, pulling her closer.

"Yes." She whispered the word as her hand wrapped around his neck, reveling in the feel of his soft hair brushing against her fingers. His lips lowered to hers, kissing her until she leaned into him. He dropped his hold on her other hand to slide his hand over her rear, pulling her against him as he deepened their kiss.

"Someone will see us."

"We are to be married. What they see doesn't matter anymore."

Married. Married to the man she loved. Her heart ached for him. Only, he had not said he loved her in return, had he? He said that he cared. He said he was mad for her. Neither of which were love. Fondness, lust even, but not love. Did he love her?

"Come with me. Surely there is a more secluded bench or something of that sort if you are going to worry about it."

"There's a gazebo in the back corner," she offered as he led her down the stone steps and into the moon-lit wilderness.

The sweet, sticky scent of the bay willow trees hung heavy in the air. Devon inhaled, memorizing the moment. He squeezed Lillian's hand as they wound their way down a path, gravel crunching under their feet. Just ahead was the gazebo, hidden from view by a veil of ivy that had been allowed the freedom to grow wild against the far corner of the garden. Lillian stepped inside first.

"It's exactly as I remember it as a child." She smiled at some long-forgotten memory as she turned toward him.

He reached out to stroke her cheek, trying to capture her smile forever. His hand drifted down the side of her neck, holding her steady as his lips found hers. He wanted to taste her, to consume her. Her lips yielded under his as her hands slipped inside his coat to encircle his waist. God, he wanted her. She deserved better than a dirt-floor gazebo, but he'd be damned if he could force himself to turn away from her.

His hands slid possessively down her back to rest low on her hips. Her breathing was unsteady, betray-ing her nervousness. He watched, fascinated by the quick rise and fall of her breasts as she tried to rein in her breathing. He moved forward, wanting to feel her against him, around him. She took a slight step back to regain her balance, bumping into the large post holding up the structure.

Holding her steady with the post at her back, he used it to press her closer. It wasn't close enough. Tilting her chin up, she looked into his face. The bright blue of her eyes shone in the dark as she pulled the coat from his shoulders with light touches. The garment fell to the ground.

He leaned into her, gently biting her bottom lip, then running his tongue over it to soothe it. Kissing her deeply, he felt her trembling hands slide to his chest and grasp at the fabric of his shirt. His need for closeness became a growing scream of demand in his ears. Her hands snaked around his shoulders to twine in his hair as he pressed her back against the post, trapping her with the force of his body grinding into hers.

Beyond hard for her, he showed her how much so with a thrust of his hips. She moaned into his mouth and began to pull fistfuls of his shirt up his back to remove another layer between them. He broke the kiss only long enough for her to pull the shirt over his head and throw it to the ground.

He began to pull the gown from her shoulders. When it hung in a loose pile of fabric below her breasts, she shimmied her arms free and ran her hands over his chest. His shoulders. His arms. He tensed in response to her innocent touch.

He ran a finger beneath the edge of her corset. Guiding her breasts free of the contraption, he weighed them in his hands, allowing her hardened nipples to slide between his fingers. Her breathing quickened as she watched him release his hold on one breast, only to dip his head and take one perfectly taut nipple into his mouth, grazing it slightly with his teeth and running his tongue around it before sucking it into his mouth. She arched into him, grabbing the back of his head, pulling him closer. She wanted more, he realized, chuckling. Good, he wanted more as well, much more. He wanted her. All of her.

He skimmed a hand down her leg to lift the hem of her gown and run slowly up the outside of her bare calf, her knee, her thigh. Her soft skin felt like fine silk under his hands. He tugged at the gown where it covered her other leg until it was compressed to a lump of cloth across her belly.

His lips skimmed the surface of her breast as he moved to her neck. He paused to catch her pulse as it throbbed under his lips. His hand lifted to her bare shoulder and he ran his fingers over the pearls where they wrapped around her throat, while he tugged on her earlobe with his teeth. Lily. God, he needed her, more of her. She must have felt the same, for she wrapped her legs around his hips, tugging him a fraction closer to where he wanted so badly to be.

Devon pulled her mouth back to his as his hand sank into her hair, scattering the last of the pins that held it in place across the ground. His other hand rounded her hip, holding her to him. He broke their kiss to glance behind him, searching for a better location to proceed with things. He spied a bench near the entrance. A bench. Lily deserved better than a bench.

Seeing his concern, she offered in a breathless

whisper near his right ear, "There are blankets inside the bench. At least there were when I was young."

"Perfect. Wait here." He set her down on her feet, holding her waist for a moment until she was steady before turning to retrieve the blankets.

When the ground was covered with soft blankets, he looked back toward her. She had removed her dress from around her hips. Her skin glowed in the silver light of the moon. He could see traces of the soot from his hands smudged across one breast and over a shoulder, marking her as his. And yet she wasn't his, not completely. He held out his arm to her and watched as she walked toward him to lay her hand in his.

"This is madness, with the ball taking place just across the garden," she said, lines of worry creasing her brow.

He looked past her for a moment, only seeing fragments of light through the vines that covered the forgotten gazebo. He could hear faint strains of music floating on the air from the open doors of the ballroom but no voices to indicate anyone had come outside. He looked back into Lily's eyes, brushing the fallen strands of hair from her forehead. He couldn't wait to have her. He needed her now. It had to be here. He opened his mouth to try and explain, but the words caught in his throat.

She laid a hand on his chest, stepping closer to him.

"The truth is, Lily, I am mad. I am mad enough to burn ships for you." He wrapped an arm around her waist. "I am mad enough to follow you to every ball in London. I am mad enough to blackmail you just to insinuate myself into your life." He looked into her eyes, forcing out the words he could barely admit to himself. "I may have had this name for a long time, but I have only truly been mad for the last year. I am mad for you." He paused to take a breath. "Because I love you, Lily."

"That's why you blackmailed me?"

"Yes, and I would do it all over again if it would bring you right back here where you belong, in my arms."

She shook her head. "All along I thought you must hate me."

"Lily, I have loved you from the moment I met you in that tavern a year ago."

A smile broke over her face like sunrise dawning over a mountain. "I love you, too, Devon."

He pulled her down with him onto the blanket at their feet, easing her to her back. Resting on an elbow at her side, he drew a line with his finger across her shoulder and down the silhouette of her slim body, enjoying the feel of her shiver beside him as he kissed her lips.

His hand moved of its own will toward the apex of her thighs, making ever closer circles as he caressed her smooth skin. The heel of his hand pressed into her, and he found the small sensitive bud with his finger and stroked it. She arched into his hand on a silent plea for more, with her fingernails pressing crescents into his shoulders.

Her eyes were bright with fire. He plunged his tongue into her mouth at the same time his finger entered her. Her eyes closed as she pressed her hips farther into him and a noise escaped from deep in her throat. He caught the sound with his lips and kissed it away as he plundered her mouth and drove two fingers into her wet heat: teasing, coaxing, and then finally demanding what they both wanted.

She tightened around his fingers, and her fingers pulled at his back as she sought her release. She shivered violently in his arms just before going limp and kissing him with more lazy passion than she had before. He withdrew his fingers, smiling at the pleasure-filled look in her soft eyes. He needed her more now than ever. She giggled as she looked up at Devon, a look of awe lingering on her face.

He ran a hand over her belly, curving it around her hip. He pulled her in to kiss her with all the passion that had built between them. He wanted her beyond reasonable thought, but he must take his time. It would not do to climb on her and have it over in one thrust in the manner his body was screaming for. She had to be ready. She needed to want him as he wanted her.

He was in the middle of regaining his control enough to proceed with her when, to his surprise, he felt her fingers dip into the waist of his breeches. In fumbling with the buttons, the backs of her fingers were grazing his skin, searing him with every brush of her hand.

"Dear God, you're going to kill me," he murmured.

She wrenched her hand around and popped a button loose, then another, as she threw a seductive gleam up at him. When all of the buttons were opened, she reached into his pants and wrapped her hand around him, stroking his length. He instantly grabbed her wrist to still her hand and carefully pulled it free and pinned it above her head. He did not want this interlude to end here while he still had his pants on. He needed her. He needed to be inside her.

"Did I do something wrong?" she asked, worried.

"A little too right, I'm afraid." He looked into her eyes, seeing his own hunger reflected there.

She arched her beautiful body into his where he hovered above her, letting her nipples glance past his chest on her descent back to the blankets. He needed no further encouragement as he ripped his pants off with an animal-like growl and rolled on top of her, finally feeling her naked skin against his.

Her arm still lay loose above her head where he had briefly pinned it and he ran his hand down its surface, watching her shiver at his touch. Her every squirm under his light touch tugged at his groin. When he reached the very outside edge of her breast, he bent to lavish one kiss on its peak while his hand danced to her side to seize her other hand where it lay beside her. He picked it up, pushing it above her head to join the other. Leaving a trail of smoldering kisses up her neck, he looked her in the eye as he pushed her thighs open with one knee.

His heart beat violently as he sat poised at her entrance. Their foreheads were touching. Their ragged breaths were mingling. And heavy-lidded eyes met in the darkened gazebo. He claimed her mouth and entered her in the same moment with one long, slow thrust.

She made a small noise of discomfort at his size. He stilled, watching her. She blinked for a moment, adjusting to him before she raised her hips to meet his.

He pushed fully into her before retreating to thrust into her again, deeper and harder.

She was tight and warm. She was his.

A year he had longed for this. He steadily drove into her without mercy. Her legs came back up to wrap around him, gathering him in with her body as he took her. She met his thrusts, gripping his back, pulling him in. She pulled him down into a world where there were only the two of them and time did not exist.

"Oh, Devon," she cried into the night.

He covered her mouth with his, tasting the desire on her lips and devouring it.

He thrust into her over and over with relentless need. She was his at last.

She shook as she shattered beneath him, tugging him with her over the edge into oblivion. He pumped into her one last time on a low growl before collapsing on her and rolling to the side, catching her up with him as he went. She lay across his chest, her golden hair spilling out in every direction as she floated back to earth with him. Her arms and legs were tangled with his in a twisted puzzle of body parts that neither wished to move.

Sometime later, he brushed her hair away from her face and kissed the top of her head. "We should return to the ball."

"I suppose so," Lily replied, twisting to look him in the eye. "I know how much you enjoy attending balls with London society."

"Yes, you know me so well."

"Or we could disappear into the night," she suggested.

"You are adept at such things," he smirked.

"Yes. Only this time, when I disappear into the night, I'm taking you with me." She smiled as she bent her head to kiss his shoulder.

"Always." He lifted her until she was level with his face as he smiled up at her. "Because I never want to lose you again, *Lily Whitby*." He laughed as he caught her up in his arms, tumbling her onto the ground beneath him.

"You never will," she returned as he kissed her again. "Although I may be forced to steal kisses from you for the rest of our days."

Epilogue

DEVON MADE HIS WAY ACROSS THE PARLOR, WATCHING his new bride as she chatted with one of the Green sisters and Roselyn. The other Green sister was standing to the side, deep in conversation with Steelings. Devon's gaze returned to his bride, beautiful in his home, their home now. The celebration was a small affair in ducal terms. Yet, after their return from Scotland, a wedding breakfast had seemed a bit late.

After all, he had broken his fast for a week in bed with Lily before their return home. But his mother had insisted. And when the dowager duchess of Thornwood insisted on anything, it was done. So here he was, surrounded by friends and family and enduring congratulations until he could have Lily to himself once again.

At the exclamation of "Holden" from across the room, his eyes narrowed on Steelings. He watched as his friend strived to make the eldest Miss Green laugh—or was there more to their conversation than that? Steelings' gaze seemed to be affixed to the girl while a faraway daze covered his face. Perhaps he had found his Suzanna after all. Devon was jolted from his bemused state by his mother.

"Thornwood, dear, have I mentioned how happy I am to have Lillian in the family?" his mother asked, impeding his progress across the floor.

"Yes, Mother. But I'm glad to hear it again."

"Your father would be proud of your choice in a bride," she added.

"I like to think so. Truthfully, I'm still relieved I was able to marry her. I didn't think it possible." Devon shook his head to banish the unpleasant memories.

"Anything is possible where love is concerned, dear. Speaking of love in the air…are you prepared to escort your sister to every ball in town next season?"

"You aren't still on about that, are you? Is it not enough that I married?" He spotted Lily and Roselyn walking his way and raised his voice so they could hear him. "Now I must attend all of the balls next season as well? All for the likes of Roselyn?" he added with a grin as his sister joined their conversation.

Roselyn jabbed him in the arm. "Yes, you certainly must."

He looked into Lily's eyes as she stepped up beside him. "As long as I get to dance with my duchess, I believe I might survive it."

"Of course," Lily replied as she wound her hand around his arm.

His mother led Roselyn off to chat with Nathaniel as Bixley sidled up to Devon, his glass of brandy resting on his large girth. Devon still didn't like the man, although if not for Bixley's greed and greater desire to have a high title in the family than Solomon's vengeance for the ships, Devon would not be wed to Lily. For that he was grateful.

"Thornwood, excellent to see you made it back into town with my sister. And even better that you returned wed. Since your disappearance from the ball, tongues have been wagging all over town."

"Bixley, tongues have been wagging over my every action for years now." Devon leaned in to offer in a conciliatory tone, "It's this damned madness, inconvenient as hell."

"Yes, I suppose you have been discussed at some length," Bixley replied, looking uncomfortable with the direction of the conversation.

Lily laughed. "I believe our family could use a little madness. Let society talk. They only dislike what they don't understand."

"That's quite wise, my love." Devon never ceased to be amazed by Lily. Her independence of thought wrapped in grace continued to make him smile—as did her slim body when in his arms. He covered her fingers where they were tucked close to him.

"Thank you. I'm happy to be the Mad Duchess on your arm any day," she said, her face wreathed in smiles. She turned to her brother with a sincere look in her eyes. "Josiah, I owe you my thanks as well. His Grace told me of how you allowed our union to occur."

"Yes, well. He made quite the argument." Bixley gave her a small nod and took a sip of his drink.

"That reminds me, Bixley. That estate manager I mentioned will be calling on you tomorrow as I promised. You should see Bixley Manor become a profitable estate within the year."

"Many thanks, Thornwood. I see you have other guests wishing to speak with you, so I will go." Bixley nodded in farewell to his sister with a murmured, "Lillian." He shook Devon's hand and left them, moving in the direction of the decanter of liquor on the table by the window.

Devon looked back in time to see Elandor entering the parlor. He watched as the marquess's eyes swept the room, coming to a rest on Nathaniel. There was only the hint of a nod and smile evident to anyone watching. No wonder they had managed to keep their relations private for so long under the eyes of London gossips. If Devon didn't already know of their involvement, he would never have guessed at it.

"Elandor," he called out. "I'm glad you could make it here on such short notice."

Devon turned to Lily for a round of introductions. "Your Grace, this is the Marquess of Elandor. Elandor, this is my duchess." He grinned, adding, "Thanks to you."

"It's nice to meet you, m'lord." Lily dipped into a quick curtsy.

"The pleasure is mine, Your Grace." He bowed. "I wouldn't think of missing this happy occasion." He handed Devon a folded piece of parchment. "It's a wedding gift."

Lily eyed the letter with a frown creasing her face. "His Grace spoke of your help with breaking the betrothal agreement. After all of your assistance, a gift isn't necessary."

Elandor leaned closer and dropped his voice,

a twinkle in his eye. "Consider it a gift from Nathaniel, then."

"Why would your gift be from Nathaniel?" Lily asked. There was only a second of silence before she continued. "Oh! You're friends with Nathaniel! You are... It's a pleasure to meet you!"

Elandor pointed to the parchment now in Devon's hand. "It's a shipping contract for the Crown."

Devon was stunned. "I don't know what to say... Thank you, I suppose. Although that doesn't seem quite sufficient."

"You won't need to chase down business overseas any longer. Of course, that puts you home more...if that's an issue..." Elandor broke off with a grin at Lily.

"No. I've decided to accept the responsibilities of my title. With some encouragement." He paused to give Lily's hand a squeeze. "I would like to become more active in Parliament and join His Majesty's Treasury. I'll miss exploring the world, but this is my life now."

"Thornwood, Parliament doesn't meet year 'round. You can maintain your life outside your title, as I do." Elandor tilted his head toward Nathaniel where he was chatting with Devon's mother.

"Ah, I suppose I never saw a way to have both." He glanced at Lily, almost chuckling at the bright look of anticipation in her eyes. He turned back to the man before him. "Thank you for such a generous gift, Elandor. It will allow my family to live without concern for funds, and I'll be able to explore without the worry of conducting business for trade while traveling." He shook his head in awe at the turn of his fate. "I'll be free."

"Only if I am free at your side," Lily stated.

"Always, my love, always," Devon returned.

"Will you excuse me?" Elandor asked, backing away from them. "I need to give my greetings to your brother, then I must be leaving."

"Thank you for coming, Lord Elandor," Lily offered before he walked away. "It was nice to meet you. I do hope you will visit our home often, especially at family gatherings."

"I would consider it an honor, Your Grace." He bowed and moved away.

Now was his chance. Devon had been waiting for everyone to complete their congratulations so that he and Lily could slip away for a minute. "Lily, come with me. There's something I would like to show you in the gallery." He tugged her out of the parlor, leaving the chatter of their guests behind.

Lily giggled as she followed him down the hall. "I've seen the gallery, but I'm not going to pass up the opportunity to be alone with you for a minute."

He led her up the stairs. For once he was not haunted by the memory of her in his arms on the staircase. He sighed. Lily was where she should be—at his side. As they walked through the door into the gallery, he stepped around behind her, slipping his hands up to cover her eyes. She laughed and leaned back into him. Guiding her forward, he stepped carefully through his exhibits of foreign artifacts.

"Devon, where are you taking me?"

"Here." He dropped his hands from her eyes and allowed his fingers to rest on her arms, holding her close. Her gaze fell upon the surface of her mother's writing desk.

"Mama's desk! Devon. How did you find this? How did you know?" She ran a hand over the wooden surface before turning in his arms to look at him in amazement.

"I learned of it the day you left me a year ago when I went back to Habersham's shop in my search for you. Although it was only recently that I purchased it."

"You searched for me?"

"Of course, Lily. As I told you, I have loved you from the moment I met you." He stroked a hand through her hair as he looked into her clear blue eyes. "When you stole my pocket watch that night, you stole my heart. And it's been in your possession ever since."

"And I will not be returning it." She smiled. "I love you, Devon."

"I love you too, Lily." He kissed her, capturing her soft lips beneath his. Pulling back, he grinned. "And I will spend the rest of my days making you pay for your life of crime, my little thief."

She stepped away from his reach with a smile. "Only if you catch me."

He reached for her and she was gone in a rustle of skirts and laughter. He gave her a second's head start, chuckling as she looked back over her shoulder halfway to the door. He'd been chasing her ever since she tracked him into that tavern, and he would follow her all of his days. Striding across the room, he closed the gap between them. Once he caught her, he would never let her slip away again.

Read on for a sneak peek at book two
in the Tricks of the Ton series

Desperately Seeking Suzanna

Torrent Hall, Kingston upon Hull
March 15, 1816

"Who are you supposed to be?" Holden asked,
adjusting the animal skin draped over his shoulder as
he attempted to settle further into the chair.

"I'm Helen of Troy, of course," his cousin April
stated as she adjusted the folds of her skirts around her
legs. "I simply adore dressing for dinner like this, don't
you?" As she straightened, her gaze turned serious and
her eyes narrowed on him. "Who are you, anyway?"

"Attila the Hun, although I'm regretting the decision at the moment."

Only the Rutledge family would concoct such a
plan for the evening of his homecoming—a historical
dinner involving costumes, no less. He finally pushed
aside the fur with a shrug of his shoulders. He'd worn
the damned thing through dinner; surely he could
remove it now without issue. "I suppose it would be
outlandish to dress as ourselves and talk of the damp
English weather."

"It would indeed." April drew back in mock

dismay, bumping into one of her sisters on the settee beside her in the process and causing a clatter of teacups and squeals.

Holden chuckled as he glanced toward Aunt Penelope and Uncle Joseph, who were sitting and chatting in the corner of the drawing room, seemingly unaware of the din of girlish voices around them.

It was nice to be back. He liked the familiar sights and sounds of Torrent Hall, even if he had to dress in a ridiculous costume sometimes. It was a price he was willing to pay, for this was the closest thing to home and family he'd ever known. He grinned and took another sip of his drink.

Piles of books lined the walls of the drawing room, stacked so high the room almost appeared to be made of a patchwork of leather. Abandoned embroidery, paints, and stationery covered the side tables, leaving only small spaces where polished wood was visible.

As it often did, the room rang with laughter as April attempted a dramatic fling of her arm, indicating the tea tray. It would have been a convincing Helen of Troy imitation had one of her bracelets not flown from her arm and hit Uncle Joseph on the head.

"Sorry, Papa!" April scurried across the thick rug to retrieve her lost jewelry, her bright pink dress swirling around her as she moved.

"No damage done, dear," Joseph replied, rubbing his balding head and shifting Caesar's wreath of leaves askew in the process.

Holden couldn't contain a chuckle over April's ensemble now that he truly looked at her. She had taken the excuse of her historical persona to wear every piece of jewelry in the family's possession. Her arms were laden with jewels. Pearls were layered on top of diamonds surrounded by sapphires, all shimmering in silver and stacked up to her elbows. No wonder she was losing them with every shift of her arms.

What gentleman would she tie herself to this season? So far she had been more interested in the ball gown she wore than the gentleman with whom she twirled the floor. That would change soon. With the Rutledge dark hair and exotic eyes, she was too lovely to remain unwed for long. He would have to keep an eye on her while in London—all of his cousins, really. Not that he minded surrounding himself with his lovely cousins. After all, Holden Ellis, Viscount Steelings, was always surrounded by beauty. Beautiful ladies, beautiful clothing, a beautifully appointed town home. He was known for it.

There was always a lady longing to be on his arm and have her name linked to his for a time, a short time anyway. His thoughts were pulled back to the present with the barking of the puppy Jan played with on the floor, the curl of her dark ringlets shining in the light of the fire. At least he wouldn't need to worry about her existence in society for a few years yet. He would have his hands full with only three Rutledge ladies in London.

"May, you're not in character. Joan of Arc would never say that." June pushed her glasses higher on her nose to level a proper glare at her sister.

"I only asked for more tea. Have you ever worn armor? It's terribly heavy. I'm positively parched from the effort." May shifted her breastplate to the side and sank further into the chair.

June's eyes darted over her sister's attire before giving her a shrug of her shoulders. "I simply don't see Joan of Arc as a tea drinker. And you need to at least speak with a French accent if you aren't going to attempt the true language."

"You aren't in character either, June," May returned, finally tossing the armor to the floor and reaching for the pot of tea on the table. "You may be wearing bed linens, but you've yet to say anything profound or insightful."

"I'm Socrates!" June countered. "I'm quite certain he was opinionated."

"Yes, and he spoke his opinions in Latin," May returned with a grin.

"That's a dead language."

"Precisely." May smiled and turned her dark head on her sister.

Holden's attention drifted to April as she asked, "Mama, is all planned for the ball?"

Aunt Penelope's eyes filled with happiness at the possibility of her daughter's involvement. "There's always much to do, if you're volunteering."

"No," April replied a bit too quickly before offering her mother a smile. "I was only asking so that I might begin selecting my gown. I want to coordinate with the décor, but not match it."

He heard May mutter into her cup of tea. "Why does it matter? It will look just as all your other gowns do—pink."

Aunt Penelope frowned in response before turning back to April. "You will look lovely, my sweet. Don't forget your mask, though." She beamed and clasped her hands together. "I already have Sara preparing mine for the event."

"It's to be a masquerade ball this year then?" Holden asked, unaware of the change in plans as he'd only arrived at Torrent Hall that morning.

"Yes, did I forget to mention that fact? I do hope you have a mask with you. If not, we can find one for you to wear."

"As it happens, I brought one." He'd discovered long ago that it paid to be prepared for all wardrobe eventualities when staying with the Rutledges.

"Oh, perfect!" Aunt Penelope exclaimed with a jump, making her Cleopatra costume catch the lamplight and cast green sparkles around the room. She grew still as she watched Holden, making him tense about what might be to come. "I feel as if I've forgotten to tell you something…"

Aunt Penelope did this often. She was a bright lady, although her mind frequently traveled in two directions at once. Down one path lay glittery masquerade masks and down the other lay her opinion on how Holden should be living his life. He didn't mind. It was actually nice to be worried over. He waited, returning her gaze. What would it be this time? His blond hair had grown too long for fashion? He needed to eat properly or drink less?

"Lady Rightworth came for tea yesterday while you were out."

"Rightworth," he repeated, trying to remember the name. "Is she the one with the hook nose?"

"No! She's quite handsome, but that's neither here nor there." Aunt Penelope waved away the comment with the back of her hand. "She asked after you, wanted to know if you would be making the rounds in London this year, since you're back in the country. I assured her you would."

"Why would she want to know my schedule? I'm not even entirely sure of whom we're speaking."

"I believe she has her eye set on you for her daughter. She's introducing her to society this year. Evangeline, I believe."

May gasped. "That's horribly unfair of her. She should be focusing her efforts on Sue, who is almost on the shelf as it is. Now, with Evangeline coming out, Sue won't stand a chance."

April rounded on her sister with a superior "I'm far older and wiser than you" voice. "May, you can't force gentlemen to dance with such an obvious wall-flower as Sue. Some ladies are perfectly content with spinsterhood, you know. Lady Rightworth cannot make her elder daughter a diamond of the first water any more than I can make flour into a cake."

"When have you ever gone to the kitchen and tried to make a cake? Which proves my point perfectly, just so you know." May crossed her arms with a frown.

Aunt Penelope intervened before anyone came to blows, which she did so often as to not be upset by it. "Girls, it is not our place to interfere with the goings-on inside the Green household. Lady Rightworth can see to her family as she chooses. I only brought this up to let Holden know he was spoken of over tea yesterday."

Holden leaned forward to regain his aunt's attention. "Why would she be interested in me? I've never met either of her daughters."

"Holden, you are getting to be of an age…"

"Nine and twenty is an age, all right. Thirty, forty, and fifty are ages as well, and I plan to see them all without a leg shackle, thank you."

Uncle Joseph leaned into the conversation, his toga draping over the arm of his chair. "Don't be defensive, Holden. Your aunt is only trying to help. Perhaps this would be a good time to peruse the available ladies."

"Uncle, I peruse ladies every chance I get. I just have more interest in young widows with no interest in marriage."

Aunt Penelope gasped and shot him a look of disapproval. "Holden! Don't speak of such things in front of the family."

"My apologies, Aunt Penelope. At this point I'm not even certain how long I'll be in England. This trip was rather sudden."

"Speak of what in front of the family?" Jan asked from her seat on the floor before the fireplace. "What did Holden say? Was it clever? What did I miss?"

Holden needed to change the subject to something far from the topic of his marriage prospects. He glanced at his youngest cousin where she sat curled on the floor in a Leonardo da Vinci costume playing with her new dog. "Da Vinci killed puppies for sport."

"He did not!" Jan pulled the puppy in her lap closer into her arms to protect him from harm.

"You're right. It was only the brown ones with white paws he favored for puppy murder." Holden laughed in response as he'd just described the ball of fur Jan was holding.

"Holden," his uncle murmured when the conversation around them turned to Jan's newest pet.

Holden turned to face him.

"I understand your reservations in regards to marriage. Every man experiences a young man's love of freedom, but what of an old man's loneliness? Look at all I have." He smiled at his family scattered around the room. "I want the same happiness for you. I only ask that you consider it."

Holden gave his uncle a tight-lipped nod before returning his attention to Jan and her puppy. It wouldn't take him long to consider the issue of marriage. There. He'd considered it. And it was never going to happen. It couldn't.

❧

Sue raked her eyes across the garden, searching for movement. All remained still. Only a slight breeze rustled the trees beyond the stone walls. They were safe.

Straightening, she started to push the sash of the window closed. *Squeak!* She cringed at the sound, although the herd of cats at her back in the darkened hallway was making far more noise than any window was able to produce. That's what she called them, for that was the way they acted—always preening, strutting about, and demanding attention as they drifted through life on a smile and a coy rejoinder. They were also known as her sister and twin cousins. Sue rolled her eyes and slammed the window shut with one swift motion.

She turned, shooting identical glares at her identical cousins through the holes in her dark masquerade mask. "Shhh…we'll all get caught if you two don't quit arguing. Does it really matter why she stepped on your toe, Victoria?"

"It matters to my toe," Victoria huffed as she adjusted the bright green, bejeweled mask higher on her cheekbones, shook out her matching gown, and took a dramatic step away from her sister.

"For goodness' sake! Isabelle didn't mean to injure your toe." Sue lengthened her stride to catch up with her sister, pulling Isabelle along with her as she hissed over her shoulder at her other cousin, "It's dark and she was crawling through a window."

"She did it on purpose," Victoria stated with a raised chin, looking like the exotic peacock she was dressed to resemble, the feathers woven into her hair trembling with indignant hauteur.

"I did not," Isabelle argued from Sue's side, her yellow mask shifting as she scrunched her nose.

They were halfway down the hall now. The farther they drew away from the window, the more Sue relaxed—which was very little. This was a terrible idea. At least she was of age, but her sister and twin cousins hadn't even been presented to the Queen or had any sort of introduction to society yet. It was only a matter of a week, since they would leave for London in a few days, but if they were caught at a masquerade ball, Sue knew exactly who would take the blame.

She'd said no when the girls first approached her about attending tonight. Yet, with Evangeline and Victoria involved, Sue knew they would have come anyway. It always fell to her to be the sensible voice of reason. Sensible, simple Sue Green. She rolled her eyes. No wonder she was still in the market for a husband after four failed seasons. Who would want to marry someone like her?

She glanced to the side, watching one of Isabelle's blond ringlets fall over her cheek in perfect bounces with every step. She would be betrothed within the month. And, of course, Evangeline would have no troubles. Renowned beauties rarely had issues capturing a gentleman's attention.

Evangeline threw her hand out to stop their journey down the shadowed hallway. Sue bumped into her sister, her nose squashing into the back of Evangeline's deep blue gown.

Sue ran her fingers over her mask, checking for dents as she peered around her sister to see what had stopped their progress. "What? Did you hear something? Is someone coming?"

Acknowledgments

I would like to thank my family for supporting me in my dream to be an author, my friends for enduring years of neglect while I write, and the amazing industry professionals who took a chance on the new girl in town. A special thanks to Michelle Grajkowski, my fabulous agent, and Leah Hultenschmidt, my awesome editor. Thank you for believing in me and my stories. Thanks to the "Bad Girlz" of Badgirlzwrite.com. You are my sisters, my critique partners, my friends; and I promise I will always have chips.

To Carolina Romance Writers and Romance Writers of America, I appreciate all that you've done and continue to do to help me grow as a writer. To my mom, who is smiling down on this right now, you are loved, missed, and appreciated for all that you did. And a huge thank you to Mike, Sylvia, John, Webb, and my dad for all that you do to keep my world spinning around. I couldn't have done this without you! Thank you!

~ E. Michels

About the Author

Elizabeth Michels blends life and laughter with a touch of sass into the Regency era. This flirty debut author turns ballrooms upside down, and challenges what lords and ladies are willing to do to get what they most desire. She lives in a small, lake-side town in North Carolina with her husband, "Mr. Alpha Male," and her son, "The Little Monkey." Elizabeth is furiously typing away at her next novel while dinner burns in the kitchen. She loves to hear from her readers; please visit her website at www.elizabethmichels.com.

Desperately Seeking Suzanna

Tricks of the Ton

by Elizabeth Michels

Coming March 2014

She had one Cinderella moment...

Lord Steelings is a charming rake and the life of every party. He always has a joke to tell and a smile on his face, all masking a dark secret. If London society knew of his mentally ill mother hidden away in the country, he wouldn't be welcome at a single *ton* event. Sue Greene has never been noticed. The older sister of an exotic beauty, she's spent her life being pushed to the side. When she has the chance to attend a masquerade ball, she seizes the opportunity. If she had only known donning a mask would change her life...

For more Elizabeth Michels, visit:

www.sourcebooks.com

How to Lose a Lord in 10 Days or Less

Tricks of the Ton

by Elizabeth Michels

Coming July 2014

**Their love sparks in the stables, but
it's bound to be a bumpy ride**

After years away from home, Andrew Clifton, Lord of
Amberstall, is attacked by a hired hit man and forced to flee
back to London. But he doesn't get far. With an injured
horse and no shelter, Andrew becomes the unintentional
houseguest of the Moore family. Katie Moore could always
be found at the stables—until her riding accident. Now,
she locks herself from Society, embarrassed by her injuries.
While Katie tends to Andrew's horse, the two are at odds
about everything, except their feelings for one other and the
danger that they're about to discover on the road ahead…

For more Elizabeth Michels, visit:

www.sourcebooks.com